NOBODY ELSE BUT YOU
Pacific Vista Ranch, Book 1
Copyright © 2019 by Claire Marti

eBook 978-1-7333046-0-3
Paperback 978-1-7333046-1-0

This is a work of fiction. Names, characters, places and incidents are either the product of the author's imagination or are used fictitiously, and any resemblance to actual persons, living or dead, business establishments, events or locales is entirely coincidental.

Printed in the USA.

Cover Design and Interior Format

Nobody Else But You

PACIFIC VISTA RANCH

BOOK ONE

CLAIRE MARTI

DEDICATION

To Kay Bennett for the inspiration,
the encouragement, and the Savasana.

ACKNOWLEDGEMENTS

WRITING A BOOK IS DEFINITELY a team effort and I wouldn't have been able to bring Samantha and Holt's story to life without assistance. I learned about the world of horse breeding directly from Kasey Bennett, Farm Manager of Ocean Breeze Ranch, in Bonsall, California. I couldn't have created Pacific Vista Ranch without Kasey's input: on my ranch visit, she taught me more than I ever dreamed of knowing about running a successful breeding operation. I may have blushed a few times.

Stephen Kane helped me come up with the name Pacific Vista Ranch and his lovely partner Amy Dulan offered invaluable insight and assistance about horses. Melissa Hardie——thanks for helping me come up with Holt's name while you put those pretty blonde streaks in my hair. Anna Bradley——I couldn't have polished this story without your honest feedback and clever suggestions. Michele Arris——thank you for listening and offering your wise advice.

Katie Lane——thank you for your mentorship and wisdom——I feel so lucky we've connected. Joanna Kelly——thanks for your advice on Hollywood movie sets and for your support. Catharine Williams——your eagle eyed attention to detail and line edits were invaluable. To my brother Robert Petretti——your support as my big brother and your talent as an editor helped me make this book the best it could be. Thank you Jessica Reed-Cancel for sharing your ballet experience. And thank you Liana de la Rosa for helping me create the dreaded synopsis.

I want to thank my wonderful beta readers and critique partners. Kay Bennett, Lacy Pope, Joanna Kelly, Leslie Hachtel, April Fink, Megan Randall, and Megan Camp—you each help me more than you could imagine. I appreciate your time and opinions.

To my wonderful editor, Lindsey Faber, thank you for helping me polish this story so it shines as bright as a diamond.

Last but not least, to Todd for being the best husband in the world. I love you. And, finally to my furry kids: Lola, Beau and Josie, thanks for providing me unconditional love.

CHAPTER 1

SAMANTHA MCNEILL WAS IN ONE of the upper rings of hell, or at least the inside of a wood-fired pizza oven. She wiped the sweat from the back of her neck, shifted her heavy braid over her shoulder, and stuffed her scratchy cowboy hat back onto her head. The Santa Ana winds were plaguing Rancho Santa Fe, California, and the dry, crackling air had transformed her state-of-the-art quarter horse breeding barn into a furnace.

She tilted her head to the high wood-beamed ceiling and huffed out a breath. Pacific Vista Ranch's prized stallion, Hercules, had duties to attend to and time was ticking. No time to contemplate the heat. She smoothed her sweaty palms over her well-worn denims and yelled, "We ready? Where's the tease mare?"

"Marco is bringing her. Is the doctor on her way?" Owen, her tall, lanky stallion manager, stood with Hercules in a separate stall space, just beyond the main breeding area.

"I'm here, I'm here. Sorry I'm late." Dr. Amanda McNeill, Sam's big sister and the resident equine veterinarian, rushed directly to the horse breeding platform, and double-checked to make sure the height of the phantom mare was correctly set up. If the breeding mount wasn't precisely adjusted for the stallion, he couldn't perform and the entire afternoon would be a waste of time. "This miserable heat is stirring up all the animals over in rehab."

"Marco, hurry up. Where's Christina? We need the tease mare pronto." Sam gritted her teeth. Without the female's influence in the afternoon romance, Hercules's contribution could be jeopardized. Why couldn't her ranch hand ever be on time?

"In Hollywood, we call the Christinas of the world fluffers." A deep voice drawled from behind her.

Hollywood? She hated Hollywood. Who was in her barn and why was he comparing her mare to a woman hired to arouse a male porn star? Seriously?

She counted to three and turned around to see who'd uttered the juvenile comment. Golden rays shimmered around a tall, rangy man standing in the open entrance of the enormous shed, creating the illusion of an angel fallen to earth. The uninvited stranger's face remained shrouded in the shadows. Probably not an angel.

"Hilarious. Never heard that one before. Yes, Christina is one of our resident fluffers. Ha ha." Sam crossed her arms, her cotton shirt sticking to her shoulder blades. *Was the temperature escalating?*

"Come on, it was pretty funny." He chuckled. "I'm looking for Chris McNeill or Sam, the breeding manager? The guy at the east gate told me to make my way to the main building. Maybe I took a wrong turn?" He sauntered toward her on long denim-clad legs. "Or are you Sam?" He called out to Owen.

Of course he assumed Owen was the breeding manager, because the breeding manager couldn't be a female, right? She hadn't liked Mr. Hollywood on sight, and now she disliked him even more. "You were right the first time," she said. "You took a wrong turn, so why don't you and your brilliant sense of humor just spin around, get back in your car, and don't stop until you've returned to Los Angeles."

"Sam!" Amanda scolded. Her sister acted more like a surrogate mom, despite being only two years her senior. She called her out when she was rude, or ruder than usual. Sam scowled. What, had that been ruder than usual?

"We don't have time to waste, especially not for amateur comedians." She pivoted back toward the breeding platform. She would fire Marco if he didn't arrive with the fluffer—*damn it, the tease mare*—in the next ten seconds.

"You're Sam?" Doubt threaded through Mr. Hollywood's husky voice, which now came from directly over her shoulder. "I thought Sam was a…"

"A man?" Damn it, she didn't need this. She had worked twice as hard to prove herself in the male-dominated industry, not to mention endured endless jokes about her dubious title.

"Look, I've got business—" Mr. Hollywood began.

She cut him off. "Listen. As you may be able to tell, we are in a horse-breeding barn. People from all over the country pay big bucks for our top stallion's bloodline. We are right in the middle of helping our stallion make a deposit with the phantom mare so we can freeze it and send it off." She enunciated each word slowly, as if she were trying to communicate with a toddler. "So I'd appreciate it if you'd just shut up and—"

She turned toward him and her breath lodged in her throat as she caught her first full glimpse of him, and a shiver of awareness prickled the hairs on the back of her neck.

Messy blond hair framed a high-cheek-boned, square-jawed, perfectly chiseled face. Piercing silvery blue eyes narrowed and his full lips pressed together when her words registered. A white scar slashed through his left eyebrow, saving him from looking too angelic. No wonder he was cocky. His face would cause any woman to forget her own name.

Any woman except for her, of course. She was immune to pretty boys. Her accelerated pulse had nothing to do with his broad shoulders or his warm masculine scent.

Of course it didn't.

She pulled her attention back to the center of the room. Her sister was biting her lip, fighting back a grin, obviously reading her reaction to the man, as sisters do. And maybe not just sisters. Owen kept his gaze focused on Hercules, but a reddish flush crept up his neck, a sign he was stifling laughter. Hercules tossed his ebony mane, pawed the dirt and seemed to roll his eyes.

"Enough already. This is business." Sam said when Marco sashayed in with Christina, the beautiful chestnut mare who always managed to get Hercules motivated for his job of sharing his superior genes.

And Christina was *not* a fluffer.

"Nice of you to finally join us." She frowned at Marco and vowed to reprimand him later.

Hercules chuffed and pawed the ground. Christina was one of his favorite ladies, but in reality Hercules liked them all. Unlike their former stallion Julius, who would turn up his velvety nose if a mare didn't meet with his approval, Hercules wasn't picky. He didn't care if the brood mare's haunches weren't well-rounded or her mane wasn't suitably silky——he was always raring to go.

The stallion made her job easy——unlike her tardy ranch hand and the tall unwelcome stranger. What business could this guy have with her dad or her? No way was he here to buy or sell horses. She squared her shoulders and focused. She was one of the best breeding managers in the country and she wouldn't be distracted by Mr. Hollywood's presence in her barn.

Sam hurried to the breeding platform and took her place opposite her sister, ignoring the irritating man behind her, at least for now. Awareness skittered down her spine——she could feel his hot gaze burning into her. She nodded to her sister and called to Owen.

"Let's do this."

After allowing Hercules a brief nuzzle, Christina exited stage left and Owen led Hercules to the phantom mare, which had the right anatomical parts of a real mare, without the legs, tail and head. Twenty seconds later, it was over. Hercules didn't waste time. The stallion manager escorted a now relaxed Hercules back to his premium fancy stall, where all he needed was a cigarette and a nap.

"I'll bring everything back to the lab for you," her sister said after Sam had collected the sample from the phantom mare.

Sam walked over to the large sink against the near wall and washed her hands. "Thanks, Amanda, is everything okay down at the rehab facility or do you need some help?"

"I've got it covered, but I'll run back down now because I still have tons to do. Are you sure you've got everything handled here?" Her sister raised her brows.

Sam had almost forgotten about idiot hot guy, but when she turned back, he remained rooted to the same spot. Damn it, he *was* as gorgeous as a fallen archangel. Too bad the effect was ruined when he opened his mouth and spoke.

"I thought I'd seen everything, but that was something else. Your stud sure doesn't seem to mind an audience, does he?" Mr. Hollywood chuckled.

"Oh please, I'm sure you wouldn't either." Okay, so maybe she should have kept that thought to herself, but he rubbed her the wrong way.

"Ma'am, if you could just tell me where I can find your father, I'll be out of your way." He aimed a crooked grin at her sister. Sam's gut clenched—this guy was trouble. She always trusted her gut.

"I'll show you where to go—" Amanda stepped off the platform and approached Mr. Hollywood.

Sam scowled and crossed her arms. "Who are you and what do you want with our father?"

"I'm sorry, my name's Holt Ericsson. I'm sure he'll fill you in, but I need to speak with him directly. He's expecting me, so if you'll just point me in the right direction..." Despite his polite tone of voice, she could swear he was smirking at her. What was this guy's deal?

Shaking her head, Amanda smiled at him. "You just take the road about a quarter-mile farther and you can't miss it. Our dad's office is in the house. You can park in front. Are you sure we can't answer any questions for you?"

"No thanks. I appreciate the enlightening scene—I'll never forget Christina." He grinned at Amanda, pivoted on his worn cowboy boots, and strolled out of the barn. And, no, Sam wasn't checking out his butt, she was simply making sure he was gone.

"Is that steam pumping out of your ears, little sister?" Amanda said. "I know it's hotter than Hades in here and the season's in full swing, but you were pretty hard on him."

"Didn't he bug you too? I'm sorry, but I don't like this one bit. A Hollywood guy looking for Dad can only cause trouble." But maybe she had been a *teeny* bit over the top.

"Who knows? If you're really concerned, why don't you go up to the house and see?" Amanda squeezed her shoulder. "You have to admit he is awfully easy on the eyes."

"Easy on the eyes. Please." Sam snorted. "You're right though. After I clean up everything here, I'll go up and make sure Mr. Hollywood doesn't get lost on the way off our property."

CHAPTER 2

HOLT ERICSSON ACCELERATED UP THE hill because he had a feeling he wouldn't get much time with Mr. McNeill if his fiery-tempered daughter interrupted them. Come on, his joke had been funny—but maybe they'd heard that one hundreds of times before. He had grown up around horses outside of Denver, but he'd never been on a quarter horse breeding ranch. Who knew stallions needed a little encouragement? He'd received a full education in less than five minutes. Fluffer horses. He chuckled.

Maybe he should have conducted a little more research on the key players before cruising down from L.A. He'd never heard of a female breeding manager and with a name like Sam, who could blame him for assuming she was a he? Although Sam McNeill smelled like sunshine and her snug jeans showcased the most perfect butt he'd ever seen, he had an assignment. No time for prickly pint-sized redheads.

When he curved around the winding road, he hit the brakes to admire the sunlight glancing off the terracotta tiled roof and enormous sparkling windows of the cream-colored, Mediterranean-style estate. No way could anyone miss this house. It resembled a sprawling Bel Air mansion or Malibu manor, accented by beds of white and pale pink roses, clusters of red and purple bougainvillea, and giant orange birds of paradise. Did people get lost when they lived in houses this huge? He'd grown up in a modest ranch-style house outside of Denver and had never become accustomed to the ostentatious estates up in Los Angeles.

Holt continued up the driveway and parked his white Ford truck next to a gleaming Land Rover, which made his five-year-old pickup look ready for the scrap yard. He got out of his truck and headed to the front door, which was twenty feet high with a large black wrought iron door handle and a huge brass lion doorknocker. He lifted it and let it drop to announce his arrival.

A few moments later, the front door opened and instead of a stereotypical British-accented butler in a tuxedo he'd been half-expecting, a striking redhead in a floaty sundress stood in the open entrance. He did a double take because there was something familiar about her.

"Hello?" Her musical voice lilted up in question and her full ruby lips curved in a welcoming smile. "Can I help you?" She tilted her head to the side.

"I'm Holt Ericsson and I'm here to see Chris McNeill. Am I in the right place? Because I already made one wrong turn. Your vet was kind enough to direct me up here."

"Oh, you must've stopped at the breeding barn. People make that mistake all the time. Come on in, I'll take you to my dad's office. It's in the other wing." She stepped back and gestured with one slender arm for him to enter.

"Your dad?" Another sister? How many were there?

"Yes, I'm Dylan McNeill. You met Amanda, my older sister, and probably ran into Sam too."

He swallowed a rude comment about Sam. "Yes, I walked in on some, umm, horse business."

"Oh no, you didn't walk in during the middle of a breeding session, did you?" Laughter tinkled in her voice.

He fell into step alongside her and they crossed an enormous biscuit-colored hallway with vast ceilings and rich hardwood floors. Open doorways revealed glimpses of colorful paintings, large furniture, and azure sky peering in through floor-to-ceiling windows. Impressive.

"That's exactly what I did. And your sister Sam wasn't too happy about it."

Dylan laughed. "That's my twin sister. She's very serious about her job and runs the operation with an iron fist. Sam can be blunt when she's working, but you shouldn't take it personally."

Her words registered and his jaw dropped open. "You're twins?" It was like *The Dark Half* by Stephen King—the evil twin had devoured the good twin in the womb.

She smiled. "We're identical twins."

"No way." No way *in hell* could this sweet, polite woman be the twin of the sassy terror in the barn.

"*Yes* way." She nodded and her dark eyes sparkled with humor. "Seriously, we are identical. Our features are exactly alike, even if our personalities aren't. We used to trick people all the time when we were kids."

"I'll take your word for it..." No need to argue, but no way. The foul-tempered woman in the barn was most definitely not a beauty like her graceful, feminine sibling.

"Here we are." She stopped in front of a closed door, rapped twice, and opened it. "Dad, I've got someone here to see you."

He followed her into a huge study. Wow, he'd never seen so many books except in a library. Along the far wall, built-in bookshelves were stuffed to the brim with leather-bound tomes. If he hadn't known the ranch was successful, he would now by all the framed certificates and trophies on the walls and shelves.

A tall, rugged, strawberry-blond man rose from behind a massive teak desk, scattered with files and papers.

"You must be Holt. Harry told me to expect you sometime today." He skirted around the desk and offered a firm handshake. "Did you find it okay?"

"He accidentally went to the breeding barn first and interrupted Sam." Dylan laughed, apparently highly entertained about the situation. If she only knew the off-color joke he'd made and her sister's furious reaction, she might not be so friendly.

Mr. McNeill barked out a laugh. "That must've been educational."

Holt nodded and smiled. No need to offend the patriarch. Who was he to judge if the man allowed his brash daughter to run his ranch operation? From what he'd seen in Los Angeles, wealthy parents indulged their children all the time.

"If you gentlemen will excuse me, I'll let you get to your business. I've got to get back to my studio." Dylan strolled out of the room.

"Holt, can I offer you anything? I've got bottled water here in the mini-fridge or we can get some coffee?" Mr. McNeill asked.

"Water's great. No need to make a fuss." Go time. His movie producer boss, Harry Shaw, had warned him to seal the deal.

Mr. McNeill returned to the chair behind his desk and gestured for Holt to sit in one of the comfortable tan leather chairs facing him. "So, tell me what's so urgent Harry insisted I meet with you today?" He steepled tanned fingers under his chin and rested his elbows on his desk.

Holt rubbed his hands on his thighs. Damn, why hadn't Harry made it clear how much he'd shared with McNeill and also the nature of the favor he was calling in?

"Well, he probably told you his new movie is a large-scale Western." When Mr. McNeill nodded, he continued. "Everything has been going smoothly in pre-production and then we lost our location site."

"And what does that have to do with me?"

"Well, the ranch in Paso Robles we were planning on using was destroyed in a fire. Without the location, Harry's worried the movie will go under. The budget is astronomical already and we can't afford to pay too much for another location."

Mr. McNeill's brows drew together. "Harry wants me to invest in the film? Are you one of the producers? Is that why he sent you instead of asking me himself?"

Holt dug his fingers into his legs, working to remain calm. Damn Harry for tossing him into this situation. When Harry had asked him to help him out, he'd agreed without asking questions—this movie had to move forward. But Harry could've at least prepped Mr. McNeill. "I'm an associate producer and investor and also the lead stuntman. Did he tell you anything about our meeting?"

McNeill shook his head, leaned back in his chair, and crossed muscular arms over a broad chest. *Shit.* Even a body language novice could see he was losing the man before he'd even asked for the favor.

"Okay, here's the deal. Harry wants to film on your ranch. Of course, he'll compensate you for the time—"

"My ranch?" Mr. McNeill surged up out of his chair. He stalked toward the French doors overlooking a huge patio and sparkling swimming pool.

Holt rose to his feet as well, but remained by the desk. Harry had mentioned his friend had a short fuse. He addressed the older man's back. "We'd just need the location for about four weeks, give or take, and we wouldn't start until your breeding season was finished. That's in about a month, right?"

"Do you know why I live here now? Why I left Hollywood? I can't have the paparazzi buzzing around here—I won't expose my family to that bullshit again." Mr. McNeill's voice rose as he turned to face Holt, his eyes narrowed.

Harry had mentioned that a decade ago, McNeill

had been the biggest director/producer since Clint Eastwood. Then, after a tragedy on the set where his wife was killed, he'd turned his back on Hollywood, except for a few film investments. He'd bought Pacific Vista Ranch, an impressive two hundred and twenty-eight acres, only five miles from the Pacific Ocean. Holt didn't know much more than that. Harry assured him Chris McNeill wouldn't refuse, but now Holt wasn't so sure.

"I'm sorry. Of course we'd have a closed set with only employees allowed on the property and security and…" Sweat broke out on the back of his neck. This movie had to happen. He'd invested every cent of his savings and if the film went under, he'd sink with it.

Mr. McNeill moved back to his desk. "Where's Harry? Let's get him on the phone." The patriarch's cheeks were red.

"He's putting out some fires back in L.A., but feel free to call him. I'm sure he can answer any questions you have." He damn well better.

Mr. McNeill picked up the phone on his desk and punched in a number. A second later Harry's voice came over the speaker.

"Harry Shaw."

Holt sank back into the cushy chair and jiggled his leg impatiently. Harry better have the answers because he was in over his head.

"What the hell, Shaw? I've got your man down here asking to film a movie on my ranch. Are you out of your freakin' mind?" Mr. McNeill braced his hands on the edge of his desk and glowered down at the phone.

"Hey, Chris. I'm sorry I didn't come ask you

myself, but I had an emergency and Holt was able to step in for me." Harry's voice sounded nonchalant.

"It sounds like your life is full of emergencies. You know I haven't been back to L.A. in over a decade and I won't expose the girls to the press and everything that comes along with filming." He gritted the words out with a clenched jaw.

"Just listen for a minute."

"You've got sixty seconds. That's it." Mr. McNeill said.

"Look, this is the biggest film I've ever made. I lost my other ranch. I only need to use about fifty acres. I need the scenery. I need the accuracy. I can guarantee we'll keep the location top-secret and hire extra security to keep out the paparazzi."

"It didn't work so well before, did it?" McNeill sat and rubbed his hand across his chin.

"Chris, it wasn't my fault. It wasn't anyone's fault." Harry's response was subdued.

"Do you need to film the stables or the horses?"

"Well, not the stables because this is a classic Western. We've got some horses we're using, but we'd want some of yours out in the pastures, more like background. I can control the schedule. We can work around you. Off-season is quiet, right?" Harry's voice remained remarkably calm.

"Yeah, yeah. But, remember I know how this goes. You can't control everything and it could spiral pretty quickly. I swore to the girls they'd never have to deal with the movie industry again, at least not here."

Holt remained silent and tried to keep up with the rapid-fire exchange. Obviously, the situation went much deeper than he'd realized.

Not that he'd really considered it.

"I get it, I do. But the girls are adults now, right? It's been a long time since everything went down and I'm sorry about it all. You know I wouldn't ask you if I had anywhere else to turn. But I could lose my ass over this film."

Mr. McNeill got up again and stalked around the room.

"You there?" Harry's disembodied voice called from the speaker.

"I'm sorry, but I just can't do it. I could make some calls to a few other ranches we work with around the country. Maybe one in Texas or Kentucky could work?"

"Texas doesn't work and Kentucky is too far. The whole story needs California topography and scenery." Harry's voice deepened a few octaves. "Chris, you owe me."

Holt dragged his fingers through his hair, suddenly wishing he hadn't cavalierly agreed to handle the meeting for Harry today. The men's shared history was none of his business.

"Damn you, Harry. You're putting me in a really tough position."

"Take me off speaker and pick up the phone."

Mr. McNeill glanced at Holt, as if he'd forgotten he was in the room. He grabbed the phone, stalked to the far side of the office, and turned toward the window. From the distance, Holt studied the man's stiff posture, tension obvious in his broad shoulders. What would Harry do if the man refused to allow them to film?

Damn, what would *he* do? He'd turned down

all other jobs for two months in anticipation of this production. More importantly, he needed the payout for too many reasons to count. McNeill had to agree.

"Alright. Alright," Mr. McNeill said. "But, I want every actor, every gaffer, and every damn craft service worker to sign a non-disclosure agreement. With stiff penalties for breach. I want this place to have so much security the damn Queen of England could visit. And, if there's one violation and the past is dredged up again, we're done. You hear me?" He hung up and spun back to face Holt.

"Fine. You've got a deal. Have the lawyers draw up the paperwork and it better be ironclad, do you understand me?" Mr. McNeill didn't look happy about it. The grooves bracketing the older man's mouth had deepened significantly over the last ten minutes.

"Look, sir, I'm just here on Harry's behalf. I didn't mean to upset you." Damn it, he felt liked he'd just kicked a puppy or something.

McNeill sat down behind his desk. "It's not your fault. Harry should've come down instead of sending you to do his dirty work. Tell me about the movie at least, since Harry didn't bother to. And call me Chris."

Holt relaxed, grateful Chris wasn't shooting him for being the messenger. "It's an epic, probably the biggest western movie in decades. Mind you, I'm just the stuntman for Jack Hanson, but I always go through the scripts with a fine-tooth comb before I commit. Jack Hanson and Ella Roche and every other big-name actor you could imagine are in it. Hell, Clint Eastwood is even performing a cameo. Harry's convinced it will bring back the glory days of Old Hollywood."

"The glory days, huh? Damn Harry knows I always wanted to bring back the Western." Chris's shadowed eyes held a faraway look as he gazed out toward the windows again. "They don't make movies like they used to anymore."

Holt leaned forward in the chair. "The script will blow you away. You won't regret it."

Sam strode into the room. "He won't regret what? Script, like a movie script?" Her hat was still tugged low, but Holt knew the question was directed at him. Well, shit. He'd hoped to avoid another confrontation with this daughter. Something about her made the hair on the back of his neck prickle. Why couldn't the angelic one have returned instead of the red devil from the barn?

Luckily, before he had to answer, her father spoke up. He used a much softer tone than he'd used with Holt and Harry.

"Samantha. I'll share everything with you tonight. We'll have a family meeting and discuss it over dinner."

Holt rose from the chair. "I should be going anyway." He addressed Chris. "Do you mind if I drive around the ranch before I leave?" He could get a tour of the stables and other buildings another time.

"Why would you scout around our ranch?" She blocked his exit. Her boots were planted and her hands were fisted on narrow hips.

In the brighter light of the house, he noticed

she was definitely as beautiful as her twin. The bone structure and creamy skin were there underneath the tan cowboy hat. But, where her sister was kind and hospitable, she was snippy and rude. Nothing inviting or appealing about this woman.

Funny how much personality could impact looks. When he was a kid, his mom had always lectured his baby sister, "pretty is as pretty does." He'd laughed hearing his mom manipulating his sister to behave, but now he saw evidence of it in the flesh.

"Samantha, I told you we'd discuss it tonight," Chris said. "Holt, feel free to drive around the ranch."

Sam frowned, but stepped aside, leaving the doorway open for him to depart.

He extended his hand to Chris McNeill. "Thanks. I'm sure Harry's lawyers will get you the paperwork and I'll be in touch to schedule another visit soon. I'll see myself out."

He skirted around the woman like she was a rattlesnake ready to strike. Unable to stop himself, he grinned and winked at her. Maybe he could charm her? She curled her upper lip and sneered at him. Or maybe not.

Holt escaped down the huge hallway and rubbed the tense muscles on the back of his neck. Nice of Harry to toss him into the lion's den. He didn't know what had been worse––dealing with the father or the daughter. Probably the daughter. Maybe he'd get lucky and the McNeills would take an extended vacation while they were filming and he'd never have to see her again. Life was too short to deal with temperamental brats, even beautiful ones.

Her sister had obviously received all the good genes.

CHAPTER 3

NO WAY IN HELL WOULD she wait until dinner to discuss this situation. Sam paused in front of her dad's desk, struggling to contain the fury threatening to boil over. Her heart was pounding against her ribs and the back of her neck was on fire. She refused to turn and watch that *annoying man* stroll out of her home after whatever "business" he'd foisted on her father.

"Samantha, you can just calm down. I'm not discussing this more than once, so you'll have to wait until dinner." Her father's expression was controlled, but she caught a glimpse of the tic in his left temple, a sure sign he was upset.

"I'm not going to calm down, Dad." Her finger-nails dug into her palms. "You have no idea how disruptive the guy was down at the barn—I don't want him here. What is going on?" Despite her thundering pulse, she managed to keep her voice level and congratulated herself at her supreme self-control.

"Look, I need a few minutes to process it all. Please?"

Her dad sank into his wing-backed office chair and rested his forehead in his hands.

"Dad?" Her voice cracked. "Now, you're scaring me a little bit." The flames of temper licking at her belly extinguished. She crossed the office in three long strides and stroked her hand along his shoulder.

He lifted his head, then reached back and squeezed her hand with his large one. "Don't worry. It'll be fine. Let's go for a ride, okay? I need a good dose of speed on Roman and would love to have my baby daughter with me."

"I'm not the baby. Dylan and I are the exact same age."

He smiled and his beloved hazel eyes crinkled at the corners. "No, you came out two minutes after Dylan, so technically, you are and will always be my baby girl."

Her heart squeezed in her chest. Her dad was everything to her: father, mother, boss, and most of all, her hero. If going for a ride would alleviate the haunted look in his eyes, she would accompany him.

"Let's do it. Why have a ranch if we can't take our horses out whenever we want?" She returned his smile.

Together they strode out of the house and down the curving stone pathway toward the stables. Her favorite two hummingbirds––Betty and Susie–– hovered at one of the numerous red feeders she'd set up. The sweet fragrance from the riot of colorful flowers and shrubbery helped her jangled nerves to quiet. If only the palm trees offered more relief from the damn heat.

When they crested one of the rolling verdant hills, she caught a glimpse of the deep blue ocean. A haze sat in the air from the Santa Ana winds, the staggering heat suspended over the horizon like a sandstorm. The breeze scorched her cheeks and she shoved her hat further onto her head. No need to fry her fair skin in this relentless sunshine. She scanned the skyline and mouthed a silent prayer to the weather gods for rain.

With the extreme temperature and powerful dry gusts, all it took was a spark to create a blaze capable of decimating homes, nature, and everything. Parts of Rancho Santa Fe still hadn't recovered completely from when the Witch Creek fires in 2007 wreaked destruction throughout San Diego County. They'd only just moved to the ranch and if she tried hard enough she could still conjure up the acrid smell of smoke. Since the Santa Ana's had kicked in unseasonably early this year, they had horse trailers ready down by the four large, thirty-stall barns, should they need to evacuate.

They ascended the incline into the smaller twenty-one-stall stable closest to the house, where the family housed their personal horses and Hercules. The wood-beamed ceiling was high and the entrances on each end were open, providing tons of natural light for the horses. Dust motes sparkled in the air and a few soft whinnies greeted them from the horses when they heard their arrival into the barn.

Princess Buttercup's golden head poked out from her stall and Sam could swear the horse grinned at her in anticipation. She stroked the horse's silky head and smiled into intelligent brown eyes. "Ready for a ride, girl?"

Buttercup whinnied and tossed her cream-colored mane in agreement. Her face was so beautiful—she was a palomino, with a white blaze on her forehead. Dark eyes always seemed to hold a glint of mischief and knowledge. Sam unlatched the gate to her stall and led her out to the aisle where she tied her and began to saddle her.

Her father mimicked her actions with Roman, his huge bay gelding. They worked swiftly and silently to prepare the horses for a ride around the ranch. Her dad would share the news in his own time. After seeing his earlier reaction, she wouldn't push him.

"The track or the trails?" One of the things she loved best about Rancho Santa Fe was the network of riding trails running alongside the roads and ranch estates. Her neighbors could be seen most days riding along the lush tree-lined paths. As a teenager arriving in the new community, she'd been thrilled to learn a woman architect named Lillian Rice had designed the Covenant of Rancho Santa Fe back in the 1920s with the horses in mind.

"Let's cruise over to the track. Roman needs speed today."

"Roman or you, Dad?" She bit her tongue, swallowed down the urge to question him, and mounted her horse.

"Both. I think you do too, right?" He levered up into the saddle. "Let's go."

"Definitely. This weather is driving me insane and the guy really got under my skin." Maybe if her only concern was with the joke he'd made in her breeding shed she could forget him, but her gut twisted seeing her father unhappy.

Her dad and Roman trotted out and she followed

him toward the three-quarter-mile racetrack on the opposite side of the property. As usual, the minute she began to ride, her blood pressure settled and all began to feel right with the world. She loosened her hold on the reins and allowed Buttercup to stretch her long, elegant legs. As they cantered along the track, her cheeks cooled and a laugh bubbled in her throat as she matched her father and Roman stride for stride.

The knots in her belly softened and she allowed the joy of riding to take precedence over the anxiety clouding her mind.

For now.

SAM STUFFED AN ENORMOUS BITE OF CHICKEN into her mouth and groaned as the delicate flavors exploded on her tongue. She was famished after such a busy, stressful day and the crispy, tender meat served as its own reward. She couldn't resist sampling the yummy meal right from the serving platter.

"Sam, take your plate to the table. I know eating is one of your favorite pastimes, but save some for the rest of us." Dylan nudged her away from the enormous pale granite island toward the giant oak dining table around which all family business was conducted.

"I don't know where you put all that food." Amanda commented as she loaded approximately one-quarter the amount of food onto her own plate. "It's not fair, you're half my size and eat twice as much."

"Oh please, you're a twig. You're just picky."

Her older sister had lucked out with their father's height and like all of them, had the slender McNeill build.

"I'm not picky, I just don't eat like a truck driver, that's all," Amanda sniffed as she plucked up a napkin and carried her mostly empty plate over to join her at the table.

"It's Angela's fault—she's spoiled us with her cooking." Sam plopped down her admittedly overflowing plate onto the homey red placemat and sank into her upholstered dining chair. Her cheerful sunflower yellow ceramic dish was piled high with two crispy chicken breasts, a mountain of red-skinned mashed potatoes, three tiny brussels sprouts, and a hunk of corn bread roughly the size of her head. Truck driver was right.

"Girls, girls, no bickering." Angela laughed, addressing them like the teenagers they'd been when she'd come to manage the McNeill household, before she'd married their dad. Angela was an incredible woman. Although she didn't replace their mom, they'd all grown to love her as much as their dad did.

"Did you invite the boys for the meeting or is it just us?" Sam asked between bites. Angela's three sons had become Amanda, Dylan, and Sam's step-brothers.

"I know Ryan, Grant, and Austin would love to pipe in with their two cents, but because none of them live here currently, it's just us." Chris joined them at the table. "We'll eat first."

Sam managed to focus on her food and remain patient until everyone finished eating. Her heart was racing and every muscle in her body was tense. Dylan, in her sweet quiet manner, cleared the dishes before rejoining everyone at the table.

"We've got a scenario. Let me share everything first and then you can ask all the questions you want and I'll do my best to answer. Deal?" He arched a thick brow at Sam and she nodded. Sam's overstuffed stomach began to churn. Maybe the last dollop of mashed potatoes hadn't been her wisest choice.

"You girls probably don't remember my old colleague Harry Shaw from L.A. He's in a bind." He paused and gazed around the table. "He's making an Old Hollywood-style Western, and at the last minute he lost the original ranch where he'd planned to film."

"But Chris..." Angela trailed off and a frown marred her lovely features. She threaded her hands together and bit her lip.

Her dad held up a hand. "He wants to film the outdoor scenes here. It wouldn't be until breeding season is finished, so the ranch will be quiet. They'd only be out on about fifty acres on the far end of the property."

"But the horses——" Sam sputtered.

"Hollywood?" Dylan asked, her chocolate brown eyes wide. "Dad, you swore we'd leave this behind. Why now?"

Amanda's usually sparkling green eyes went flat. "It sounds like you've already made up your mind. Do we even get a say in this?"

Sam's stomach dropped. Amanda was the calm, mature one, but on the rare occasion when she lost her temper, it was a sight to behold. Her dad wasn't thinking straight. How could he be oblivious to how this could destroy the safe haven they'd created over the last twelve years?

"Nobody associated with the movie will set foot on our ranch unless they have signed a non-disclosure agreement about the location. No exceptions. Harry will also provide additional security to keep the press away." He paused and took a sip of his longneck beer.

"Do you think the confidentiality will really hold up, Chris? Just how large is this production anyway?" Angela always played the peacemaker, but the furrow between her brows belied her calm tone. Sam deduced her father had sprung this on Angela too. None of it made any sense.

Over Sam's dead body would they film a movie here. She remained silent, unable to trust herself to enter the discussion. She gripped the wooden edges of her chair, digging her fingers in until her knuckles turned white. She'd known the man would be trouble, but she never could have imagined the Pandora's box he'd unleash on her family.

"I know I did and for the last decade, we haven't had anything to do with L.A. or the industry. It's not ideal, I know. But, we've got the space and it's helping out an old friend."

"But Dad, the mares will be foaling. It'll be noisy and disruptive. What if some of the animals are harmed?" Sam said. Weren't the horses as important to him as they were to her?

He was the one who declared Hollywood the enemy and uprooted the family after everything went down with their mom. Her perfectly ordered world could crumble down if the paparazzi resurrected the past. The mountain of mashed potatoes in her gut churned like an ancient volcano ready to erupt.

Dylan shoved away from the table and ran out of the room. "I can't believe you'd do this. I won't stay here."

Amanda caught Sam's eye across the table. They needed to go after their sister. Sam pushed away from the table, leapt to her feet, unable to contain the energy coursing through her veins a second longer.

Tears welled in Amanda's eyes and her voice caught on a sob. "If you don't care about the animals, what about us, Dad? How can you turn our home, our refuge, into a movie set? I don't understand."

"Of course I care about our horses——" Chris began.

"No, Dad. You need to find a way to fix this. Help this guy find somewhere else to film. This will tear apart our family. Don't your remember?" Amanda's clear, calm delivery emphasized her powerful words. She pivoted and marched out of the room.

"Of course I remember. I haven't directed a movie since that day." Chris sank back in the chair and Angela laid a hand on his forearm in comfort.

Blinking back tears, Sam stormed out to find her sisters to figure out how to stop this juggernaut from ruining their world. Adrenaline pumped through her body as she ran on shaky legs to catch up with her sisters.

Sam found them in the bougainvillea-shrouded patio on the east side of the house, kind of a secret garden. Her twin was curled up on one of the carved wooden benches at the far end, her slender arms wrapped around her legs, and her forehead resting on her knees. Amanda and Sam flanked her.

Thank goodness Amanda was generally even-keeled, often the voice of reason who maintained the balance. Now, however, Amanda's visible distress stoked Sam's rage. Her fingers curled into her palms, the sharpness of her short fingernails a welcome relief from the tears threatening to spill.

Dylan's palpable sorrow pierced her own heart and battled with the anger housed there. Although they were mirror images on the outside, inside they were polar opposites. Her sensitive twin's default was melancholy, while her go-to was irritability and fury. Although the trembling in her limbs and ache in her chest didn't feel like the pure cleansing anger she needed right now. This felt more like fear.

"How can he do this? What in the hell is going on? He promised us—" Sam's blood began to simmer all over again.

"Shh, Sam. You know Dad would never harm us on purpose. There's got to be more to the story. Let's talk about this." Amanda's practical voice slid into the fragrant evening warmth. At least one McNeill could be cool, calm, and collected regardless of the situation.

Sam chewed on her bottom lip. A gust of evening breeze cooled her skin, and she closed her eyes for a moment, savoring the relief. She flashed back to that awful afternoon when she'd been on the movie set, doing her dreaded Algebra homework. She'd had on her headphones, listening to

Stevie Nicks' crooning about the edge of seven-teen, when her world shattered. A loud crash, piercing screams, and sounds of someone sobbing. Later, she'd realized it had been her weeping because she'd seen her mom tumble from the set and realized she'd never get up again. Her eyes popped open and she swallowed the lump rising in her throat.

If losing their mom in a freak accident on the set of a movie their dad was directing wasn't earth-shattering enough, the days and weeks that followed devastated her family. The paparazzi had destroyed any semblance of a normal life they could have hoped to regain.

"My biggest concern is the paparazzi. If A-list celebrities come here, the media will follow. The obsession with fame has only gotten worse in the last ten years with all the reality TV junk." Sam despised reality television.

Amanda nodded at Sam and wrapped her arms around Dylan. "Good point. If we can keep the location a secret, I think it will be okay. A decade ago it was the most dramatic story around, but times have changed and the story probably wouldn't be interesting these days."

"But what if it is? Old scandals come up all the time. It was so ugly. The rumors about Mom having an affair with one of the producers. The insinuations against Dad. Those monsters chased us at school, camped on our lawn, and almost ran us off the road. We were basically prisoners in our house and we can't go through that again." Dylan looked up, her brown eyes drenched with tears and her voice wavering.

Amanda grimaced. "And my boyfriend dumped me because his parents didn't want him to be involved with our notoriety. That period of time was hell."

"We've worked too hard to live a normal life. If one grip or gaffer can't resist extra money to provide a photo op or a story?" Sam shook her head. Not on her watch. "I refuse to allow our lives to be ruined again. We've created a perfect refuge from that nightmare. Don't worry."

"What kind of favor could Dad owe Harry? It has to be something big, because I can't believe he did this lightly," Amanda asked.

"Who knows? It has to be personal. Didn't they work together back in the day?" Sam racked her brain, but she'd purposely relegated her father's former big shot director career and everyone associated with it to the past.

"I don't remember," Dylan said.

"Me neither. We'll ask him in the morning. And Angela will help keep Dad steady, heck, probably help all of us stay steady like she's done since we were kids." Amanda reached across and caught Sam's hand.

"I hope you're right. It's a lot of pressure on her too. She never mentions it, but she's lived in mom's shadow, even though she and Dad are totally happy and right for each other." Sam squeezed Amanda's hand in return.

"Well, I'm dead serious. One disruption to our horses or our life and they are out of here. I don't care what Dad owes this Harry Shaw guy." Sam jutted her chin and rolled her shoulders back.

"What about the hot guy?" Dylan gave a watery

smile.

Sam wrinkled her nose. "What about him? If he comes into my barn again, I'll kick his smart ass all the way back to Hell-A. Hopefully, he'll perform his little dog and pony show and we won't see him at all."

Mind made up, she nodded her head. Running the breeding operation and the ranch would keep her plenty busy. No need to run into Mr. Too Hot Hollywood and if he had a brain in his muscular body, he wouldn't disrupt her busy schedule.

Not that she'd noticed his body or face or hair.

Not at all.

CHAPTER 4

"SERIOUSLY? YOU WANT ME TO waste my afternoon giving the guy the full tour of the ranch? Why can't Dylan do it?" Sam rolled her eyes, but managed not to stamp her foot.

"Because Dylan is an artist. She doesn't run the ranch. You do. You know every blade of grass, every animal, every length of fence. Don't you want to make sure no detail goes unexplained?" Sam's dad appealed to her from across his massive desk with raised brows and a crooked grin.

So he was buttering her up so she'd do what he asked, and receiving praise from her father never grew old. But she really didn't want to waste her afternoon babysitting the man.

Two could play the flattery game. "I don't know, maybe you should do it, Dad—you're the real expert, right?"

"Nice try, pipsqueak. Look at it this way, if you do it, you'll have all the control and isn't that what you want at the end of the day? To make sure everything goes off without a hitch and they get out as soon as possible?" Her dad shrugged.

"Okay, okay. But I don't get why it has to be *him*. He's just the stupid stuntman, not even an Assistant Director or actor." *And he's rude and cocky.*

"Look, he knows horses. It's part of why Harry hired him—besides the fact he's the best in the business. It makes me feel better to know a true horseman will be on set 24/7."

Her dad did make a valid point. "I guess you're right." Sam sighed, and then stiffened. "24/7? What do you mean 24/7?"

Her dad fiddled with some papers on his massive desk. "Oh, didn't I mention it? Holt will be staying in the first guesthouse since Grant's traveling. It will be easier for him to be there in case anything happens. Harry insisted upon it."

"The guesthouse? For the whole time? Who appointed Harry god? None of this makes any sense, Dad." She shot to her feet and paced over to the oversized window and stared out at the bright blue cloudless sky. Having the guy on her ranch during shooting was infuriating enough, but living here?

It was annoying enough to have the filming happen every day and be invaded by strangers for weeks on end. But, to have someone stay in the guesthouse? *Him?* Mere yards from where she rested her head on her pillow each night? Ridiculous.

Her dad joined her at the window and laid a large hand on her shoulder. "It's not such a big deal, Samantha. Remember we'll be stabling the actors' horses and it'll be good for Holt to be close. Your life really won't be altered too much. Okay?"

"Don't push it, Dad. Like you said, I know every inch of this ranch. I'll know every second they're here. But fine. So, when do you need me to do this? My schedule's pretty tight right now with end of the season." She angled her gaze up at him. Come to think of it, she always had to slant her gaze up, except with her equally vertically challenged twin.

Her dad's smile was sheepish. "This afternoon? Around two?"

She narrowed her eyes and glared at his beloved face for a full thirty seconds. "Fine. I'm not happy about it, but for you, I'll do it."

And when she was finished with Mr. Too Hot Hollywood, he would know who was the boss around here

"YEAH, YEAH, I'LL LISTEN TO HER, ALTHOUGH I don't understand why McNeill can't show me around." His fingers tightened on the steering wheel. Spoiled little rich girls drove him nuts, just like his ex-girlfriend and every other actress/model in Los Angeles who expected special treatment.

"She runs the damn ranch, Holt, so you'll treat her with respect. I'm certain Chris raised his daughters to have the same type of work ethic and attitudes he has." Harry's disembodied voice warned from the car's phone speaker.

"Sure." He snorted. "She's a kid. How much could she know?"

"You should know better than to make snap judgments on external appearances. She had to grow up fast. From what I understand, she's one of the top breeding managers in the country and their stallion Hercules is one of the most sought-after studs."

"Yeah, whatever." He'd believe it when he saw it. Daddy's little girl—playing with ponies. He'd been on the receiving end of one of her temper tantrums, hadn't he?

"Be professional. I'd hate to take you off the movie. I won't have Chris upset, especially by offending his family. We're straddling a precarious line and I won't lose this location and you can't afford to either. Use a little of your pretty boy charisma. Got it?"

He snorted and forced his hands to soften the death grip on his steering wheel before he crushed it. Not only did this movie need to be his last stuntman gig, it had to have a huge payout. He couldn't afford to allow one annoying person to jeopardize his future. "Pretty boy charisma, right. Don't worry. I'll be professional."

He would be mature, but it didn't mean he had to be friendly or charming.

He'd ride the ranch with her and focus on the logistics.

After today, he'd simply avoid her.

How tough could it be?

From her hostile attitude, he doubted she'd hang out nearby. The ranch was over two hundred acres and the movie would only be filmed on less than a quarter of it.

"Call me on your way back. I want to hear how it goes. Be nice."

"Sure. Talk to you later." Holt forced his shoulders to relax.

He flashed his ID for the guard at one of Pacific Vista Ranch's four guarded gates and drove up to

the main house. Hell, the place was already fortified like a medieval castle; all they needed was a
moat and drawbridge. Extra security seemed like
overkill, but Harry was paying the bills, not him.

He gave a low whistle as he cruised along the
curving road and admired the rolling hills and
dappled sunlight reflecting off the clusters of trees.
In the distance, chestnut mares grazed in the
sprawling pastures and not a single cloud marred
the brilliant blue San Diego sky. The mountains of
Colorado would always be home for him despite
leaving years ago, but these green hills and lush
foliage appealed almost as much.

Did the McNeills appreciate how lucky they
were to call this place home? It sure beat the tiny
studio where he crashed in the Los Feliz neighborhood of Los Angeles. Los Feliz was cool, but
he was rarely home, so it was more of a place to
stow his suitcase and guitar between jobs.

When he pulled into a parking spot in front
of the courtyard entrance, his tour guide for the
afternoon sauntered toward him wearing faded
jeans, an equally faded t-shirt, and a cowboy hat.

"Are you ready to see the ranch?" Her voice was
clipped.

"That's why I'm here." He gritted his teeth.
Damn it, he'd try to be polite. No need to start
out this visit at odds with her. "Lead the way."

"Let's head over to the stables, it's best to see it
on horseback. My dad said you were an experienced rider?" She asked as she strode past him.

His step hitched when he glanced down and
saw how her jeans highlighted her perfect heart-
shaped ass. *Whoa.* He shook his head and hurried

to fall into step alongside her, careful to keep his gaze on the path. "Grew up riding horses outside of Denver."

"You had horses? On a ranch, or...?" She looked up at him from underneath the brim of her tan hat. He caught a glimpse of smooth creamy skin and unpainted naturally rosy lips. Her eyes were hidden behind mirrored aviators. She smelled like sunshine and the outdoors. His gut tightened.

"Not exactly. I grew up next to a ranch and helped out in the stables. Everything from mucking out stalls, to grooming and exercising the horses. I ride every chance I can since then." His neighbor's horses had been one of his primary joys and reasons to smile growing up.

"Yeah, I couldn't imagine life without my horses and riding every day." She smiled, revealing straight white teeth.

Stop noticing her perfect ass and her equally perfect smile, damn it. "How many horses do you have here? I saw five barns?"

"Yes, five barns and close to one hundred horses between Hercules, the mares, foals, and yearlings. We've got one barn for the family's horses and that's where we're headed now. Are you up for a challenging mount or an easy ride?" One dark brow lifted.

"I'm always up for a challenge." No way would he get stuck on a slow horse. "So, the other barns are all your breeding mares?"

"Exactly. We also house Hercules, our stallion, at the far end of our personal stable."

"Makes sense." His shoulders relaxed. What do you know? When she wasn't sneering or snarling

at him, they were actually carrying on a civil conversation.

They reached the modern, meticulously maintained building with stalls running along the full
length and stopped inside the open doorway. Sam
waved to one of the grooms who was cleaning
some tack, "John, can you please saddle up Rocco
for him?"

Holt frowned. "I can saddle the horse." Did she
think he was incompetent?

"Don't worry about it. John knows where
Rocco is and it'll be faster. Come with me while
I saddle my horse."

He kept his gaze honed on the stables, resisting
the urge to look at her. They stopped in front of
one of the stalls on the right side and a gorgeous
palomino poked her head out and whinnied.

"Hi sweet Princess. Ready to go out?" She
crooned and leaned in to stroke the horse's face.

"Princess?" His first instinct was right—spoiled
little girls and their ponies.

"Her full name is Princess Buttercup. Didn't you
see *The Princess Bride*? She's the ultimate heroine."
She whipped off her sunglasses and her enormous
chocolate brown eyes widened.

He chuckled, his jaw softening. "Best movie
ever and you're right, Princess Buttercup stole the
show." Robin Wright was still one of the most
powerful, beautiful actresses in the business.

He couldn't fault the way Sam expertly saddled her horse before the groom approached with
Rocco, a grey gelding. Together, they led the
horses out into the sunshine and mounted. She
practically leapt onto her horse, as agile and grace-

ful as a jockey.

"We'll cover the whole ranch and finish over where we have sectioned off for the movie set." She turned her horse and trotted off, obviously used to people obeying her commands.

He followed her lead and admired her obvious athletic prowess. *Suck it up, Ericsson.*

Rocco proved to be the perfect mount, full of energy and spirit. He couldn't recall the last time he'd ridden simply for pleasure and not just as part of a scene in a movie. Stables weren't exactly abundant in his neighborhood and it wasn't like he had much free time.

Sam loosened the reins and cantered toward the gate where he'd entered. Damn, she looked like some kind of goddess. He loved speed, so he followed suit. The wind cooled his cheeks and the knots around the base of his neck dissipated with the fresh summer air and the freedom of flying unencumbered on the back of the powerful animal.

Watching her ride wasn't too tough of an ordeal either.

So he could ride.

So he was an absolute natural on Rocco.

So he was definitely a genuine horse lover. She would know.

The tight ball of tension in her belly uncoiled. The positive quality could help balance out his personality, because the arrogance set her teeth on edge.

Although he didn't seem too annoying today.

More like mildly bothersome. She could at least try to be civil while she showed him around.

Her shoulders softened, and she reined in by the enormous mahogany wood and wrought iron gate and paused while Holt joined her.

"This is where you came in. This entrance is primarily for the family and for those working with us on the breeding operations. Since you'll be staying here, you can use it." She gestured to the large wooden door set into the twelve-foot-high stone gate. "You shouldn't need to walk through, but I can give you the security code later in case Edgar or another guard isn't on duty. Okay?"

When he nodded his tawny head, she ticked off the points with her fingers. "Anybody affiliated with the movie besides you or Harry must use the south gate. Each person will be screened by security every time they arrive. If they fail to show proper identification or aren't on the list, they will not be allowed in. No exceptions. Got it?"

He nodded again. His large bronzed hands, crisscrossed with faded scars, were loose on the reins. "Sure. They're used to it. Every movie set has varying degrees of privacy and they'll know this one is tight."

"We'll ride along the perimeter so I can show you where the trails are and how the ranch is set up." *Stop focusing on those rugged hands.* She trotted along the protective fence covered with green winding vegetation and riotous fuchsia bougainvillea. Fragrance from expansive beds of scarlet and pure white roses floated around them.

They rode along in comfortable silence for a few more minutes and she assumed he was surveying the beauty of the property, just as she was. The pure splendor of the emerald hills and lush foliage had captured her soul when she'd first seen it as a heartbroken fifteen-year-old girl. More than a decade later, she never took it for granted.

They crested a large hill and she stopped and pointed down to the now-empty racetrack. He reined in next to her, his strong denim-clad leg mere inches from her own. The heat from his body caused the fine hairs on the back of her neck to prickle again.

Her tummy didn't flip flop. Definitely didn't tingle either. *Yeah, right.*

"Wow, a racetrack? I thought you just ran a breeding operation? Do you train the yearlings too?" His sculpted lips parted and damn, was that a slight dimple in his square chin? The tingling on the back of her neck traveled south.

Don't stare at his perfect chiseled, devastatingly handsome face. "The track was already here when my dad bought the ranch, so it made sense to keep it. We'll use it when the horses feel like flying and we've been playing with the idea of starting to train some of the foals born here. Pretty cool, right?"

"It's awesome." He grinned and another dimple winked in his lean cheek. "Does Rocco like it?" He shifted his gaze toward her, his expression lit up like someone who'd just received free front row seats to the Super Bowl.

Her pulse accelerated and her nipples hardened. "Yes Rocco likes it and no, we aren't racing on the track today. This is business, remember?" Her body apparently forgot that important tidbit.

Please don't let him notice.

"Okay, boss, whatever you say." The grin remained on his face. Maybe he wasn't such a jerk after all.

She laughed. "That's more like it."

"So, once we reach the other side of the track, we'll approach where you guys will be set up. There's room for some trailers and equipment. No night filming, no bright lights late because it will disturb the mares' circadian rhythms and it can mess with their fertility."

Business, this was all about business. Being civil was one thing, but skirting the edge of flirtation was unacceptable. She gripped the reins, seeking her composure. *Focus on the ranch.*

"Don't worry, no night scenes planned. They'll build a few structures for the outdoor set, which they can break down when those are done. And, the background shots of your horses can be filmed with a skeleton team. Harry said he'd make sure to only have the necessary actors and crew for each scene so it shouldn't ever get too crowded." His husky voice assured her as he easily matched her pace.

"I'm so glad you understand. You're making me feel better about all of this." She nudged Buttercup forward, determined to re-establish some distance between them. A red-tailed hawk soared overhead, iridescent turquoise dragonflies flitted about, and the quiet scene warmed her as it always did. To the west, pastures rolled out as far as the eyes could see, with mares peacefully grazing on the verdant lawns. When they reached one of the lines of split rail fences, her heart warmed.

"I'm looking forward to filming this movie here. It will be great. This place is just incredible. Can you show me the rest of the property?" He smiled, relaxed in the saddle.

"Sure. You've already seen the breeding shed, I'll show you the other stables, the rehabilitation facility, the foaling sheds, and where Amanda's vet practice is housed." Pride surged in her chest; Pacific Vista Ranch was the best in the country.

"Must be nice to keep it in the family."

Her spine went rigid. Surely she had misunderstood his overly bland tone. "Excuse me?"

"I said it must be nice to keep it in the family." His gaze was scanning the horizon, not even paying attention to her.

Heat suffused her cheeks and she whipped her head to glare at him. "What's that supposed to mean?"

"Well, you run the breeding operation and your sister is the equine vet, right?" He shrugged. "Not everybody is so lucky to have a dad who owns a ranch like this. No offense, but some people actually have to apply for jobs."

"There's no *luck* involved. My sister is a frickin' genius and graduated top of her class from Virginia Tech Veterinary School. And, I'm one of the best breeding managers in the country because I work my ass off." She wheeled Buttercup around. *Total asshat.* "Some of us have real jobs and don't just play make-believe all day." She snapped over her shoulder and let Buttercup fly.

Arrogant baboon. The breeze helped cool her cheeks, but the anger bubbled up into her throat. He wasn't the first man to assume she was in her role because her dad handed it to her on a platter. How dare he question Amanda though? Nobody insulted her family. This is what she got for ignoring her initial gut instinct. And she'd actually just been flirting with him? *Rude, Hollywood jerk.*

She'd done her duty and shown him where the movie would be filmed. Someone else could show him the rest of it. Or he could scurry back to L.A.

"Wait up." Rocco's pounding hooves were closing the distance between them. No way in hell would she finish the tour—she'd fulfilled her duty by showing him the gates and movie location. She clucked at Princess Buttercup to speed up.

She reached the stable first and leapt to the ground, her jaw set, and steam puffing out of her ears. Dylan was walking up the hill toward her, looking cool and lovely in one of flowered sundresses. Not even her sweet twin could soothe her fiery temper right now.

"Sam, oh, and hello, Mr. Ericsson." Dylan smiled up at the idiot.

"Call me Holt, please." The rude baboon jumped off Rocco and flashed his pearly whites at her sister. Probably veneers. Come to think of it, his messy blond hair was probably highlighted.

"Holt." Dylan's smile remained in place. "Did Sam show you everything you needed to see?"

"Well, she was going to show me the other stables and the rehab and vet building, but if you're available maybe you can show me?" Holt's tone was honey sweet, completely opposite of his sharp comments a few moments ago. Why was he standing so close to her sister?

"You've seen what you need to see. Just go back

to La-La Land, where you belong." She ignored Dylan's gasp and wide eyes.

He addressed Dylan, all innocent charm. "I drove down to see everything today before we arrive for filming. I'd hate to go back to L.A. and not be able to tell Harry I'd seen the entire ranch."

"I can do it. I've finished work for the day. We can just walk over from here if that's okay?" Dylan had always been the polite one.

He smiled and took a step closer to her twin. "If you're sure it isn't too much trouble?"

"No trouble at all. See you at dinner, Sam." Dylan's brow creased momentarily, sensing the tension. They strolled off toward the other barns, like they didn't have a care in the world.

Why was her sister being so friendly toward Mr. Hollywood? Wasn't he the enemy?

"Perfect. You two go. I'll take care of the horses." She muttered to Buttercup and Rocco.

Because that's what privileged little rich girls do.

CHAPTER 5

"THE RANCH IS AMAZING. YOU'RE lucky to live here." Holt smiled, the knots of tension gripping the back of his skull relaxing in Dylan's agreeable company.

Why was Sam so damn sensitive about him simply stating the truth about working for her father? It was a fact, right? Even though she'd been handed her job, she was smart, passionate, and an expert on horses and her ranch. His respect for her had grown throughout the ride. For a while there, he'd actually enjoyed her company. Sure, he'd been blunt, but shouldn't she be able to handle it?

"We are. It's truly been our safe haven since we moved here after—" She hesitated, but continued quickly, "After we moved from Los Angeles."

"Look, Harry will bend over backwards to make sure you won't even notice we're here. Only necessary crew will be here when we film." He softened his tone. Why couldn't Sam be more like her sister? Even-tempered and polite?

"You're nice to say so. I hope that's the case. Anyway, here is the first stable and the other three are basically identical, with thirty stalls each. I believe my dad's cleared out some stalls for the movie star horses you're bringing."

They stepped into the entrance of the enormous terracotta-roofed structure. High wood-beamed ceilings, huge stalls running along each side, and a well-groomed dirt floor appeared to be impeccably maintained. Soft whinnies and snorts punctuated the mild summer breeze and the familiar scent of fresh cut hay reached his nostrils.

"Wow. These horses have it made and the Hollywood ones will be spoiled." Everything here was top-of-the-line and expensive. The smells might be the same, but nothing else here remotely resembled his neighbor's ancient wood barns he'd grown up close to in Colorado.

Through the open entrance on the far end, he spotted a few single-level structures, which weren't as massive as the stables. "What are those buildings to the west?"

"Come on, I'll show you. Amanda might be around too and we can say hello." She seemed to float over the ground, unlike her twin who stomped like an angry toddler. *Damn it all to hell, stop comparing them*.

"So, those are the vet buildings?"

"Exactly. The clinic, offices, and the rehabilitation facility. It's state of the art."

"Of course it is." Damn, he needed to watch the sarcasm around Dylan. She didn't deserve his snark. "I mean everything looks like it's the best."

Her brows drew together, but either she was too well mannered to acknowledge his rudeness or chose to ignore it. "Why wouldn't we have the best for our horses? Come on in." She pulled open a glass-paned door leading into a single-story cream stucco building.

An empty pale green waiting room with a long reception desk and plenty of natural light greeted them. "Amanda, are you in here?" She smiled at him. "We're really formal around here."

"Dylan, is that you?" Dr. McNeill hurried in from a room on the far end of the sunny space. She jolted and halted mid-stride when she saw him.

Her smooth golden brow creased. "Oh, hi Holt. I thought you were touring the ranch with Sam?"

"Yeah, we were, but she had to finish something up, so Dylan offered to show me the rest." No need for the two nice McNeill sisters to hear about his scene with Sam.

"What did you think? Maybe it isn't right for the film after all?" A hopeful note lifted the vet's voice.

"Actually, it's absolutely perfect."

"Good to know. It's just tough. I hope you can understand. We'd really prefer anything to do with Hollywood and the movie industry stay in the past. It brings up a lot of negative memories." The eldest McNeill sister wound her long slender fingers together.

His jaw tightened. Damn it, their past wasn't his fault and he needed this movie to be a blockbuster hit to protect his investment and set up his future. But, his conscience prickled. "I'm sorry."

Dylan moved to her side and slid a slender arm around her older sister. A united front. "We know it isn't your fault. If the press gets wind of a movie being filmed here, it could get really ugly," Amanda said.

"Look, I know Harry will make it work and

I'm sure your dad will kick his ass if he doesn't." Sweat popped up on the back of his neck. Harry damn well better have it under control.

Desperate to change the subject, Holt swung his gaze around the room. "So, where's the rehab facility?"

Amanda nodded. "Let me show you. We can cut through the back way because a lot of it is attached."

He exhaled and followed them into a long hall-way, which opened into a huge space with various stalls. Just like the clinic, the vast area was bathed in plenty of natural light. Assorted contraptions lined the walls, some recognizable and others looking like something from a *Star Trek* conven-tion.

"So, this is the primary rehab facility where we treat injured or sick horses. Off-season and some-times even during the season, I also work with other local animals. We've helped many of them get new jobs as dressage or jumpers or pasture horses."

"That's great you work with all kinds of horses. And I'm assuming you're referring to ones that can no longer race?" He knew the McNeill ranch specialized in quarter horses specifically for rac-ing.

Amanda nodded. "Exactly. Many of the horses you see in our pastures never raced for a variety of reasons, but they have great bloodlines and are excellent for breeding. They also can work as nannies for the foals."

Holt cautiously approached a huge, bizarre-look-ing device. "Is this one of those horse treadmills?"

Amanda laughed. "It's called the Equisizer and yes, it helps the horses walk to get exercise and build strength so they can hopefully return to normal."

"Okay, this is pretty amazing. How big of a horse can it hold?" It looked big enough for an elephant to stroll along on its wide track.

"Well, we've gotten Hercules on there before and he weighs twelve hundred pounds." Dylan piped in as she moved to the next giant piece of equipment. "This is my favorite: the theraplate. The horse just stands on it and it vibrates. It helps just about everything from increasing circulation to curing tummy aches."

"You know horses can't vomit, right, Holt?" Amanda asked.

"Right and they also never stop eating. The plate helps?" The old school ranch where he'd helped out certainly didn't have one of those. In fact, it didn't have any kind of rehab equipment at all. Another difference between the wealthy and the rest of the world.

"It can help prevent colic—pretty incredible. And my favorite is the saltwater bath on the other side. Thirty-five-degree water helps soothe and encourage the healing process."

"All of this is incredible." Everything in the facility was shiny, clean, and looked brand new.

"We're really proud of it. We've also got the Pegasus laser, it's infrared and can heal wounds faster." Amanda smiled. "We love the horses and we make sure they get the best of everything."

"Wow, you've got quite the operation here." They were using their money for admirable purposes. As an animal lover, he approved.

"Do you work with the horses too, Dylan?" She always seemed to wear dresses, so it seemed unlikely.

She shook her head. "Only if I'm sketching them. I love horses and I ride, but I don't work for the ranch. I'm an artist."

"That fits. What type?"

"I'm a painter, but I love to work with charcoal too. Landscapes, portraits, a little abstract, a little old school impressionism. It all depends." She waved a slender arm.

"She also writes poetry and plays the piano. We joke she got all the ladylike talent and Sam and I are the dudes." Amanda laughed.

"Strong women don't have to be dudes. My mom is the most incredible woman on earth and she doesn't have to act like a guy to do it." Maybe someone could alert Sam to be more like her sisters. Damn it, why did she keep popping up in his brain?

"Oh, that's so sweet. Are you close to her?" Dylan asked, her tip-tilted chocolate eyes wide.

"I am. And to my little sister. They mean the world to me." His chest tightened. He would move heaven and earth for them.

"Are they up in Los Angeles too?" Amanda asked.

He shook his head. "No. They still live in Littleton, just outside of Denver."

"That's so far away. Do you see them often?" Dylan's dark brows drew together.

"I travel so much, I don't see anyone often. I visit when I can." He ignored the hollowness under his breastbone. Once he received the payout for this movie, he hoped to convince his mom and sister to relocate to California.

"Aren't most of the movies shot in LA anymore?" Amanda said.

He shook his head. "These days a lot of movies and TV shows are filmed in Atlanta, Vancouver, North Carolina, and all over the world because Southern California is so expensive. I go where the work takes me."

"That sounds like a tough life." Dylan frowned.

"I make great money, there's always something new happening, and I get to see the world on someone else's dime. What's tough about that?" He injected enthusiasm into his voice.

Lately, the shine had worn off the planes, trains, and automobiles. Playing the guitar or reading books in interchangeable, generic hotel rooms or grabbing drinks with the crew in another dive bar no longer appealed.

Amanda tilted her head. "Are you trying to convince us or yourself?"

He forced a laugh, but her question struck a nerve. "Not trying to convince anyone of anything." He'd worked his tail off for the last twelve years to become the top stuntman and the money he'd amassed would set up his new future. Nothing else mattered.

"Of course, I didn't mean to give you a hard time."

"No worries. I need to head back to L.A." He couldn't call it home, especially after seeing how the McNeills lived. "Thanks again for the tour, I appreciate it. Good day, ladies." He lifted his hand in a half-wave.

He strolled back to his truck, and hopped in. Flicking on the ignition, he scratched the day-old scruff on his chin. This movie symbolized the turning point for his adult life. As long as Harry ensured everything ran smoothly, he'd play a challenging role in an intriguing movie, benefit from a little peace and quiet on a dream ranch, and achieve freedom once his highest paycheck to date hit his bank.

How hard could it be to avoid one bad-tempered little redhead?

CHAPTER 6

SAM STRETCHED UP ON HER tiptoes and pecked Angela's cheek, then grabbed a shiny green apple from the cheerful striped bowl on the kitchen counter. "I won't make it home for dinner tonight, because I'm going to try to make ballet after I knock out a few errands."

"Oh, good, I love to see you dancing again. You're a vision on toe shoes. I'll save you a plate, sweet girl—I'm making tamales and I know how much you love them."

Sam snorted. "Not so sure I'm a vision, but I do love going back. And yes——a heaping plate. You make the best tamales in the world." Sam grinned in anticipation of stuffing her face after ballet. Not that she was eating her feelings about the movie shoot starting tomorrow—no, of course not—she just had a healthy appetite, that's all.

Angela's dark eyes twinkled and the dimple in her full cheek appeared as she smiled indulgently at her. "I know how you can eat more than your dad, don't worry, I'll load it up for you."

"You're the best. See you tonight." She twirled out of the kitchen and started down the wide, biscuit-colored hallway.

Sam adored Angela and couldn't imagine any

of their lives without her peaceful strength. Back when they'd first fled Hollywood and moved to Pacific Vista Ranch, they quickly realized they were in over their heads. Her dad hired Angela to manage the household and ranch. Her police officer husband had been killed the year before, in the line of duty. She'd moved into one of the guesthouses with her sons and assimilated into the McNeill's lives.

After the first year, the business relationship turned romantic between her dad and Angela. By that time, it had been two years and the initial grief of losing their mom had dissipated, but their scars ran deep. Having a caring, warm, strong woman as a role model helped immensely. Angela was the opposite of their fragile, artistic mother—practical, no-nonsense, yet warm and caring too. By the time Angela and Chris fell in love, the girls were comfortable with it and happy to see their dad feeling loved and supported by such a great lady.

"Samantha." Dylan's voice was practically a whisper, yet it stopped her in her tracks, two steps out of the kitchen.

"What's going on? Why do you have a suitcase?" Her breath caught in her throat and dread filled her when she raked her gaze over her usually ethereal sister.

Instead of one of her floaty ensembles, Dylan was dressed in slim black pants, a black t-shirt, and Converse tennis shoes. She had a roller-bag with her artist supply case propped on top of it. Her hair was slicked back from her pale, make-up-free face.

"I can't stay here while they film. It's stirring up too many memories. I'm afraid to go to sleep." Her usually glowing complexion looked dull, and bluish circles marred the underneath of her sister's brown eyes. For years, Dylan had been haunted by nightmares, particularly from one incident when Sam had been late to meet her to leave school and one aggressive reporter had chased Dylan down the sidewalk, causing her to trip and slam into the pavement. Sam still felt guilty for not protecting her sibling.

Sam's stomach clenched into knots. What would she do without her twin's calming influence to soothe her own jangled nerves? "You seemed fine. I need you here. We need you here."

Angela glided into the hallway, wrapped a strong arm around her sister's narrow shoulders, and led her back into the sunny kitchen. "Dylan, sweetheart, are you sure? Where are you planning on going?"

"I'll be fine. It just hit me yesterday and I know we'll all be better off if I'm not here. Sam—I think you'll be able to focus better without having to cheer me up." Dylan's eyes pleaded with her.

"But where are you going? For the whole shoot? That's a month or more." Panic began to bubble in her throat. How could she deal with damn Holt Ericsson without the buffer of her sister?

"One of my girlfriends from art school lives in Paris now. It's right in the middle of the art scene and will be an incredible opportunity for me to paint, to be away, to immerse myself. It's an opportunity I can't pass up."

"Paris? What's this about France?" Their dad

stepped into the kitchen.

"I need to focus on my work. It's impossible with a movie crew on our property. You chose to allow the movie to be filmed here despite none of us wanting it. I thought I would be okay, but I'm not. It resurrects too much about mom's death. So, I'm going." Dylan's cherry red lips flattened into a mutinous line. Uh-oh. Sam recognized the look. Dylan didn't share her short fuse, but when she dug her heels in, she was as stubborn as a donkey and nobody could change her mind.

Sam silently applauded her sister's brave speech. She rushed forward and enveloped her sister in a bear hug. They'd been apart for longer periods of time back when Dylan had gone to art school and Sam remained behind and studied biology at San Diego State University, but this was different. Her twin was leaving without giving Sam a choice but to stay. Then again, she hadn't lived anywhere else––the ranch was her refuge. Or, had been before this movie debacle.

"Are you sure? Do you have enough money? What arrondissement are you staying in? Is it safe?" Her dad peppered her sister with the questions at a gunfire pace.

"Of course, Dad. You know Lily's family has owned a place in Paris for years. It's in the Marais and it's lovely. Sam, you should come join me for a few weeks. She needs a vacation and the stuntman guy really rubs her the wrong way." Dylan smiled for the first time since she'd entered the room.

"What? Ericsson? Did he do something? I'll have him kicked off the film, Harry be damned." Her dad pierced her with his hazel eyes, his cheeks flushing in what she recognized as the beginning of the famous McNeill temper about to ignite. She should know–– she'd inherited it from him lock, stock, and barrel.

"No, Dad, he didn't do anything. I just think he's an arrogant Hollywood blowhard." Sam scowled. "I need to stay here and make sure everything stays safe." *Please, like she could leave the ranch while it was under siege by a movie crew?*

"I've actually got an Uber coming for me now. My flight is later today and I want to get to the airport early." She smoothed one hand back over her topknot.

"Okay, okay. Now, have you written down the address and Lily's phone number and her parents' number and––" Their dad frowned.

"Dad, I'm going to Paris, not the high school prom. Please." Dylan laughed. "I've written it all down and my cell will work there. It will be fine"

"We'll all walk you out. Did you say goodbye to Amanda?" Chris and Angela flanked Dylan as they exited the kitchen and headed to the front door.

"I already did. She's the easy one to tell—not the emotional ones like you guys." Dylan smiled to soften her words.

They accompanied Dylan to the circular drive-way and helped load her belongings into the driver's silver compact car.

"Promise me you'll come visit," Dylan whispered in her ear.

"We'll see. Please take care of yourself." Sam squeezed her one more time.

"Okay, I'm out of here. I hope there are no

more surprises today. I don't know if I can deal with it." Sam waved at her dad and Angela and headed to her white Land Rover.

Damn it, this movie filming on the ranch was causing ripples from the past to morph into pounding waves. She would not relive everything with her mom right now. Or ever again. Once was enough. Thank goodness she was heading to ballet later. She'd hopefully be able to work out the lump in her throat and the prickling behind her eyes.

CHAPTER 7

HOLT RETURNED PETE'S WAVE AS he drove through the South gate entrance onto the McNeill's ranch. The security guard had recognized his truck immediately, so he got express entrance now. That had to be good, right?

He whistled as he pulled up to the main house to meet Angela and get the keys to the guesthouse where he'd be staying for the next several weeks. After being on the road for more than a decade, packing was a cinch, at least when he wasn't somewhere like the hills of Hungary in January or the swamps of Louisiana in August. A couple duffel bags and his guitar and he was good to go. His shoulders relaxed when he didn't see the white Land Rover he'd learned was Sam's. He was in too good of a mood today to wrangle with her.

Everything was falling into place for his secret plans for the future. Not that he was keeping it a secret on purpose. He'd just hung up with his accountant and she'd confirmed he was on track. His mom and sister heartily approved. This film would be the last one and it needed to go off without a hitch.

He hummed as he sauntered up to the house. Maybe Dylan would answer the door again.

Although he'd realized the other afternoon, despite her sweetness and loveliness, he didn't feel any spark of attraction to her. It made no sense. No, when he was on McNeill property, the primary sensation evoked was anger, annoyance, or impatience, all at the hands of one Ms. Samantha McNeill. Not today, though, nothing could bother him.

The door swung open before he could ring the bell and Mrs. Angela McNeill smiled warmly at him. She was an attractive brunette in her fifties, tall, with an athletic build. Thus far, she'd been nothing but welcoming to him.

"Hi, Holt. I'm glad you made it. I've got the keys, so why don't we walk over to your new home away from home?"

"Great. Should I move my truck or leave it parked there?"

"Let's walk over and then you can come get the truck. The guesthouse isn't far and it has its own parking. But, this way you can see the path so when you come up for dinner and such, you'll know the shortcut." She stepped out of the doorway and pulled the enormous wooden door closed behind her.

"Dinner?" He fell into step with her long strides.

"Of course, we'd love to have you over for Sunday dinners—you're our guest." She smiled at him, as if this were the most normal scenario in the world.

His eyes widened. Family dinners? Guest? "It's really kind of you, but I wouldn't want to get in the way. The hours are crazy…"

Her easy smile remained in place. "You come

when you feel like it. 7 p.m. It's an open invitation."

He shrugged and followed her through the sun-drenched courtyard framed with giant palm trees, birds of paradise, and lush clusters of fuchsia and violet bougainvillea. The Santa Ana winds had finally dissipated and a cool Southern California breeze ruffled his hair as they strolled along the gray-stone paved path.

Had he stepped into a Disney movie? Shimmering hummingbirds flitted over tidy rows of fragrant pink and white rose bushes planted along the cream-colored stucco walls. Water gurgled from the spouts of a pair of dolphins gracing an azure-tiled fountain.

After they turned the corner, the open space widened dramatically and an Olympic-sized swimming pool sparkled in the sunshine and a white-canopied cabana beckoned. An enormous built-in barbeque, bar area, and outdoor dining set signaled this was party central at the McNeill mansion. Because he'd seen tons of estates in Bel Air and the Hollywood Hills, he managed not to gawk. The way he'd gaped when he'd arrived in L.A., back when he was a relatively innocent eighteen-year-old.

But damn, nothing like luxury mansions to remind him he'd grown up one step away from the neighboring trailer park. And no matter how hard he worked, he'd never live like this.

When they crested another sloping green hill, he caught the panoramic view of the ranch and in the distance, a peek of the Pacific Ocean. He paused. "Whoa."

"Pretty spectacular, isn't it?" Angela patted his shoulder. "The first time I saw this view, my mouth dropped open. I couldn't believe a refuge like this existed so close to San Diego proper."

"It's as beautiful as any view I've seen in all my travels. You McNeills are lucky." He shook his head. What would it be like to see this view every day and know it was yours? He'd lived like a nomad for so long, he'd adjusted to not caring where he laid his head at night. He snorted. As if he could afford anything like this, even with his future plans.

"I've been here more than a decade and I'll tell you, it never gets old. Okay, we'll take the left fork in the path here. Almost there."

"What is on the right?" Good thing he had a decent sense of direction.

"The stables. I'm sure you'll be there a fair amount."

"Thanks. I will. It's nice to know the shortcut." Was Sam down there now? Damn. Where had that come from?

Angela paused in front of a single-story house bigger than Holt's childhood home. Hell, it was bigger than the new house he'd purchased for his mom and sister five years ago. "Okay, here we are."

"Wow, can my whole family move in?" he half-joked.

"You have a family?" Angela turned her head toward him as she twisted the large pewter door-knob.

"My mom and my younger sister, Jenny. I guess when you said guesthouse I figured it'd be a cottage." *Idiot.*

"Well, the house definitely holds a family of eight comfortably." Angela laughed and entered the house. "My son Grant preferred living here to being with us in the main house. He stays here when he's in town."

"Wow." He halted and looked around. Pretty sweet digs.

He followed her along the wide marble-tiled hallway which opened into an enormous great room, with soaring wood-beamed ceilings, a kitchen fit for a chef on the right side of the room, and a pale grey granite island surrounded by several navy upholstered bar stools.

To the left, a fireplace tall enough for the McNeill's prized stallion to stand in occupied the wall. Two large L-shaped charcoal gray couches, a couple over-sized black leather chairs, a dark coffee table, and a widescreen television made up the perfect man cave.

"Right? I love this place." Angela grinned. "Let me show you the bedrooms and then I'll take you to the back patio so you can see the Jacuzzi and the fire pit."

He was definitely moving up in the world.

"This is the master bedroom. This room should work for you, right?"

"Uh, yeah. This will work." This place rivaled some of the nicest hotels he'd stayed anywhere in the world.

Was this for real? The bedroom was enormous, with the same wood-beamed ceilings and pale gray oak floors as the great room. A huge king-size bed dominated one wall and a nook with a large desk and chair served as a mini-den or workspace. The far wall was a set of French doors opening to the back patio.

"Great. There are three more bedrooms on the other side of the house, but you can explore those on your own. The fridge is stocked and you can call up to the main house if you need anything at all."

"You're being more than generous. I am truly grateful, Mrs. McNeill." He followed her back into the kitchen.

"Call me Angela. So, you're from Colorado? Are your mom and sister still there or did they come to California with you?" She bustled around the kitchen, adjusting a dishtowel, peeking in the fridge, and generally making him miss his mom.

"Yes, we grew up right outside of Colorado, a little suburb; well, not so little anymore, called Littleton. They're both still there."

"Your mother must be proud of your success. Chris mentioned you were the top stuntman in Hollywood?" Angela leaned against the counter.

"I've been successful and sure, my mom is proud of me."

"Well, I hope everything goes smoothly with this film. It's tough on the family and I hope you can understand and not take it personally if anyone seems to take it out on you." A slight frown marred her friendly face.

"I was the messenger, but at the end of the day, I'm just the stuntman for the lead actor. No, I don't take things personally, but Sam sure seems prickly." Usually he could smooth things over with anyone. Apparently not her.

"Oh good. I know Samantha can be..." She paused and glanced skyward before looking directly at him. "Over-protective, but she has a warm heart. So, anything else I can answer for you before I let you settle in?"

"Well, actually yes. This might sound kind of—" He ran his tongue around his teeth. "Funny. Is there a local ballet studio around here?" The words tumbled out of his mouth. Damn it. Guys did ballet all the time. Hell, NFL players did ballet. He wasn't apologizing for his training regime.

"Ballet studio?" Angela's dark brows soared up to her hairline. "You study ballet?"

He cringed. "I wouldn't call it study. Look, I've got to stay in peak shape. Brazilian jujitsu, running, weights, but ballet helps me with agility like nothing else can. When I'm doing some of the hairier stunts, it's probably saved my life." He wasn't defensive, not at all. Right. His baby sister teased him mercilessly about it and had even sent him some pink tights last Christmas.

"No need to explain. It makes perfect sense to me. I'm just surprised, that's all." She raised her hands off to stop his excuses and grinned. "You don't usually see the guys wearing cowboy boots at the barre. Ballet has several different purposes besides performing *The Nutcracker*. As a matter of fact, there's a studio tucked into Rancho Santa Fe."

"Yeah, I don't exactly advertise this part of my training plan. So I can drop in?" Perfect. He could be discreet and nobody would be the wiser, unlike L.A., where he could run into someone in the industry at any given time. Never fun.

"Absolutely. We know the owner, since the girls…"

"The girls?" *Shit.*

"It's just a local studio and the girls danced when they were younger." Her eyes twinkled and her smile broadened. "It's called The Dance Studio and I happen to know there is a 5:30 class today. Just tell Cecile that Angela sent you over." Angela waved and left.

CHAPTER 8

SAM PARKED HER CAR IN the hidden spot around the back of The Dance Studio and shut off the engine. She'd run on autopilot all afternoon, but she'd finished her errands. Anytime thoughts of Dylan running away to Paris surfaced, she ruthlessly squashed them down. Of course it would be fine. She would be fine. She was always fine.

But damn——the yin to her yang would be gone and she had a feeling Dylan's soothing influence would be missed over the next month. Not like her sister lacked inner fire, but her twin had received the lion's share of softness. So, she'd just have to ride Buttercup more, dance more frequently, and heck, maybe even work to step up her practically non-existent dating life.

Not that she was against having a boyfriend, or even a casual friends-with-benefits situation, but who had the time? Maybe a fling with a surfer boy could be a distraction. Heck, she could call up a few of her SDSU girlfriends and even drag Amanda out for a girls' night. She hadn't seen her old friends recently, but everyone knew she went underground during breeding season.

"Enough" she muttered to herself. No need to ruminate. When she danced, all of her emotions lifted up and out of her tissues and the sensations were the language of her body.

Grabbing her bag containing her leotard, tights and shoes, she headed into the back entrance of the studio. She'd known Cecile since they'd moved to Rancho Santa Fe and was able to come and go as she pleased. Time to sweat everything to do with the movies away.

Samantha stuck the final pin into her sleek bun and smoothed down her plain black leotard. Her pale pink tights and ballet slippers always transported her back to her childhood, when dancing was her whole world. She loved this studio with its no nonsense layout and no frills approach. For the next hour, she prayed she'd find some solace.

She slammed the black metal locker door shut, spun the combination lock, and hurried out into the large square room. Sunlight filtered in from enormous rectangular windows on the west wall, reflecting off ruthlessly polished light oak floors. Usually she arrived early and staked out her favorite spot away from the gleaming mirrors, but tonight, only a few spaces remained along one of the three wooden ballet barres. Oh well, she wasn't so rigid she couldn't dance in a different area of the studio. She was flexible. Flexible, ballet—ha ha. She snickered to herself as she extended one leg up onto the barre and folded forward, stretching her hamstrings.

Her eyelids closed and she focused on her breath. Time to channel quiet, calm, and grace. Nothing more. The crisp scent of ivory soap alerted her another student filled the empty spot beside her, but she filtered out the pleasant smell and kept her nose pressed into her shin. When she danced, everything except the music and the ballet faded away.

The instructor, Cecile, clapped her hands. "Ladies and gentlemen, first position, left hand on the barre."

Sam's eyes popped open. Gentlemen? There was a guy in class? Curious, she swept her leg down and glanced around. Her mouth dropped open.

Him? Too Hot Hollywood in *her* ballet studio? Her fingers curled into fists and heat rose into her cheeks. "You. Did you follow me here?"

"Huh?" He gaped at her.

"Samantha. Silence. First position." Cecile snapped with a frown.

She swallowed a scream of frustration and whirled back to face the mirrors and there he was, lurking directly behind her. Six feet of ripped bronze shoulders and sinewy biceps were highlighted in all black exercise pants and a tank. Damn it, she didn't want to be impressed. Or affected. Or have her safe haven intruded upon. Again.

She gripped the barre with her left hand and squeezed. Good thing it was sturdy or she might just crush the wood to dust. She'd pretend it was his smirking face. He'd chased off her sister with his news. Well, it wasn't his movie and he'd just delivered the message, but the proverb about shooting the messenger didn't exist for nothing.

How was she going to immerse herself in the music and the movement with him breathing down her neck? Was this man going to single-handedly ruin her life?

Her body automatically obeyed the teacher's commands, plié, tendu, degage. The fine hairs on the back of her neck stood at high alert, and her eyes kept darting to the powerful limbs moving in perfect synchronization behind her. Instead of measuring her own alignment in the mirror, her gaze was drawn to the perfect shadow behind her, every sweep of his arm performed with flawless precision. She shook her head to stop her surreptitious or not so surreptitious staring.

He represented everything she hated about people from Hollywood. Cocky, too good-looking—well, she wasn't blind, was she? Damn Holt Ericsson. *Focus on the ron de jambe, girl.*

She angled her body and Holt intruded into her peripheral vision. As if she'd been able to ignore him from her current spot. Inhale and exhale. She absolutely was not distracted by his cat-like grace.

Much too close to her.

She peeked from under her lashes. Surprise registered when his leg sweep extended almost as far as hers. Impressive flexibility. Most men couldn't come close to that level of suppleness, especially the athletic muscular ones. His golden head was turned away from her, so she gave him the side eye for another millisecond. His long, sleekly muscled arm stretched overhead and a light film of perspiration gleamed on his skin. Okay, he might be an arrogant L.A. boy, but he was flawless.

A pity he would most likely open his mouth again.

Abruptly, he turned his head and snared her gaze. Busted. When his sculpted lips quirked into a knowing smile, she cursed his ego. With a huff, she whipped her head to face the mirror.

HOLT STRUGGLED TO MAINTAIN STEADY BREATH-
ing, but his usual self-control was failing him.
Had Angela sent him to this ballet studio on purpose? What was she trying to pull?

The last seven minutes and sixteen seconds had
been exquisite torture, standing directly behind
Sam. In a modest black leotard, pink tights,
and innocent pink ballet slippers, she no longer
resembled the bony, persnickety hooligan from
the ranch.

No, now she looked elegant.

Graceful.

Powerful.

In the bright lights of the studio, her abundant
auburn hair shimmered like polished bronze. Her
traditional dancer's bun revealed the milky pale
skin at the nape of her neck, usually obscured by
her hat or heavy braid. He caught himself before
he leaned forward and kissed it.

When she'd turned to the side, her profile transformed into one of the old-fashioned cameos his
mother collected. A blue vein ran from her smooth
forehead to the top of her high cheekbone, revealing a hint of vulnerability in what he'd believed
was an impenetrable fortress.

He'd been wrong.

She was just as beautiful as her twin sister.

He glimpsed the calluses on one small palm,
evidence of the work she performed each day.
Not the manicured hands of a spoiled girl, but a
serious woman. His entire body stiffened when

he contemplated those palms sliding over his skin.

How long was this class again? He'd never survive.

Her sinuous, mesmerizing dancing revealed another layer to Ms. Samantha McNeill. Underneath the tough shell lived an artist, a true ballerina. He came to ballet to work on agility and control, but she became one with the music, like he did when he played his guitar. Accustomed to working with and observing performers, he recognized her connection to the dance, even from the warm-up exercises. Sam wasn't just a horse-woman; she channeled the emotion of the dance from inside out.

Un-frickin' believable.

She smelled like heaven and the beads of perspiration along her upper shoulders beckoned. How would she taste? Sweet, like she looked now or tart, how she acted the remaining ninety-nine percent of the time? The yearning to stroke her rosy porcelain skin surged through him––would the flush spread to the rest of her skin when she was aroused?

"Mr. Ericsson. Attention." Cecile snapped.

He jolted. Busted. He glanced around to see what the rest of the class was doing and caught Sam's smirk. Now that expression he recognized. Somehow her attitude now seemed endearing instead of annoying. Yes, he'd been too quick to judge her. He would apologize.

When class ended, Holt wiped the sweat from his forehead and the back of his neck. The punishing pace suited him and he understood why Sam came to this studio. He'd have to return while he was in town.

"So, if someone had told me a guy like you would go to ballet, well, I would have laughed. You're full of surprises." Sam angled her head toward him as she slung her damp towel over her gorgeous shoulders.

He didn't detect a note of sarcasm from her, simply curiosity. "So you've got me figured out? Yeah, yeah, I know it might seem unexpected, but my ego can handle the jokes. I found it a few years back to help with the agility and control I need for certain types of stunts."

"Makes sense. You don't usually see the big macho guys in ballet." A hint of humor threaded her tone. They walked together toward the small entryway of the studio where the locker rooms were located.

"Big and macho? I'll have you know almost half of the NFL teams send their guys to ballet." Why didn't everyone know this?

"Defensive much? I've never seen one here, but you did okay. For a guy." Her rosy lips curved up.

"Wow, a compliment?" He pressed one hand over his chest. "I'm flattered."

"Seriously. You were legit. I've got to respect that. Do all stuntmen do ballet?" Her cheeks were as pink as her lips and with the soft smile on her face; he couldn't fathom how he'd ever missed how sexy she was.

"No idea. Some, I guess." He shrugged. "We aren't exactly a fraternity. But you're a ballerina. Do you perform?"

Her smile evaporated and she froze. "I'm not a ballerina."

"Of course you are. I know a performer when I see one." Huh. Interesting reaction.

She bit her plump lower lip and shook her head. "Well, I used to dance when I was a kid. Now I just come to stay flexible. It helps me with the horses."

They stopped in front of the locker rooms.

"Why'd you stop?" What wasn't she saying? Emotion simmered beneath the surface. An urgent need to know gripped him.

She froze again. Abruptly pivoted and ignored the question. "I need to grab my stuff. Are you headed back to the ranch?"

"Yeah." He exhaled.

"I'll show you a shortcut. Locals only. I'm in the back parking spot, so give me a second and when you see my car pull up, follow me." She turned and strode away.

No longer the ballerina, she'd morphed back to the bossy tomboy. How many layers were there? The ranch it was. Curiosity piqued, he climbed into his truck and turned the key. Samantha was out of her mind if she believed this was the end of the discussion.

He hit the accelerator and caught up to her.

CHAPTER 9

SAM GRIPPED THE STEERING WHEEL, will-ing the tingles in her belly to settle. Was he hot and bothered from ballet class too? Mr. Too Hot Hollywood threw her off balance with his insightful comments and his perfect physique. His unexpected perceptiveness about her dancing troubled her. Only her family knew of her passion for dance and how difficult returning to a studio had been after she'd hung up her toe shoes.

A few minutes later, she clicked her remote control and the wrought iron gate silently slid open. She cruised up to the house at a snail's pace so Holt could follow her through the entrance, shut off the engine, and hopped out. Holt pulled up, his truck's engine purring quietly, and rolled down the window. He beckoned to her.

"Yeah?" Wary, she stopped a few feet away from him. As a smartass he was dangerous, add the layer of sensitivity and this guy could be lethal.

"Well, the crew will start rolling in tomorrow and if you want me to fill you in on the schedule in advance, come down to the guesthouse later." He spoke faster than his usual husky drawl, his fingertips drumming on the window frame.

She hesitated and worked to steady her breathing.

"Come on, I won't bite." He grinned and the damn dimple in his cheek winked at her. The tingling in her stomach morphed into a long, slow roll.

"Umm...okay. It's probably the smart thing to do for the horses, I mean I should be prepared and know everything in advance, right? Let me grab dinner and I'll be down. Angela made tamales and they are to die for. Should I bring you down a plate?" She sucked in a shaky breath and willed herself to stop blathering like an idiot.

"She mentioned them. If there are leftovers, that would be great." His silvery blue eyes glimmered like aquamarines in the dim light.

"Great, see you in a bit." She turned and forced herself to saunter back to the house, while his hot gaze seared through her thin leotard.

When she reached the front door, she peeked back and he hadn't budged. He waved and departed down the drive. She quickly wrenched open the door and bolted inside, pausing to sag against the solid wood and catch her breath.

"So, you sent Holt to my ballet studio?" Sam patted herself on the back for her calm, even tone as she loaded her plate with mouthwatering tamales.

"Well, Samantha, he asked me for a studio close by and you know it's the only one in the Ranch. I didn't want to send him all the way down to Solana Beach." Angela's voice was neutral.

"The whole five miles down to Solana Beach?"

She snorted. "Anyway, I was surprised, that's all." More like distracted, aroused, and fascinated. Pesky details.

"Is he any good?" Her stepmom's voice held a hint of laughter.

"Actually, yes. He's graceful as a cat." Her stomach performed another dive and roll as a visual of his sinewy bronzed forearm flashed before her eyes. "Like I said, just surprised. He seems to be everywhere all of a sudden."

"Ericsson was at the ballet studio?" Her dad piped in when Sam joined him at the huge dining table.

Her sister echoed their father from the doorway, "The stuntman was at the ballet studio?"

"Yes, he was the only guy there, but it didn't seem to bother him. Go figure." She shoveled in her first bite and closed her eyes and moaned.

"The tamales are that good, aren't they?" Her dad laughed. "Well, Harry said he's the best at what he does. I hear lots of athletes are doing ballet these days. Top stuntman in the country. I know he's got a brown belt in Brazilian jiu jitsu."

"Brown belt? Not a black?" Her eyes widened and she stared at her dad.

"Actually, I think the brown is the highest in Brazilian—requires at least five years of dedicated practice." He nodded.

Sam forked in another bite and the spice and savory taste of the shredded beef exploded on her tongue. *Focus on dinner, not on how delicious Holt looked in a black tank top.*

She didn't want to appear too interested. She didn't want to be interested at all. But, dammit, he was interesting.

"Christopher, how in the world do you know that?" Angela laughed.

He grinned at his wife. "Just one more random fact I picked up somewhere. Who knows?"

"Any updates on the movie? Is everything still on schedule?" Amanda wasn't laughing as she stared at their father.

"Yes, the crew begins coming in tomorrow. Harry will be down and you can finally meet him."

"Where's he staying? I'd imagine you'd have invited him to stay at the guesthouse. It's kind of strange the stuntman is there instead." Her sister raised delicate light brown eyebrows.

"Well, Harry has a beach house on the cliffs in Encinitas. He said he wanted someone he trusts staying here and he sees Holt as a surrogate son." Chris shrugged. "This is a unique situation apparently."

"Well, I think it's weird." Sam said. A surrogate son? "Does Holt not have a father?"

"I actually don't know about his family, but I know Harry gave him his big break when he was a teenager and they've been close ever since." Her dad frowned. "I know you two got off on the wrong foot. Just try to be civil. He knows horses and movie sets. As long as the press stays away, I think we'll be fine."

"Okay." She stabbed another bite. No need to mention she was going down to the guesthouse. It wasn't a big deal.

"Dad, do you really think the press will be interested after all these years? Are we overreacting?" Amanda posed the question lurking in the back of everyone's mind.

"I hope we are." Chris's face was now solemn and he gripped his wife's hand on the table. "It's old news. We'll be fine."

Sam caught her sister's gaze across the table—her dad's baritone wasn't as confident as either of them would have preferred.

After they finished the meal, Sam cleared her empty plate and pulled out some tin foil to cover the heaping meal Angela had prepared.

"Sam dear, will you please bring a plate down to Holt? I promised him my tamales earlier today." Angela smiled serenely.

Sam jumped. "What?" Why did she feel guilty?

"Can you please bring a plate down to the guest-house for Holt? I already put it together for him." Her stepmom repeated, one eyebrow raised.

"Fine." She shrugged. Now she didn't have to sneak down there. Not that she needed to sneak, but…

"Do you want me to take it down to the guest-house? Holt doesn't bug me like he does you and he is awfully easy on the eyes." Amanda laid a slender hand on her shoulder.

"Easy on the eyes, seriously?" She shook her head. "It's fine. I need to talk with him anyway."

"Hmmm…will you be discussing playing the leads in Swan Lake?" Amanda teased.

"Very funny." She laughed despite the quickening of her heartbeat imagining the outfit he'd have to wear if he portrayed the prince. "He mentioned he could share some intel before the movie crew arrives over the next couple of days. I want to be prepared, that's all." She gripped the plate tightly.

Her sister smirked. "Hmmm...I thought you found him arrogant, annoying, and frustrating? Rude and offensive?"

"Look, he was a total idiot in the barn. But, if I'm going to protect our horses, our ranch, and our privacy, I need to stay close to the action and the more I know, the better. Right?" Who was she trying to convince?

"If you say so." Amanda's smile was angelic, but her eyes danced.

Clutching the plate in both hands, she whirled to face her sister. "That's all it is. Cut out the teasing."

"You're just being sensitive, which isn't like you at all. I think you might have a little crush on the blond god." Amanda's green eyes twinkled with mischief. Although she was the sensible sister, she had the McNeill sense of humor.

"Blond god?" Sam sniffed.

"He's better looking than the star he's stuntman for and that's saying a lot. Just be careful—he's a Hollywood charmer."

Her pulse kicked and she gripped the tamales like a lifeline. "You're totally overreacting. I'm an adult, I can handle him."

"I know, I know. It's just fun to watch your red-head complexion give you away. You and Dylan can never hide your blushes." Amanda hugged her. "And it's better to joke than stay upset the entire time of the shoot. I'm glad you're being so vigilant. I will be too. I just wish Dylan hadn't run away."

"It's probably for the best. I'll worry about her less in Paris than here on the ranch during the filming. Okay, I'm heading over for a bit." She bit her lip, and then shook her head.

That's all it was, right? Watching out for the ranch? Her unprecedented reaction to Holt's masculinity was irrelevant. She had a duty to her family and said duty included her horses.

"Don't do anything I wouldn't do." Amanda called after her, the laughter bubbling through her voice.

She refused to dignify the ridiculous comment with a response. Her sister wasn't exactly daring, so the list of potential risks she would take by going to see Holt was limited.

SWALLOWING A FLUTTER OF NERVES IN HER throat, she rapped on the door. She was simply going for business. Ranch business. Bringing him dinner was simply being polite, like her father had raised her to be. So why was her heart hammering against her ribcage?

"It's unlocked." A muffled voice called. So much for manners. Holt apparently didn't seem to bother with them.

She hesitated a moment. She smoothed back an errant strand into the ballet bun she hadn't bothered to unravel. Although she'd changed out of her dance gear into her favorite old pair of jeans and a super-soft t-shirt, she hadn't been in the mood to mess with her hair. Briefly, she regretted not being more like her twin sister, talented with makeup and hair. But, nope, Dylan had received the lion's share of feminine genes.

Whatever. She opened the door, and then froze. He was rubbing his hair dry with a white towel slung over one shoulder. The pristine white material emphasized his bronzed skin. Tiny beads of moisture clung to chiseled pecs and the light sprinkling of golden hair on his chest was the only thing preventing him from looking like a marble statue. Barely. Shredded eight-pack abs and sharp V-cuts of muscle converged at the waistband of a pair of jeans as faded as her own. Her mouth suddenly parched, she swallowed. Hard.

"Sorry, I got stuck on the phone." He grinned and tossed the towel onto a nearby chair.

She jerked her gaze up to his face, which had to be safer, right? Her pulse thrummed in her temple and heat descended to her belly. Damn. His face was definitely not safer than his gorgeous body.

"How'd you get that scar?" She blurted out the words, desperate to distract herself from his pure physical presence. He really needed to put on a shirt. Pronto.

"Scar? Which one?" He laughed, seemingly oblivious to her reaction, thank goodness.

"Forehead. The one across your forehead." A flaw. Weren't scars flaws? Why did it make him look just a little dangerous? And it did save him from utter perfection. Didn't it?

"Oh, that one. A bar fight. Got cracked over the head with a beer bottle." He rubbed his forehead with a rueful smile.

"Bar fight? You get into bar fights?" Actually, she wasn't surprised but her mouth seemed to be moving without her mind engaging at all. At least if she were talking then she wasn't drooling, right?

He shrugged. "Well, sure. Here or there. But this one happened on set when another stuntman got a little too eager and actually broke the bottle over my head."

His wintry blue eyes snagged hers and she couldn't look away. Her mind blanked.

"Something smells delicious." His shimmering gaze didn't waver from hers.

Was he complimenting her on her perfume? Wait, she didn't wear perfume. Her soap? She bit the inside of her lower lip, willing her brain to resume functioning.

"Are those the tamales?" He gestured with one hand toward the foil-covered plate she held.

"Tamales. Of course, the tamales smell as good as they taste." She marched toward the kitchen and the microwave. Idiot. She brushed his bare shoulder when she passed him and goose bumps erupted down her arm. *Control yourself, girl.* Simple animal attraction, that's all.

"I'll heat it up in the microwave while you put on a shirt." Oh crap, had she really said it out loud? She squeezed her eyes closed.

"Great, thanks. I'll be right back." He sounded totally unperturbed. He was probably accustomed to running around shirtless.

Wiping her damp palms against her jeans, she blew the pesky tendril of hair off her now warm forehead and reviewed the rulebook for how to act like a normal person.

Heat up food like a friendly neighbor.

Discuss the movie like a professional.

Go to bed.

Alone.

She peeled off the foil, placed the plate into the microwave, and punched in the time. What the hell was wrong with her? Men never shook her composure—she'd succeeded in a masculine-dominated field and never lost her self-control like this.

Maybe because she either acted like one of the guys or established authority in her role as breeding manager. If some of the ranch hands couldn't handle having a female boss, their time at the ranch was cut short. Holt was neither her buddy nor her employee. Since he didn't neatly fit into a category, she'd try to treat him like one of her stepbrothers. She grimaced. No, she definitely couldn't look at him like a sibling.

The bell dinged and when she reached to open the microwave her fingers brushed Holt's strong hand. She snatched hers back, but the damage was done. How was he always able to sneak up on her? He moved as silently as a mountain lion. She scooted to the side. Space, she'd just maintain the space between them.

"Oh my god, this looks amazing." Holt's eyes lit up like a little boy's right before the school bell rang at the end of the day.

"Forks are in the far drawer." She pointed to the second drawer from the sink. No way would she risk scorching herself against his smooth skin again.

He grabbed silverware and sat on a stool at the granite island and shoveled in an enormous bite of tamale. The only sound in the room was his fork scraping the ceramic plate. Would he ignore her until he'd inhaled the entire plate? He'd invited her down here and now it was as if she weren't even there.

Fine. She wanted the information he was supposedly going to share so she'd wait him out. She sat across from him and folded her hands in her lap. When he continued to stuff his face—not so perfect now—she gazed around the familiar room. A guitar case propped against the hearth caught her attention. He played the guitar? She swung her head back to look at him, just as he stuffed the last bite into his mouth. Pure joy radiated from his face. Grudgingly, she acknowledged he apparently worshiped food just like she did.

"Wow. Those were the best tamales I've ever had." He dropped his fork onto the plate and leaned back in his chair. "I've got to get the recipe."

"You cook?" Seriously, who was this guy? Stunts, horses, ballet, guitar, cooking? No wonder she wanted to jump his bones.

"No, I just love to eat. It's not for me." He laughed.

She narrowed her eyes. "Who is it for?" Crap, way to sound like a jealous girlfriend.

"My mom. She's an amazing cook and loves Mexican food. Her tamales are good, but these are on a whole different level." He grinned and patted his flat belly.

Sam's shoulders softened and she returned his smile. "Well, as long as she doesn't live in San Diego, my step-mom has a reputation to protect."

"My mom and sister still live in Colorado, in Littleton, just outside of Denver." He slouched back on the stool, his eyes warm.

"She'll probably help you out then. What made you leave Colorado?" Was he close to his mother?

"Well, I'm not a big fan of snow and freezing temperatures." His eyes cooled and he stacked the fork and knife onto the now empty plate.

"So is your dad there too?" Suddenly she wanted to know.

Without a word, he stood up, grabbed the dishes, and headed to the kitchen sink.

And, the rude guy from the barn had returned. "Umm, hello?"

"Yes, just my mom and sister and no, I came for work." He kept his back to her and began washing the dishes.

Was his short stint at friendliness over? When a few minutes passed in awkward silence, Sam gritted her teeth. She knew better then to let her guard down—he'd made his opinion of her clear. Guys like him dated models and actresses and didn't go for tomboys like her. The pull of pure animal attraction she'd felt in the ballet studio had simply been a mistake. And obviously one-sided.

"So, did you have something to tell me about the movie or did I come down here as a dinner delivery service?" *Keep it all business.*

He grabbed a dishcloth and took his sweet time turning around to face her. Where his expression had been friendly before, now his face was an impassive mask.

"Well, if you're going to snap at me, maybe I won't."

Heat rose in her cheeks. Snap? Seriously? "Fine, I'm sure I'll be able to figure it out. Give me the plate."

She stepped forward to grab the dish. He lifted the plate out of her reach. "Don't be in such a rush, brat. Harry did want me to share some information with you."

She refused to dignify his behavior by straining to reach the plate. Her stepbrothers used to tease her mercilessly for being vertically challenged. "Don't call me brat. And Harry can go jump in a lake. Give me the damn plate." Her fingers itched to grab it, but she managed to stand her ground.

"Ask nicely."

"Oh, get over yourself. Bring it back yourself and make sure it's when I'm not around." He was infuriating. She pivoted and marched to the doorway.

She'd deal with Harry tomorrow and avoid Holt. They were oil and water and she kicked herself for lowering her guard and believing anything different.

"Wait, I'm sorry..." Holt's husky voice was almost a whisper.

The doorknob was cool against her overheated palm. She opened the door and jolted when one large tanned hand pushed it closed. She froze and the hair on the back of neck prickled.

"Look, I'm sorry. Sometimes Colorado brings up bad memories." His warm breath caressed her ear. Her pulse accelerated. The white scars crisscrossing the back of his hand stood out in stark relief against his bronzed skin.

He was too freakin' sexy and now he was actually apologizing for his behavior? His proximity and his hot and cold routine were dangerous.

She blew out an unsteady breath. She didn't dare look over her shoulder––he was too close. "Don't worry about it. I've got to go."

When he didn't budge, she tugged on the door-knob again and this time he stepped back. She retreated up to the house, muttering to herself. She would maintain a professional distance from Holt. She would make sure not to be alone with him. She would take a cool shower and absolutely not allow images of his rock-hard, lean body to pop into her mind.

This evening confirmed keeping her distance from Mr. Too Hot Hollywood was her only option if she was going to survive the next month.

CHAPTER 10

PINK AND GOLD RAYS THREADED through
the gap in the plantation shutters, alerting Holt
dawn was breaking. He flipped onto his back and
stared at the high wood-beamed ceiling. He'd
tossed and turned all night, Sam's words echoing
in his brain. Last night when she'd asked about his
dad, he had reverted to defensive mode. And acted
like a total ass.

But he refused to discuss why he'd left Colorado.
It wasn't her business. It wasn't anyone's business.

The day he'd been forced to become a man, he
and Jenny were with their mom in the "infusion
lounge." The hospital had nerve referring to the
place where the brutal poisonous sessions stole the
patients' energy as any type of lounge. Infusion
lounge sounded more like a beach bar in Cancun,
where you'd ask for tequila with an infusion of
lime. Bullshit.

When he'd driven his mom home after she'd
endured the fifth of six aggressive chemotherapy
treatments, his sister had helped set their mom
up in the small master bedroom for a nap. Holt
had gone to the dim galley kitchen to grab a cool
drink of water and something in his peripheral
vision alerted him.

He'd scanned the cramped living room—his dad's ratty red plaid recliner dominated the room, a stack of auto racing magazines overflowed from a small side table, and…wait. No remote control. His dad dictated the remote control always be in one of two places: his hand or on his beloved magazine pile.

His father's most prized possession, the television, wasn't in its place of honor on the old faded console table. A chill flashed down his spine. Maybe his dad took it in for repairs? He certainly hadn't been available to take his mom to the hospital for treatment. Again.

He'd glanced up at the clock over the ancient four-burner gas stove: 5:30 p.m. His father lived by his 8 to 5 schedule at the garage where he was the lead mechanic, and by 5:15 sharp he was always settled in his recliner, icy can of domestic beer in hand. No deviations to his routine tolerated. Not even for his wife of eighteen years and her battle against cancer.

"Holt?" His sister's strained voice called from the narrow hallway.

"What's wrong? Is it mom?" He pivoted away from the empty living room and rushed toward the bedroom.

Jenny grabbed his arm, halting his progress. "No, she's resting. I think dad's gone." Her dilated pupils almost obscured her cornflower blue eyes.

"Gone, what do you mean gone?" His gut clenched and he swallowed down the bile threatening to spill from his throat.

"I…" Her eyes welled with moisture and she furiously blinked back tears. Her narrow shoulders were trembling and her cheeks had gone chalk white.

"Let's sit down." He led her to the hideous olive green lumpy couch.

"I got mom into bed and she fell right to sleep." She paused and swallowed. "When I hung her sweater up in the closet, it was half-empty. Dad's clothes are gone."

"What the hell?" He surged to his feet, hands curling into fists. "Where would he go?"

"I don't know, but the TV is gone too." Tears streamed down her pale cheeks. "Why would he do this? Mom's sick. Where would he go?"

"Damn him. Mom is in the middle of treatment. Shit, they've been married forever. What a bastard." He slammed a fist into the living room wall, wishing it were his dad's face. He welcomed the sharp surge of pain where the skin split on his knuckles.

Where was his dad? He'd simply disappeared.

Sleep eluded Holt as he wrestled with how he would break the news to his sick mom in the morning. Confirmation arrived in a phone call at 8:13 a.m. from Mike of Mike's Automotive. He'd asked if his dad was on the way because there was already a backup of cars to be serviced and Mike couldn't finish all the lube jobs himself. Holt had played dumb with some bullshit answer that he'd spent the night at his buddy's house and thought his dad was at work.

He'd hung up and stared sightlessly out the tiny kitchen window, a pit heavy in his belly. When his mom emerged from her room, looking exhausted and frail, heaviness flooded his limbs and his heart. What now?

Jenny made peppermint tea and dry wheat toast and they sat together around the table covered with the plastic daffodil-patterned tablecloth their mother insisted brightened up the drab room. Once his mom had managed to nibble half a piece of toast and sip some tea, Holt shared his suspicions.

"I think Dad left." He kept his hands clenched in his lap.

His mom closed her eyes and took a deep cleansing breath. "I was afraid this would happen. Your father isn't really one to stick around when the going gets tough." She shook her head, but her eyes were dry and her demeanor tranquil.

"How can you be so calm? I'll find him and make him come home." His hands curled into fists again, his voice shaking with fury.

She laid one fragile hand on his arm, "No, you absolutely will do nothing of the kind, Holt. Promise me you will not seek him out."

"Mom, are you kidding? How can you act so calm?" Tears poured down his sister's cheeks.

"Honey, we won't chase after someone who doesn't want to be here. I don't have control over much right now and I have to do what all these doctors dictate. I don't have any damn hair, and my legs feel as wobbly as a newborn deer's. But I will maintain my pride. I can control that. I forbid either of you to ask him to come back. It might be selfish of me because both of you deserve to have two parents, or at least one healthy parent, but we're better off." His mom's voice was steady and sounded like she was discussing whether they would have rice pilaf or scalloped potatoes for dinner.

Holt shook his head. Had he been blind? He didn't have any illusions his parents were madly in love or anything, but they'd seemed normal. No huge fights like his best friend Billy's parents, who'd actually had the cops at their house a few times. No, his parents just seemed like, well, parents. Now, his mom sounded like she didn't care his dad was gone, potentially forever.

"He didn't even say goodbye. What are we going to do?" Jenny's lower lip wobbled. She'd been daddy's little girl.

"I'm sorry he wasn't man enough to tell you kids. Now, we'll be fine. Your father wasn't much of a saver, but I am and we'll be okay. Plus, I've squirreled away enough for community college funds for you both. We'll get by until I'm back at work full-time. Our house is paid off; thank goodness I inherited it from my parents. We'll be okay." She clasped her hands together and the contrast of her delicate translucent skin against the fluorescent yellow flowered print emphasized her ailing health.

He would drop out and support his mom and sister. Since his dad was too much of a loser to do it. "I'll ask Mike if I can have dad's job. I'll take care of us." No way could he go to school today and pretend everything was normal. School wasn't his favorite place anyway and he'd never grasped why he needed to learn Algebra. What if his mom couldn't go back to work? Insurance didn't cover all her medical bills either.

His mom pushed herself to her feet, her hands

gripping the edges of the battered table for support. "You will do no such thing, Holt Ericsson. You will finish your education with straight A's, just like you started it."

"Mom, I can do it. The garage is open early and I can finish school with the night degree program. I've helped out there for years. I'm the man around here now and I'll make sure we're all fine." He clenched his jaw.

"But Holt—" Her pale blue eyes, a mirror of his own, revealed the pain she was so bravely fighting.

"Mom, you can't talk me out of it. I won't waste time on stupid classes when it's more important you and Jenny are taken care of." He'd never told her, but college didn't interest him. No, he wanted to experience life and be around action and adventure, not trapped in some musty classroom.

"I could babysit more." Jenny piped in, her voice as watery as her eyes.

Now his mom's eyes filled. "Oh, sweetie."

Jenny popped up and enveloped their tiny mother in her slender arms. Holt hugged them both and rested his chin on his mom's rose-colored knit beanie. He squeezed his eyes shut. He could do this. His mom and his sister wouldn't have to worry about money.

Raking his fingers through his hair, Holt pulled himself back to the present and climbed out of bed to brew coffee and start the day. After this movie shoot ended, he'd have the money to start his business and ensure his mom and sister's security.

Nothing would prevent this film's success, as long as he had any control over it.

CHAPTER 11

SAMANTHA BLEW OUT A SIGH of relief when she entered the empty stables. No sign of the unwanted guest—Mr. Fire and Ice. And they called women moody. She snorted as she saddled Princess Buttercup.

Determined to enjoy her usual morning ride despite the impending arrival of the movie crew, she trotted out into the crisp summer morning. No sign of the movie horses that would be housed in the family stables. The animals were welcome guests. The *only* welcome guests as far as she was concerned. Damn it, she missed Dylan. Not having her twin nearby for moral support was rough.

She and Princess Buttercup sailed together over her beloved rolling verdant hills, savoring the kiss of dew in the early morning breeze, and the power of her horse's graceful stride. She grinned up at the golden Southern California sunshine bestowing its warmth on her and her home. Although she thrived during breeding season's hectic pace, she appreciated the down time during off-season.

Sam frowned. This dumb movie would ruin her peaceful summer. Even though her dad was acting like filming a Western on the ranch wouldn't disturb their lives, she didn't buy it. She ran this

damn ranch and refused to accept his seemingly
casual acceptance of Harry's proposal. She'd judge
for herself.

When she crested the hill, she jolted to a stop.
The usually serene quiet end of the ranch where
they'd decided to shoot the movie was bustling
with activity, and it wasn't even 6:30 in the morning. Half a dozen huge 18-wheeler trucks were
parked in a semi-circle along the perimeter of the
tall tree-lined fence. Pairs of men were hefting
expensive camera and sound equipment from one
of the vehicles, and the sparkle from the metallic apparatus reflected off the shiny white of the
truck's cab. She shaded her eyes with one hand
and scanned the transformed space. The usually
empty pastures were filling up with not just modern paraphernalia, but also a wood-frame shell of
what appeared to be a log cabin or house.

More trailers rolled up and one was emblazoned
with the Wardrobe sign. Flashbacks to playing
with Dylan and Amanda in the wardrobe trailer
on the set of her mom's favorite period piece
assaulted her. She sucked in her breath and a sharp
pain pierced her heart. Tears brimmed in her eyes
and she blinked to prevent them from overflowing.

The costume designer had loved children and
always welcomed them with warm embraces,
bowls of colorful candy, and the chance to
play dress-up with the fancy costumes. A bubble of laughter escaped at the memory of Dylan
attempting to keep her balance with an enormous
powdered wig, complete with a full-sized bird-
cage containing a scarlet and emerald stuffed bird

inside, threatening to topple her. Marie Antoinette she was not. Buried somewhere in the dusty boxes of old photographs, was one of Sam's favorite photos of their mom and all three sisters in their borrowed aristocratic finery.

A visceral sob tore through her and she stuffed a fisted hand in her mouth to stop the scream threatening to escape. Tears streamed down her overheated cheeks, but she remained silent, careful to avoid alerting anyone down in the hive of activity of her presence.

The photo was tucked away somewhere, along with all of the movie-related pictures of their mother. Would her mom have wanted them to abandon all the joyous times they'd shared watching her live her dream as an actress? Pretend it hadn't existed? They'd hidden not just the photos, but also the happy memories. Maybe it was time to dig them out?

She hadn't been on a movie set since the freak accident killed her mom. She'd vowed never to set foot in the environment again. When they'd realized the paparazzi would never allow them to live in peace, her father promised them they'd never have to be exposed to the whole movie-making business. He'd promised they would be safe in Rancho Santa Fe, protected on their ranch, safe in their bubble.

He'd broken his promise.

Princess Buttercup tossed her golden head and her stoic strength broke the remainder of Sam's self-control. She buried her face in her beloved horse's silky mane and the floodgate of tears unleashed. After a few minutes, she hugged Buttercup's neck, wiped her face like a five-year-old after a tantrum, and sat ramrod straight in her saddle. She cautiously scanned the scene below her to make sure nobody had witnessed her bout of weakness.

She didn't do tears.

Oh who was she kidding? With the noise and bustling about, nobody could see or hear her from where they were creating the movie set. As long as *he* didn't see her in a vulnerable position, she'd be fine. Like a burr under her saddle, he rubbed her the wrong way.

Damn it. Would anything be the same again? This movie had broken open a seal and Sam hated it. Unwanted and unwilling attraction to a man she didn't even like. Memories of her mom long hidden away rising to the surface. She didn't want these unwelcome feelings interfering with her perfectly organized life.

She didn't want to wonder why her dad chose to allow the filming. Didn't want to care. Didn't want to be involved beyond ensuring the ranch's safety. Safety was paramount.

She slammed the vault shut, wheeled her horse around, and galloped to the house.

She wasn't running away.

No, she simply savored the speed.

HOLT RELISHED THE LAST SIP OF HIS COFFEE, OR sugar rocket fuel, his mom's nickname for his morning beverage of choice. A mountain of sugar in the blackest black beverage he could brew. So he had a tiny sweet tooth, who cared? Certainly not his boss.

His phone buzzed and Harry's name flashed on the screen. Speak of the devil.

"Morning. I was just headed to the stables. Are you here?" Holt asked and hit the phone's speaker button.

"Yeah, we've got the semis with the grips, sound, wardrobe, cameras, and props starting to unload. The stars' trailers should be here in a few hours. The talent won't be here until tomorrow. How soon can you get down here?"

"It depends on if the horses have arrived yet. If so, I'll make sure they are stabled and ride down. If not, I'll be there sooner." He pulled on jeans, a long-sleeved thermal, and shoved a Rams baseball cap onto his uncombed hair. Showtime.

Time to survey the set, and make sure the small portion of the ranch where they would shoot the movie was transformed into the Wild West. Holt shut the heavy wooden door and started to lock it and then snickered.

"What's so funny?" Harry asked.

"Nothing. Was just leaving this guesthouse and started to lock the door. Like anybody would break in." He chuckled again. Not like he had anything worth stealing, except for his Martin guitar.

"That would never happen. Is everything going okay with the McNeills so far? You didn't tick off Sam again, did you?"

"What?" Holt froze. "Why would you ask?" His boss couldn't know about last night, could he?

"I know you two weren't getting along and just need you to make sure you don't make this situation tougher than it already is." Harry warned.

He was not having this discussion with Harry, no matter how close they were. "It's fine. I'll be down as soon as I leave the stables."

"Okay, okay. Damn, my old friend Chris really did this ranch thing right. I couldn't have asked for a better place to shoot this movie." Harry changed the subject and sounded pleased with himself.

"Yeah, it's pretty perfect. See you in a few." He swallowed away the niggling guilt at how unfair he'd been to Samantha last night again. She brought out the worst in him.

He arrived at the stables, but the Hollywood horses hadn't arrived. He saddled Rocco and rode across the ranch that was quickly spinning a spell around him. Of all the places he'd visited around the world, nothing compared. Simply put, Pacific Vista Ranch rocked.

When he had almost reached the movie set, he paused to admire the view again. Suddenly, the hairs on the back of his neck prickled. Although the air was blessedly silent this far from the trucks and trailers, something alerted his instincts and he whipped his head to the left.

The early morning light threw her pristine profile into sharp relief and he was struck again by how much she resembled one of his mom's prize cameos. She sat in her saddle as if she and her horse were one. Just as her natural ballerina grace had sparkled through when she danced, her natural affinity for her horse was powerful. Why did it make her sexy?

A loud sob burst from her lips and tears poured

down her pale cheeks. She wrapped her arms around her horse's neck and buried her face in Princess Buttercup's mane. Her petite body vibrated as she wept.

Holt remained rooted to the spot in the shade of the enormous cedar tree, but couldn't tear his eyes away, even after she'd wiped her eyes and ridden back toward the house. He rubbed the stiffness from the back of his neck and blew out a quiet breath. Damn it. Talk about being in the wrong place at the wrong time. Not his fault.

But he'd been cold to her last night when she'd actually been friendly. Definitely his fault. Witnessing her break down stirred something unfamiliar in his gut, something he didn't care to explore.

When she'd been so hostile toward him, he'd figured she had a chip on her shoulder. He wasn't stupid; he knew he could be an obnoxious ass. He hadn't figured on how deep her resistance to having the movie filmed on the ranch went. Now he'd seen her crying, he felt shitty for being well, so shitty.

Damn it. She'd been a kid when her mom was killed and avoided anything to do with the movies ever since. So, maybe he needed to treat her like a little sister. Wouldn't that make it all much safer and smoother? Yeah, it would. He'd treat her like she was his little sister from now on.

But, she'd be suspicious if he was suddenly Mr. Nice Guy, especially after he'd frozen her out last night. All the way around, it was probably smarter for him to avoid her as much as possible. How hard could it be?

No more ballet studio when she was there. If he could erase the vision of her grace and sensuality when she danced, it would be a hell of a lot easier to act like a big brother. No more guesthouse visits. No more stables or rides across the ranch.

No problem.

Dilemma resolved, he squared his shoulders and trotted down to the set, ready to focus on work. At thirty years old, it was taking longer and longer to recover from the beatings he took on the job. His body couldn't sustain the current punishing pace he'd handled for the last decade. This movie would be grueling and he'd shut off anything to do with the youngest McNeill and begin the mental and physical preparation necessary for a successful shoot.

Industry outsiders usually assumed stunt people were reckless show-offs, when the total opposite was true. Successful stunts required mathematical precision, bordering on obsession. A bar fight, for example, was more like a choreographed ballet performance than a wild punching match. Mental preparation and exquisite control were vital to performing some of the dangerous work without succumbing to injury.

He shaded his eyes with one hand and surveyed the scene. The area was abuzz with activity and as far as he could tell, everything was moving along according to schedule. Workers were unloading the exorbitantly expensive and state-of-the-art cameras and lights. Although they had stipulated not to film at night, often natural light wasn't adequate to create the images on film, even on a sunny summer day.

He spotted Harry, who was gesturing animatedly with his hands, standing next to Chris McNeill. Sam's father was shaking his head and frowning. Shit, would he throw a wrench into the movie production after all? No way could this gig go south now.

He dismounted from Rocco and tied his reins on the temporary split rail fence. He sauntered up to Harry and Chris, who were so engrossed in their conversation they didn't even notice him until he addressed them directly.

"Morning guys, so how is everything looking? Start date on schedule?" It better be.

They turned to look at him. Holt couldn't read Harry's poker face and didn't know Chris well enough to gauge what was going on, although his scowl indicated he wasn't thrilled.

After a moment, Harry nodded. "Yes, we're good to go."

"So what should we do first? Do you have the schedule outlined yet?" Holt had worked with Harry many times and knew the director's planning bordered on obsessive-compulsive.

Harry ran his tongue around his teeth. "Well, I'm trying to talk Chris here into coming on board and helping me out a little bit with the directing. He was the best in the business back in the day." He slapped Chris on the back.

Chris remained silent. The grooves on either side of his mouth deepened and his eyes remained hidden behind his dark shades.

"You're going to direct?" Holt's jaw dropped open. Sam would freak out. And why the hell was *that* his first reaction?

Sam's dad shrugged one broad shoulder.

"Just hoping I can convince Chris to lend his eye and input on some of these scenes. Right?" Harry grinned, showing even rows of white teeth, kind of like a shark before he chomped on fresh prey.

Finally Chris's fierce expression softened. "I don't know what you're trying to pull with all of this. It's just too damn hard to be on set after everything——"

"It's been more than ten years. It wasn't your fault. It wasn't anybody's fault." Harry gripped the taller man's shoulder. "Pamela loved what she did. Losing her was a tragedy. But, you've moved on and I know you're happy."

Holt remained rooted to the spot, an unwilling witness to another McNeill's pain.

"Don't you miss it, even a little bit?" Harry's voice was almost a whisper.

"Yeah, damn it, once in a while I miss the excitement and the energy, but it doesn't mean——" Chris scanned the busy movie set. Blew out a breath.

"Look, all I ask is you come down for a few of the pivotal scenes. Observe only the way you can. Offer some feedback." When Mr. Harry Shaw, two-time Academy Award winner, wanted something, very few could deny him.

Chris whipped off his glasses and his hazel eyes were hot. "Fine. One scene. Maybe two. But you make sure the security remains air-tight, you make *damn* sure every piece of equipment is triple-checked, and you make double damn sure no harm comes to my family, or my horses. Got it?"

Holt caught himself before he whistled through

his teeth. Had Chris McNeill just agreed to direct for the first time since he'd lost his first wife? Harry was persuasive, but Holt hadn't anticipated this plot twist.

What would Samantha do when she learned of her father's capitulation? She'd obviously inherited not just the McNeill backbone but also the fiery temper. And damn it, why did his thoughts keep jumping to her? Oh yeah, because he regarded her like a little sister to be protected.

Right.

"I'm heading back to my office. Let me break the news to my family my way. We'll figure out the scenes later. And by the way, Angela invited you for dinner tonight, Harry, so don't try to weasel out of it." He pointed at Holt. "You too. My wife has taken a shine to you. 7 p.m. Don't be late. Either of you." With that, he marched off toward his own horse, leapt up onto its back, and cantered back toward the estate.

Harry grinned and slapped Holt on the back. "Come on, let's check everything out."

"Anything else you want to tell me about your plans here? I'm not a big fan of surprises."

"Nope, son. Nothing you need to worry your pretty blond head over." Harry snorted.

"Screw you." Holt lightly punched his arm as they headed over to the camera truck.

CHAPTER 12

A BSOLUTELY UNACCEPTABLE.
Food was the answer. Only a crunchy, salty snack would do. Better her jaw worked crushing something tough into tiny bits than experiencing the blow of pain she'd suffered looking down at the movie set.

After her crying jag, she'd ridden Princess Buttercup for another hour in a desperate attempt to calm the hell down. Anger was an easier default. Today, she would have preferred stewing in the pure dark energy of righteous fury, but instead she'd sobbed like a toddler who'd dropped her favorite toy into the toilet.

Dylan tended to be the one who shed the tears in the family, while Amanda was stoic and had an incredible ability to remain calm and unruffled, at least on the surface. Sam preferred everyone stick to her assigned familial role, thank you very much.

Sam foraged through the fully stocked walk-in pantry, seeking something to help numb her over-wrought nerves.

Cashews? Nah, too sweet. Barbequed potato chips? No, too salty.

Jackpot. She plucked an unopened bag of her

favorite blue corn tortilla chips off the shelf and wheeled around to the fridge to select the perfect salsa. She fist-pumped when she found the caliente extra-spicy salsa and reminded herself to hug Angela. The woman had the best shopping skills and always found the hottest, most potent salsa at the weekly local farmer's market.

She plopped down in the breakfast nook and ripped the bag open with her teeth. Shoveling the first few chips into her mouth, she pried open the salsa with her other hand. The chips crunched with a satisfying pop and she heaped an enormous mound of salsa onto a few more and stuffed them in. Her eyes floated closed and she chomped in utter bliss as the savory flavors exploded on her tongue.

Suddenly, her eyes watered and she wheezed and choked. She jolted upright and coughed and struggled to draw in a full breath.

"Angela bought the salsa with the habanero peppers again, huh?" Her dad laughed and he thumped her on the back.

Sam opened her mouth and no sound emerged except for a slight squeak and maybe some blue flames like a fire-breathing dragon.

Her dad guffawed and went to fetch a glass of water. By the time he handed her the icy liquid, her throat felt like it had been blow torched. After she guzzled the entire glass, she managed to speak.

"Apparently I've lost my touch or they doubled the number of peppers in the salsa for this batch. Oh my god, it was like trying to extinguish a campfire with my mouth." She wiped her eyes and joined his laughter. Served her right for trying to bury her feelings with junk food.

"You okay now?" Her father's tone turned serious and he slid into the booth across the reclaimed wood table.

Uh-oh. When her dad looked this somber, something was up. What now?

"Yes…" She drew out the syllable and braced herself for bad news.

"Don't look like that. I've got something to share with everyone and I wanted to share it with you first." He reached across the table and patted her hand.

"Yes…?" Every muscle in her body clenched as if anticipating a blow.

"So, I was down on the set talking to Harry. So far so good. It's far enough away from the rest of the ranch and shouldn't impact the family or our horses."

Sam nodded her head, unwilling to share what had happened this morning. Her dad didn't need to know she'd lost it and indulged in the biggest crying fit she'd had since her mother died. He needed her to be strong.

"Anyway, Harry asked me to help him out." Her dad clasped his hands on the table, his knuckles white against his sun-weathered skin.

Her eyes widened. What now? "Help him out? You mean more than allowing him to invade the ranch and film a movie here? What do you mean?"

"He asked me to consult on a few scenes." He gazed down at the table.

"Consult? What does that mean?" Her belly clenched.

He paused for a moment and swallowed.

"You mean direct again, don't you? But you swore you'd never work on a movie again. Seriously?" Unwilling to face him, she surged to her feet, stalked to the other side of the kitchen, and stared out the window over the huge white farmhouse sink.

"Sam." He followed her and placed his hands gently on her rigid shoulders. "Please just listen for a moment."

She shrugged, and braced her hands on the familiar granite countertop, the cool stone a comfort.

"I told Harry I would direct one or two scenes. If it's too tough, I told him not to ask me again and he agreed." Her dad's voice was even.

"And if it isn't too tough?" She bit her lip, unfamiliar emotions simmering too close to the surface.

"If it isn't and I direct a few scenes, what's the worst that can happen?"

She blinked furiously, she would *not* cry again today. "We've lived through the worst, Dad, but––"

"Exactly. That's what Harry said. And he reminded me it's been more than ten years since your mom passed. He asked me a question and it changed my mind."

"What?" She dug her fingers into the unyielding counter.

He squeezed her shoulders and his deep voice cracked. "He asked me if she would have wanted me to forsake my passion for making movies forever."

Sam squeezed her eyes shut, willing the pain to dissipate. Was she the only one who still felt like it was yesterday her mom died? What could she say without hurting the man she loved and trusted most in the world?

"Sammy?" Her dad whispered her childhood nickname.

She released her death grip on the granite and reached back and squeezed his hands. When she turned to face him, his eyes shimmered with emotion.

"Are you asking me or telling me?" She searched his face for clues.

"Sammy, if you really don't want me to do this, I won't." As usual, sincerity radiated from her father.

"Do you really want to do this?" Why was she asking? His expression revealed how much he yearned for it.

"I do. God help me, there was something about the set being built and the moment I was surrounded by the grips and the crew and the excitement in the air, it pulled at me. I'd been planning on making a big Western like this one right before…" He shook his head. "If you will be too upset, I'll respect your feelings."

She closed her eyes again. "I'm still so scared what will happen if the paparazzi find us again. And what if there's an accident? What if—" Her stomach clutched and she blinked her eyes open.

An unreasonable terror gripped her heart. What if he loved it and suddenly they were all plunged back into the Hollywood nightmare? Not just the loss of her mom, but also the callousness of the paparazzi relentlessly hounding them until they'd moved to the ranch.

"What if it's fun like it used to be? What if everything is normal? You used to love being on set with us. You loved performing once."

She swallowed the fear rising in her throat. "Dancing was a different life for me, and it's over. But I can see this means a lot to you. If it's permission you want, you've got it. I just hope this isn't opening up Pandora's box for you. For all of us."

He enveloped her in a warm hug and she rested her cheek against his solid chest. Maybe it would help him move beyond the past once and for all. The final memory of his lifelong passion and career was a tragic one. Perhaps working on this film would serve as a bridge for him to move on and let go.

For the whole family to move on and let go.

What if Harry were right and this whole situation could help them? Her dad had sacrificed everything for her and her sisters; she wouldn't be the one to cause him any more pain.

"Like I said, I'll know after I direct the first scene. Maybe you could come down and watch like you used to love to do?" He smiled tentatively.

"Don't push it, Pops." She lightly pressed him away and sauntered back to her chips and salsa. "Don't push it."

THE COOL REFRESHING WATER SOOTHED SAM'S skin. She'd spent the remainder of the day in the rehab center, helping Amanda work with one of their neighbor's horses who had a mild ligament sprain. Not that she minded getting dusty and dirty, but nothing beat a long shower. Because Southern California was officially in drought season for the umpteenth year in a row, she forced herself to shut off the water sooner than she would have preferred.

Her stomach grumbled and she hurried to her closet to find something to wear down to dinner. Angela preferred everyone clean up before the evening meal. Not dress fancy or anything, but she drew the line at dirt-encrusted boots, dusty shirts, or straw-filled hair. She tossed on an aqua and lime green striped sundress and slid on her favorite flip-flops—her official fancy dinner ensemble. She snorted. Dresses were fine once in a while.

She combed out her nearly-waist length hair and decided to allow it to air dry naturally instead of bundling it up into a braid or knot. She'd never admit it to anyone, but her long silky red hair was her one true vanity. No need to restrain it for a family dinner.

"Headed downstairs?" Amanda poked her tawny head into the bedroom and whistled. "Oooh, someone is dressed like a girl—ready to flirt with the stuntman?"

"What?" Sam's head snapped toward her sister. "Holt is here?" She ignored the kick against her ribcage.

"Yeah, Dad invited Holt and the director to dinner tonight. I figured that's why you got all gussied up." Amanda's eyes widened.

"Gussied up? Please. Can't I wear a sundress

once in a while?" Once a century was probably more accurate.

"And your Titian mane flowing down your back like the goddess Aphrodite?" Amanda's dimples showed in her fair cheeks.

"Oh that's me, the goddess of beauty. Very funny." Dylan and Amanda were the beauties, not her.

Amanda stepped in and enveloped her in a hug. "You're so easy to tease, Sam. I can't help myself. You *are* as beautiful as Aphrodite and probably more so because you just don't seem to know it."

Samantha's chest tightened. For a moment, she rested her forehead on Amanda's shoulder and savored the connection with her kind, loving sister. Guilt tickled her throat, should she warn Amanda before they went downstairs? She hugged her tight, knowing Amanda would be upset when her dad shared the news about his plans to direct again.

Sam doubted her usually even-keeled sister would react any better than she had initially. Amanda played her cards close to the vest and always seemed to radiate a serene calm, but underneath she was a McNeill through and through. Maybe she was the one who had inherited their mother's acting talent. Lord knows Sam and Dylan couldn't hide their feelings worth a damn.

"You're the beautiful one. Princess Amanda." Her sister's willowy golden beauty befitted royalty.

Amanda snorted. "Right, that's me, the princess. The only princess around here is your horse. You and I both know Dylan is the one who got the princess genes in the family." Amanda threaded her slender arm through hers and they headed downstairs together.

Showtime.

CHAPTER 13

"THERE ARE MY BEAUTIFUL DAUGHTERS," Chris McNeill called from the dining room table, where they were all already seated. "Come join us."

Holt rose to his feet at the same time Harry did. Manners. His breath caught at the vision Sam made and something unfamiliar tightened in his chest. Her hair was unbound and tumbled like a fiery silken blanket around her bare shoulders. Her creamy skin glowed and her dark eyes were fixed on Harry. He raked his gaze lower and saw she wore one of those floaty sundresses. She looked delicate.

"So you're Harry." Sam's tone was flat, breaking the spell her beauty had been weaving.

Holt squared his shoulders. What the hell was wrong with him? Delicate? Maybe he'd gotten too much sun today. He shook his head. He'd resolved to be more polite to her after witnessing her crying, but every time she opened her mouth, his hackles rose.

Just because she looked sweet like her feminine sister Dylan didn't mean she acted like it. Not even close.

"Samantha. Amanda. It's so good to see you

both again." Harry's tone was smooth and charming.

"Again?" Amanda asked and raised a slender brow.

"Harry——" Sam's dad cautioned.

"I knew you girls when you were running around in diapers. So I remember you even if you don't remember me." Harry wasn't a large man, but his intense obsidian eyes, sharp Roman nose, and wolfish expression lent him a huge presence. Add in his instinct for discovering talent, his charismatic voice, and smooth charm and you had a man most people never forgot. He was one of the top power brokers in show business and Holt would never forget how he'd given him his first big opportunity when he'd arrived in L.A. broke and eager to work.

"Were you ever over at our house? I think we would have remembered meeting you." Amanda's brow furrowed.

"Harry used to come to our cocktail parties when you girls were little, so you were usually heading up to bed," Chris said.

"Huh." Sam picked up her water glass and sipped, studying Harry from across the table.

For a moment the room was silent.

Angela stood with a smile, breaking the ice. "I doubt you've ever faded into the background, Harry. I'll grab the appetizers. Chris, will you pour the wine, please?" She swept back to the kitchen.

"Yeah, you're not really a background kind of guy." Holt elbowed his boss and friend.

"Why did you send Holt down here to ask about

the movie instead of coming yourself?" Amanda asked, her polite tone saving her questions from bordering on rude.

Harry smiled. "I was managing some other aspects of the movie. Holt's got an interest in this film and had the time."

"What do you mean 'an interest in the film'?" Sam set down her wineglass and leaned forward in her seat, her auburn mane falling over one creamy shoulder.

"Just a little investment, that's all." Holt shrugged. She didn't need the details of his personal business.

"No wonder you were so gung-ho to push this on us. Money talks." Sam glared at him. What a surprise––she assumed the worst.

"Nothing wrong with investing in movies, Samantha." Chris admonished her as he poured chardonnay into their glasses. "Have you two known each other long, Harry?"

"Yes, I helped Holt get his first gig when he arrived in L.A. fresh off the bus from Colorado. He's a good kid." Harry beamed at him.

Holt shifted in the upholstered chair and rubbed the back of his neck. Time to change the subject–– the last thing he wanted was to be the center of attention, although he appreciated McNeill distracting his daughter.

"Really? How long ago was that?" Chris eased back into his chair and sipped his wine.

"About twelve years ago. And I'm not a kid." So why did he feel like one right now? Harry had been the closest thing he'd had to a male role model, a kind of father figure.

"Aren't you girls curious how long Harry and I have known each other?" Chris steered the conversation away, thank god.

"Well, since we were in diapers obviously. Your name sounds familiar. You weren't at our mom's funeral," Sam said.

"Yes, we worked together for years and I'm actually the person who introduced your dad to your mom. We go way back and it's simply the case of an old friend helping an old friend out of a bind. Nothing more." Harry remained unperturbed, but didn't address the funeral.

"*You* introduced our parents? Dad, I thought you guys met at the beach?" Sam gawked at her father and Amanda's mouth dropped open.

He looked down at his hands and cleared his throat. "We did meet at the beach, but it was a bonfire party Harry threw and he actually…"

"I was actually interested in your mother first, hell, everyone was. But the moment she set eyes on Chris, I faded into the background. It was love at first sight." Harry's tone remained even. They could be discussing the weather.

Holt snagged the bottle of chardonnay and re-filled Amanda and Sam's glasses before taking a generous pour himself. Maybe the crisp, citrusy liquid would cool down the undercurrents of tension now permeating the air. Both women continued to stare at their dad.

They hadn't even had the first course and who knew what other bombshells would be dropped before dinner? Harry had been in love with Sam's mom? Did that little tidbit of information have something to do with why Chris agreed to allow them to film here? Had he stolen Harry's girl?

Amanda stared at Harry and Sam vibrated in her seat and a flush of color rose up her slender ivory neck. Did her rosy glow extend down her chest too? Every muscle in his body stiffened and he shifted in the chair again. Damn it, how could he be aroused seeing a woman blush?

Stop looking at her, that'd be a smart first step. Sam was off limits. He struggled to pay attention to the unfolding soap opera.

During the awkward silence, Harry's lips thinned almost imperceptibly. One of his tells when he was irritated. He was accustomed to everyone falling in line with his requests and demands, no questions asked.

"Here comes my lovely wife." Chris rose from his chair to help Angela with the two delicious smelling platters of food.

"Thanks, darling." Angela looked around and pinned Sam with her gaze. No way could she miss the rosy skin and pinched expression. "Sam, are you feeling okay?"

"I'm fine." Sam grabbed her glass and guzzled the wine like it was lemonade on a hot day.

"How is everything going on set so far?" Mrs. McNeill smiled and joined them at the table. Obviously, she was the family peacemaker.

"Set up is on schedule so far and the talent arrives tomorrow. Being able to film here is saving my movie. Thank you all for agreeing to it and please know I will do everything in my control to make sure it goes smoothly. You won't even know we're here." Harry smiled, his usual charming expression firmly back in place.

"Not likely." Sam muttered under her breath as she poured the remainder of the second bottle of chardonnay into her glass.

Holt dared another glance across the table. She was drinking her second glass of wine like it was the first drink she'd had after crossing Death Valley. Why had he had to witness her breakdown this morning? Against his better judgment, she was no longer just a spoiled, bad-tempered little dictator––a heart lurked beneath her tough surface.

Stop watching her. Stop thinking about her. Stop. He sipped more wine. Wished for an ice cold beer instead.

"Have you tried the bruschetta yet, Holt?" Angela asked.

He nodded and bit into a piece of bruschetta and almost groaned out loud. Plump tomatoes, crisp fragrant basil, and crusty baguette combined to create perfection. He gestured with thumbs up.

"Enjoy. I'll grab the rest of the plates. Finish up everyone." She headed to the kitchen.

"I can't believe you didn't tell us he introduced you to mom." Sam hissed at her father. "And why have you never mentioned him?" She flicked her dark gaze at Harry.

"Not now, Samantha." Her dad whispered back. "Later."

Angela returned with two mouthwatering platters with a large roast on one and vegetables, carrots, potatoes, celery, and green beans on the other. He hadn't enjoyed home cooked meals like this since before his mom got sick and his father bailed on them.

Focus on the food. Ignore the ornery redhead.

The ornery redhead heaped her plate to over-flowing and began scarfing down her meal without another word. Where could she possibly put all the food? She probably burned it off along with all the steam she loved to pump out of her ears.

"I've got some news I'd like to share with every-one now we're here together." Chris set down his fork and knife and gazed around the table.

Sam didn't lift her head and continued eating. Holt breathed a sigh of relief he was safely out of the line of fire in his spot diagonal from her across the table. Oh shit, would there be an epic explosion when she heard her dad's news. At least he wouldn't lose a shin if she kicked out, but she could still toss her knife across the table. He scooted a little farther away from Harry.

Just in case.

Amanda's eyes widened and Chris's wife's dark brows knit together. Sam kept chewing and star-ing at her plate as though she hadn't heard a word. Harry also kept eating without a care in the world.

Chris cleared his throat. "Well, Harry and I were talking about the production and I've decided to accept his offer of directing a scene or two." He looked around.

Amanda frowned and her fork dropped from her fingers, the metallic clatter the only sound in the room. Sam kept eating. Did she have earplugs in or something?

"Chris, you haven't directed since…" Angela began.

"Since before Pamela died." He clasped his

wife's hand and gazed into her eyes. "There, I've said it. She's been gone for more than a decade and we've all paid the price."

Harry remained as motionless as a hawk honed in on its prey. The color drained from Amanda's face and she continued to stare at her father without blinking. Nobody said a word.

Astoundingly, Sam continued to chew her food and didn't look up from her plate. What the hell? Where was the fiery temper now? The erupting volcano? Had she and Dylan swapped places like they had as children and this unruffled woman in front of him was Sam's twin? That would explain the unbound hair and feminine attire.

"Amanda?" Chris squeezed his wife's hand.

"I'm just surprised, Dad. All of this is out of the blue and unexpected. Are you sure?" Her calm expression didn't give anything away, but the pulse fluttering in her throat revealed her distress.

"I know. I thought it was all in the past, but now I recognize I do miss it. I miss directing, and the energy of the set. Look, I agreed to direct a few scenes and if it feels off to me, that's it. As long as you all agree. I promise I'll be careful. With all of it." He offered a half-smile across the table and squeezed Angela's hand again.

"Sam, did you know about this? Is that why you aren't pitching a fit?" Her sister asked.

Sam set down her fork and dabbed her rosy lips with her napkin. "For the record, I don't pitch fits. And yes, Dad told me about it earlier this afternoon. Probably because if anybody would cause a scene at dinner, it would be me." She shrugged.

She pinned Holt with glittering dark eyes, then

glared at Harry. "I don't like it any more than I like having a movie filmed here. But I can't stand in Dad's way, especially if this is something he feels he needs to do. But know if anything happens to my horses or the media invades our privacy, I will do everything in my power to stop it."

"I appreciate it, Sam. I know you run the ranch. You should come down to set and observe. All of you." Harry smiled and glanced around the table as if the tension wasn't as thick as the morning fog over the Pacific.

Amanda placed her napkin down carefully next to her untouched plate. "I'm sorry, but I'm a little too busy with work to hang out on a movie set like I did as a child. If you'll excuse me." She gracefully rose and marched out of the room.

Her dad started to rise from the table to follow her.

"No, let me go talk to her, Dad. She'll come around. You need to tell Dylan too." Sam dropped her napkin onto her shiny clean plate. She'd managed to consume the mountain of meat and vegetables during the entire scene. She walked over to her father and dropped a kiss on his forehead before following her sister out.

Silence settled in the room again and Holt longed to return to the guesthouse and escape any more uncomfortable scenes.

"I would have appreciated some warning, but I am glad you spoke to Sam first." Angela's eyes showed concern.

Chris turned to Angela and kissed her tenderly. "Thank you, my love."

"Yeah, I get the feeling I would be wearing that

roast as a hat if you'd surprised your youngest."
Harry's tone was dry. "Thanks for warning her."

"Well, time will tell. I am serious, Harry. One
slip-up impacts my family; I'll have your trailers
out of here faster than a lightning bolt. Permanently. You got it?" Chris's jaw was set.

"Got it. It'll all be fine. Right, Holt?" Harry
grinned over at Holt.

"Um, sure. Of course." What now? Could he
escape?

"Oh, you poor boy. Caught up in the middle of
all the McNeill drama. Can I get you some dessert?" Angela smiled at him from across the table.

"Thanks so much, but I'm stuffed. Dinner was
incredible. I'll just head back to the guesthouse if
you don't mind." He rose to his feet, nodded at
Chris and Harry and beat a hasty retreat.

Damn, he missed his own mom and home
cooked meals, but the price at the McNeill's table
was too steep.

Solitude and his guitar were safer and simpler
companions.

CHAPTER 14

"TRY TO GET SOME SLEEP. I love you." Sam closed Amanda's bedroom door and exhaled a long shaky breath. When cracks showed in her stoic older sister's generally placid composure, the world had definitely tilted on its axis.

Because riding Princess Buttercup this late in the evening wasn't an option, a lengthy swim was in order to blow off steam and hopefully organize the myriad of thoughts tumbling around her mind. When she reached her bedroom, she stepped out of her sundress and grabbed her ancient navy one-piece. Racing sprints were one of her fondest memories from high school swim team. As long as the baggy, now shapeless, suit still hadn't disintegrated, who needed a new one just to swim laps?

Not bothering to toss the discarded dress into the clothes hamper, she padded down the quiet hallway to the back door. On the way to the Olympic-sized swimming pool, she wrestled her hair into a practical French braid. Otherwise, it would engulf her like the enormous beds of seaweed and kelp did when she paddled out too far into the Pacific Ocean. No need to slow herself down while she took out her frustration on the innocent saltwater pool.

When she reached the sparkling swimming pool, the smooth paver stones were blessedly cool beneath her feet. The evening breeze carried the soothing scent of roses and jasmine and even a hint of sea air. Usually the anticipation of a swim lowered her blood pressure, but tonight her pulse continued to thrum.

Her fingers curled into her palms. What the *hell* was going on behind the scenes with her dad and Harry? Did her dad feel guilty for winning Pamela and that was why he had agreed to provide the temporary movie set? Was there something else? More importantly, had her father been missing his film career for all these years? Why hadn't he told his family? Or had they all been so engrossed in starting new lives, they never noticed?

She stepped to the edge of the pool and dove cleanly in. The crisp water might not provide answers, but at least she could work off some of the questions burning up her brain.

HOLT FROZE.

Would he ever find any privacy? What he wouldn't give to be alone in either his generic apartment or a soulless hotel room in Anywhereville.

He'd been reclining on the chaise lounge closest to the pool cabana, ready to strum his fingers against the familiar guitar strings. Minding his own damn business. The splash jolted him out of his almost relaxed state.

Please don't let it be *her*.

After the awkward scene at dinner, he'd retreated to the guesthouse and the nearby deserted pool beckoned to him. Playing some music in the mild Southern California evening appealed to him, especially after he'd been stuck inside 24/7 during his most recent job in a remote corner of Canada.

The lights from the main house illuminated her slim, lithe form slicing through the water. Slender toned arms silently stroked and uniform kicks propelled her from one end of the pool and back. Of course she swam as well as she rode, barely leaving ripples in the glasslike water's surface.

Adrenaline started pumping through his veins. But damn—all he wanted was a little peace and quiet. His music calmed him and served as part of his pre-film preparation for all of the upcoming intricate stunt work. Definitely not the time for a confrontation with a gorgeous half-naked woman who was also dealing with a lot of upheaval. He didn't have the energy to fight.

He didn't want to fight with her, but it just seemed to happen.

Should he just bail and find another secluded spot on the property? The ranch was certainly big enough.

Maybe he could slink off without alerting her to his presence. It certainly would be a hell of a lot easier.

He nodded his head decisively, grabbed his guitar, and sprang to his feet. There had to be another spot on the other two hundred plus acres of ranch where Samantha McNeill was not nearby in a bathing suit. If luck were with him, she never needed to know he'd been at the pool. He remained in the shadows, crept toward the stone path, and prayed she kept swimming. Not that he was skulking away or anything.

Yeah, right.

"Hey, who's there?" A sharp voice barked from the swimming pool.

Shit. Shit. *Shit*.

Running his tongue along his teeth, he pivoted to face her. Damn, he'd almost made a clean getaway.

"It's just me. Uh, Holt. Just leaving. Sorry to bug you." He backed away from her, the guitar gripped in one hand.

Her voice rose an octave. "Hold on a second. What are you doing down here?"

He stopped and sucked in a deep breath, exhaled it slowly, and prayed for patience. Because he was far from sainthood, his prayers were ignored. His grip tightened on the guitar's neck.

She emerged from the pool, and in the dusky light, she resembled a shimmering mermaid rising from the sea. Every muscle in his body stiffened. Oh yeah––mermaids lured the sailors to their deaths against the hungry, perilous rocks.

"I was just getting some fresh air. I'm leaving now. Carry on." He stepped back and would have escaped, but her whisper floated toward him on the breeze.

"You startled me, that's all." Her voice had softened, the razor sharp edges blunted.

He retreated another step. Sweet Samantha was too tempting.

She snatched up a plush striped towel from the chaise lounge next to her, wrapped it around her shoulders, and sank down onto the chair without uttering a sound.

"Are you okay?" Her silence was out of character. He inched closer. How could he leave her now?

Her heavy sigh carried across the short distance between them. "I'm sorry. It's just all of this is giving me flashbacks."

Oh shit. He took another step. "No, I'm sorry. Did your family really have paparazzi spying on you?" She'd just been a kid when her mom passed away.

She swallowed. "You don't want to hear all of this. I'll head back to the house and let you do…" She waved around one slender hand, "whatever it was you were doing."

"Tell me." He sat on the other end of the lounge chair and set his guitar down next to him. "What happened?"

She hesitated and her pale fingers clutched the towel even closer around her. The thick fabric enveloped her petite frame, all the way down to her slender ankles. She looked vulnerable. Young.

He held his breath, needing to know. Wanting to help her feel better. Unable to leave her now.

"I don't really talk about it, but the period of time almost destroyed our family. My mom died in a freak accident on the set of a period piece my Dad was directing. She fell and broke…she fell and broke her neck. I was on set that day and…" She squeezed her eyes closed and exhaled a loud breath.

Damn it. Why had he pushed her? "Sam, I'm sorry. You don't have to tell me——"

"Let me finish. I'd been doing my homework and it sounded like a car crash or an explosion. I'll never forget that sound as long as I live." She gave a tiny shake of her head. "Some jerk sold a story to one of those gossip rags claiming my mom was having an affair. And that there was a major screw-up with the equipment and claimed there should be an investigation for negligence or worse, foul play. They even said my dad was involved. After that the harassment didn't stop, even though it was all a pack of lies. You'd think my mom was Princess Diana or something the way they stalked us. They'd camp out in the front yard, line up along our street, plant reporters and cameras everywhere. Helicopters.

The paparazzi lurked at our school and Dylan even got hurt running away from a stupid reporter. The neighbors began to complain, and mind you, this was Bel Air and it's chock full of celebrities. They just kept coming with ugly innuendos and lies designed to sell more magazines and papers." Sam's voice was low and her gaze remained down at her clasped hands. Even in the dim light, the white of her knuckles signaled her distress.

"I had no idea. I'm so sorry—" His stomach clenched and the urge to console her coursed through him. No wonder she'd freaked out about the movie. What if the paparazzi caught scent and tried to resurrect the story?

"It all jumbles together, you know? Her death. The movies. The damned media. We wanted to mourn and couldn't do it until my dad packed us up and we left it all behind." She raised her face to him and the bright moonlight reflected off of the crystallized tear traveling down one flawless cheek.

He reached across the distance and brushed away the solitary tear with his thumb. Just to comfort her. He slid his hand across her silky cheek and gently cupped her jaw. Unable to stop, he leaned in and pressed his lips against her perfect full mouth.

She jolted the moment Holt's strong fingers brushed across her face. The heat of his touch seared her icy skin and the tenderness in his expression froze her breath in her throat. How had this happened? She'd confessed things to him she'd never discussed with anyone but her sisters.

Her mind blanked when his firm sculpted lips captured hers in a whisper of a kiss. He changed the angle of the kiss, coaxing her lips apart. Both of his hands framed her face now, holding her immobile, unable to escape his dangerous mouth. Her lips parted helplessly beneath his assault and a hum escaped her throat when his tongue tangled against hers. Hot sparks shot straight down to her center and any water droplets still clinging to her from her swim evaporated in the charged air.

Her protective towel slid away and she wrapped her arms around his neck, thrusting her fingers into his thick, unruly golden hair. He tasted delicious, a hint of the citrus from the chardonnay mingled with something darker, forbidden.

More. She wanted more.

As if he'd read her mind, he yanked her closer and molded her against his muscular torso. His clean masculine scent surrounded her. She was losing herself in the sensation of his lips, his arms, and his presence, just as she did in the music and the flow in ballet. No longer thinking, simply experiencing. Living. Savoring.

An inane thought burst through her foggy brain––she was soaking his shirt with her wet bathing suit. She managed to lift her heavy eyelids halfway. Was her vision blurry or was steam pumping off of them now? Did it matter? Flames licked along her skin and their shared heat continued to rise.

Time ceased to exist as he explored every corner of her mouth, every nuance in her kiss. His focused attention and the single-mindedness of his embrace pulled her deeper. She was drowning and sliding further beneath the surface, reveling in the descent.

He pulled his mouth from hers and trailed kisses along the side of her neck, the stubble from his square jaw eliciting a violent shiver down her spine. When he pressed an open-mouthed kiss on her collarbone, her head lolled back. A moan split the air. Was that her? Every single spot where his lips connected with her burned.

"Samantha." His breath seared against her flesh. He brushed his mouth along her collarbone and one hard palm curved over her breast. She arched into him, her nipples leaping to attention, chafing against the rough material of her ancient bathing suit.

His hand tightened on her taut nipple and he yanked her top down and paused, gazing at her breast. He groaned. Stroked her. Once. Again.

She squirmed, unable to catch her breath when his tawny head shifted down and his hard warm tongue scraped against her sensitive skin. Her back bowed and she bit back a scream at the intensity of the pleasure.

He growled and one arm snaked around her, pulling her in even closer. His hot mouth covered her breast and he raked his teeth across her nipple. Her head fell back again and heat permeated her being, the dampness no longer just from her bathing suit. He jerked his head away from her breast and captured her mouth again. The languid exploration vanished and his kiss turned hard and wild. With one hand possessively cupping her breast, he lifted her to straddle his lap. Her hips rocked against his of their own volition.

She dug her fingers into his thick, silky hair, abandoning anything other than the powerful sensations flooding through her. His hands were everywhere——roaming down her bare back, sliding up her waist, cupping both breasts. His rough calloused palms captured her hips, molding her against him and leaving no question of his iron-hard arousal. She stroked her hands down his beautiful carved biceps and back up to curve around his powerful neck. She arched against him, hungry for more.

His hands curved around her hips and slid inside the loose edges of her bathing suit, his long fingers cupping her bottom.

"You're a perfect handful everywhere. So beautiful. So perfect." He buried his face against her neck again and his breath seared against her skin. "I want you."

"Holt." She arched away from him, but couldn't leave the temptation of his embrace. "This is crazy. We don't even like each other."

He slowly lifted his golden head and his heavy-lidded gaze roamed across her face and then pinned her own.

For a moment, only their panting punctuated the evening air. Was her chest heaving? Was heaving a thing outside of historical romance novels? Her heart thundered against her ribcage like she'd just sprinted from one end of the ranch to the other. She licked her suddenly dry lips.

His gaze dropped from hers and fixated on her mouth again.

She pressed one hand against his chest. "Holt." Her voice came out breathier than she would have liked. Breathier than it had ever sounded before.

"I don't know, sweetness, it feels like we like each other. A lot." His sculpted mouth curved up into a half-smile.

His wicked, dangerous mouth.

Space, she needed to put some space between them before she did something she regretted. What was she doing? Holt was only here for a few weeks and could she afford to complicate things more than they already were? She'd already revealed too much. She scooted off his lap and landed with a hard thump on the chaise. She snatched her towel up of the ground and wrapped it around her. Protection. A layer of protection.

She peeked over at him. Even in the dim light from the pool house, the imprint of her body stood out against his pale grey T-shirt. A giggle escaped her.

"Are you laughing at me?" Holt quirked a blond brow. He looked down at himself and chuckled. "Nice, I look like I went swimming myself."

"Sorry about that." Not *too* sorry.

He angled toward her and she hopped off the chaise, wrapping her towel more tightly around her. If he touched her again, she'd be lost. No, she needed to think. She needed to slow this down. Whatever *this* was.

"Are we going back to hating each other now?" He leaned back, his damp t-shirt stretching across his broad chest, revealing the chiseled muscles. She bit the inside of her lower lip to prevent herself from drooling. Or worse, throwing caution to the wind, tossing off the towel, and climbing back onto his lap.

"I never hated you." Should she cross her fingers on the little white lie?

"Oh please. Two words—tease mare." He straight white teeth flashed in the dim light.

"Okay, you were pretty obnoxious. And I don't want the movie here." She shrugged one shoulder. "But maybe you aren't all bad." She could flirt right back with him. That's what they were doing, right? Flirting?

"Yeah, I'm obnoxious. But you're temperamental and blunt." His voice maintained the thread of humor, belying the insult.

"I am not temperamental. I prefer quick tempered." She laughed. "I've got to be blunt. Breeding horses isn't exactly a role governed by Miss Manners."

"Truce?" He stretched one powerful hand out toward her.

"Truce." She clasped his warm hand for a moment, savored the rough texture, and then retreated a step.

They stared at each other, the silence comfortable now. Her pulse still raced and she willed it to slow. *Change the subject.*

"How long have you played?" She pointed to the guitar leaning against the chaise.

"Ever since I was a kid. Just for fun. I was just going to play a bit until you yelled at me." A mischievous grin played across his face.

"I didn't yell. Do you sing too?" Please no, it would be too sexy. Why did the picture of him strumming those long fingers across the strings make her heart slam against her ribcage?

"Not well." He stood and picked up the guitar in one fluid motion. "Look, I understand more now why protecting the ranch is so important to you. To your family. I can't imagine what it must have been like for you. If that had happened to my mom or sister, I would have gone nuts."

He stepped closer to her, his eyes solemn. "We didn't experience anything like that, but my dad bailed on us when I was in high school. I swore I'd never let anything harm them again. Don't worry, I'll make sure no press gets anywhere near your home, okay?"

Sam's stomach took a long slow roll. "I'm sorry about your dad. That's rough. It's just a lot at once. Everything's happening so fast and with my dad directing too…" She shook her head. "It's just a lot."

"Don't worry. I'm going to head back. Want another hug?" A dimple winked in his lean cheek and his eyes darkened.

"Hug, yeah right." She snorted. "That wasn't a hug and you know it. Let's sit on this for a while. It's safer."

If he touched her again, he wouldn't be going back to the guesthouse alone and her frayed emotions couldn't handle the complication. What else didn't she know about him? He cared about his mom and sister—his protectiveness made him more appealing. Although, he lived on the road. Did he want to be a stuntman forever? Had he been in love before?

"Playing it safe is over-rated, Samantha." He brushed the pad of his thumb across her swollen lower lip, turned, and sauntered away.

She touched her mouth, still swollen and tender from his kisses. Had today really happened? From her breakdown on set, to her father's shocking decision, to Harry's bombshell about her mother, to Holt. The decade of blessed serenity at Pacific Vista Ranch and freedom from the past was finished.

No matter what happened, she had changed already and the movie hadn't even begun filming. Would her family ever be the same again? What would happen when the crew loaded up and shipped out?

When the movie ended, it meant Holt would leave too.

Going back to her room alone was her only option.

CHAPTER 15

HOLT CAREFULLY PLACED HIS BELOVED Martin guitar onto one of the large leather recliners without bothering to attempt a chord. He strode to the gleaming stainless-steel refrigerator, grabbed an icy cold bottle of water, and pressed it to his overheated forehead. What the *hell* had just happened?

One minute he was savoring the quiet evening, ready to settle his mind by playing some music, and the next moment, he'd lost himself in the sexiest woman he'd ever met. Her lips were the sweetest he'd ever sampled. Her sleek, compact body and her perfect little breasts with their sensitive nipples and silky skin plastered against him thrilled him. When she'd been on his lap and he'd slid his hands under the blessedly loose elastic of her wet bathing suit, he'd almost cried when her heart-shaped bottom fit into his hands, as if she was made for him.

He'd almost tossed her back onto the chaise lounge and taken her there with the moon shining down and the mild Southern California breeze washing over them. Almost crossed a line he couldn't afford to cross. His body stiffened again as he remembered––her mouth, her passionate response, her openness.

He ripped the lid off the water bottle and chugged half of it, willing the frigid water to cool him off. He smacked the bottle onto the granite countertop and listed the reasons why touching Samantha McNeill again was a terrible idea.

Movie.

Investment.

Retire and start agency.

Move mom and sister to California.

No room on the agenda for a bad-tempered, bossy, irritating, independent, resilient, absolutely seductive woman. Her strength and backbone impressed him.

Damn it.

What now?

He couldn't have an affair with Sam. It was too messy. Harry would kill him. Well, if Chris McNeill didn't rip him from limb to limb first. Samantha belonged on Pacific Vista Ranch and he belonged…well, maybe nowhere.

He chugged the rest of the water. Hell, he should dump it over his head. He prowled around the guesthouse. Why her? If anything, Dylan was more his usual type. Sweet, artistic, and kind. Why was he attracted to Samantha when the twins looked exactly alike?

Was it seeing her vulnerability this morning when she'd cried? Hell, was that actually only this morning? Was it because he was finally getting a clue about the hell she and her family had endured in addition to losing their mom? What had seemed like an over-the-top reaction before made sense now. Why the hell hadn't Harry given him more of a warning?

Damn it. He'd just have to avoid her. That's all. He'd be leaving in a few weeks, like he always did. Friends. He'd act like friends with her if he saw her. He'd sworn to himself he wouldn't be an asshole any longer. He could handle it, right?

And he was stalking around his temporary home muttering to himself. Thinking too damn much.

His guitar. He'd play his guitar. Playing always allowed him to channel whatever was happening around him or at least escape from it. His faithful guitar had saved him during those years he'd dropped out of school after his dad left. Although he worked and finished school at night, he had found time to play whenever he could. Thank goodness he'd never needed more than four to six hours of sleep.

He picked up his treasured guitar and settled back into the deep couch cushions. He closed his eyes and began to play one of Chris Cornell's most melancholy songs, "Like a Stone." Holt couldn't sing, but he could play. The familiar notes slipped through his fingers and the heartbreaking beauty of the tune softened the stiffness around his shoulders.

Pictures of Samantha's face, soft and aroused, still wouldn't fade away.

He'd play a little longer, but he needed a cold shower to relegate Sam to the friend zone.

An icy cold shower.

Sam flipped over onto her stomach and yanked her fluffy pillow over her head, but the soft down failed as a barrier against the incessant buzzing tormenting her. It stopped. Silence. Blessed silence.

She rolled over, flopped onto her back and prayed for sleep to find her. She'd tossed and turned all night, memories of Holt's kisses sending flashes of heat through her body. She'd tried counting sheep, she'd tried counting backwards from one hundred—what a stupid exercise *that* was—but cool, calm and quiet eluded her. Imagine that.

The last time she'd glanced at the clock it was 2:36 a.m., and damn it, she needed more sleep. She pulled her soft duvet cover up to her chin, snuggled deeper into her comfortable queen bed, and sighed. Her muscles relaxed and she settled into her comfy nest and...

Bam. The phone rang again. What the hell?

"This better be an emergency or I'll make it one." She grumbled, snatched up her phone, and did a double take.

No, it wasn't her reflection, but her mirror image calling on Facetime. At 3:42 a.m.

"Do you have any idea what time it is?" She attempted to soften the snarl, but at this hour, she didn't have her usual impeccable self-control. Ha.

"Isn't it around 6 a.m.? When you usually get up?" Dylan offered a sheepish smile. "Did I wake you up?"

"It's 3:42 a.m., so yes, you did." Brilliant blue sky, explosions of scarlet, pale pink, and lilac flowers framed her sister like she was the center of a colorful portrait. "Where are you?"

"I'm over in the Luxembourg Gardens and just had the most delicious ham and cheese baguette.

With butter and these little cornichon pickles. The food here is amazing—you'd be in heaven. Boulangeries and Patisseries on every block, and I swear they blow the smells out onto the street to tempt you inside." Dylan's words flooded out in a rush.

"Did you call me at 4 a.m. to tell me about the food in Paris? Seriously?" She didn't bother to cover her mouth when she yawned.

Her sister frowned. "No, of course not. I miss you. Won't you come visit me? Just for a week?"

Something was up. Sam huffed out a breath, punched her pillow again and propped herself into a half-seated position.

"What's going on? You're with Lily and I know you two have a blast together. You can't possibly be bored of Paris. The museums, the artists, the cafes—I don't understand." So much for getting any more sleep tonight. More like this morning. Her sister needed to talk this out.

"Paris is incredible, but it would be so much more incredible if you were with me. Aren't you ready to get out of there?" Dylan's eyes widened. "And what's going on, you ask? I had a message from dad to call him, but I wanted to talk to you first."

Sam bit her lip. She filled in Dylan on her dad's momentous decision.

"What? He's never talked about directing once in the last ten years. Not once." Dylan's face had paled and panic threaded her usually melodic voice.

"Calm down. He really misses it." She shook her head. "I had no idea. Movies were his first love and he gave it all up to protect us. Seeing his face made me understand he not only lost mom, but the career he'd built."

"What if he loves it and wants to sell the ranch and move back to LA, then what? And what about Angela? What did she say? She'd hate Hollywood."

"He's not going to sell the ranch. Their life is here. Our life is here. And Angela believes in him and trusts him. It can't be easy for her to live in the specter of mom's shadow." She'd stand by her father. His pain and his excitement had been palpable. He loved the horses and the business and the ranch, but movies were in his blood.

Dylan looked away and remained silent.

"Dylan?" Her sister could be stubborn.

She sighed. "Okay. You've got a point. I'm just shocked though. I had no idea he missed it. He's never said anything…"

"I feel a little guilty now, to tell you the truth. He probably never mentioned it on purpose."

"It all feels like a soap opera. Speaking of drama––have you been able to avoid the thorn-in-your-side stuntman?"

A warm flush crept up her cheeks. "He's not a thorn in my side." Busted.

"Ooooooh, now you like him? Do tell." Dylan grinned. Her twin's moods could flip minute to minute. At least she'd distracted her sister.

"It's not a big deal." She crossed the fingers on one hand. This white lie business was becoming a habit. "I've just gotten to know him a little better and he's making up for the negative first impression a bit. He's not so bad." She crossed her toes.

Dylan pursed her lips and made smooching sounds. "Oooh la la. Is that why you don't want to come to Paris? Kissing the sexy stuntman?"

"Well…" She paused and adjusted the duvet cover. Avoided looking into the phone. She'd never been able to prevaricate with her twin.

Dylan jolted up straighter on the ornate black wrought iron bench. "Wait, I was just joking around. You kissed him? What?"

"Well, it just happened last night. I was going for a swim and he was there and then somehow I was telling him about how awful it was in L.A. after mom died and he was so sensitive and understanding." Nope, definitely couldn't keep secrets from her sister.

"You *told him* about mom?" Dylan's mouth dropped open.

"I know. I know. I can't explain it to you, but yes. And then I guess I cried——" Anytime she could shut her pie hole would be great.

Dylan's eyes practically popped out of her head. "You *cried* in front of him? You *never* cry."

Sam closed her eyes and instantly a vision of the archangel Holt flashed behind her lids. How had everything changed so quickly? "I don't know. I saw the trailers being unloaded yesterday morning and it brought it all back. Those years of being on set with mom, the accident, the frickin' paparazzi, the move. Like a waterfall thundering down on me. Then dad's bombshell just sent me over the edge. I can't seem to catch up. I figured I'd swim it out when I heard a noise and he was creeping away with his guitar———"

"Oh no. The set? Oh Sam, I'm sorry I ran away

and left you to deal with this all on your own." Dylan sighed.

"Amanda's here. Everyone's here. The horses help, but I won't lie. I do miss you."

"I miss you too, which is why you should come here. Back to this kissing business. I thought you despised him. How did you end up kissing?"

"I don't know. He wiped away my tear and then the next thing you know I'm on his lap and we were steaming up the chaise lounge."

"You didn't…?" Her sister's brows were getting a regular workout, what with all the flying up and down on her forehead.

"No, of course I didn't." Although ripping off his clothes and making love on the lounge chair had seemed like an excellent idea for a hot minute. "Don't be silly. It was just a few kisses."

Dylan shook her head. "Well, he is gorgeous. And he plays the guitar? That's dreamy. And he was kind to you? Even so, I'm just afraid it's all too complicated and you'd probably kill each other."

"Complicated is right. I'm just going to take this day-by-day. He'll be gone when the movie is over and I get the impression he lives out of a suitcase. So, there's nothing to worry about." Why did the thought of not seeing his gorgeous smirking face again create a tiny ache in her chest?

"Right. Nothing to worry about. You don't need a broken heart from a guy who probably seduces a woman on every set and leaves without a backward glance. Like a rock star on tour."

"Whoa, where did that come from? He's a good guy, Dylan." He might not have roots, but he wasn't a player. Was he?

"Defending him again. I was just testing you. You like him." Her twin looked like the cat that'd swallowed the cream. Did she look equally obnoxious when *she* was being a smartass? Ugh.

"Yeah, I like him. But I'm a big girl. If we end up having a fling and he leaves, what's the big deal? I can handle it." Why did the words feel forced?

Ha, because she was full of crap. She had no clue if she could handle it. Or him. Maybe their attraction would dwindle.

"Okay. If you say so. I still think you need to come visit me." Her sister's mischievous smile faded.

"Well, were you calling just about dad's message or is something else going on? Are you just homesick?" Time to turn the tables and put her sister on the witness stand.

"I'm fine. Just feeling emotional, that's all. This city epitomizes romance and beauty and although my painting is going well, sometimes I wish I had a handsome Frenchman to walk arm in arm with along the Seine."

"I'm sure you could meet someone in a heartbeat if you looked. Why don't you and Lily go out? There are a million cafes and clubs there."

It was her sister's turn to shrug. "Maybe. But I want love at first sight. I don't want to look. I want my knight in shining armor to find me. Like Holt found you in the breeding shed." She chuckled.

"I wouldn't call him a knight in shining armor. And definitely not love at first sight." Sam shook her head. What was all this talk of love? More like pure lust.

"Whatever you say. Okay, I'm meeting Lily and need to run. Keep me up to date on everything."

"You too. Love you."

After they hung up, Sam tossed off her royal blue comforter and swung her legs over the edge of the bed. No way she could fall asleep now. A few gallons of coffee would have to fuel her through the day. At least it was off-season. Not that she didn't enjoy visiting the young foals and their moms out in the pastures now, but nothing beat the excitement of breeding season.

Between January and July she often worked from 5:30 a.m. to 11:00 p.m., depending upon how many mares they were foaling out, how many requests for Hercules' progeny needed processing, and how many million other tiny little details she needed to handle. God, she missed it.

Her life was perfect. Well, it had been before Holt stepped into her barn. Would he be down at the stables early?

She hurried toward the bathroom to shower and go for a ride. If Holt happened to be there, well…

CHAPTER 16

SAM SLID OUT OF THE quiet house as dawn was breaking in streaks of rose and tangerine across the sky. Early morning was one of her favorite times, when the world seemed pristine and clean and innocent. Her boots crunched along the dew-covered grass and she grinned as she surveyed the beauty of her ranch. Even though it was summer, the mornings were cool and crisp and every single branch, leaf, and flower looked perfect. She hummed as she approached the large stable.

"Hello, beautiful girl, did you sleep well? Blink once for yes, twice for no." She crooned to Princess Buttercup, who blinked once and tossed her silky mane.

"I didn't sleep a wink, but I feel amazing. It's going to be a perfect day." Sam led her horse out and saddled her. Maybe one day Buttercup would reply. She was brilliant, as well as beautiful.

She mounted and trotted out toward the pastures to check on the mares and foals. Then, she'd ensure everything was going smoothly down on the movie set. Running into Holt would be a bonus.

If someone had told her she'd be embarking on a fling with the obnoxious idiot who'd mocked her tease mare, she would have laughed until her sides ached. She'd assumed he was a callous, cocky jerk. Not that she was overly sensitive, no; she was accustomed to being the only woman in the man's world of horse breeding. Her skin was thick as a rhino's and she could joke with the best of them, even when the humor was lowbrow. She was one of the guys—Sam McNeill.

Somehow Holt saw beyond the surface. He'd recognized her dancer's soul. Most people didn't have a clue. She liked the fact he was confident enough in his masculinity to go to ballet. Most men couldn't or wouldn't even try. Certainly nobody else she had dated.

Her breath caught in her throat.

Dated?

They were most definitely *not* dating. They'd argued. She'd taken him tamales and watched him scarf them down. Then gotten angry at his aloof attitude. He'd shared dinner with her family, and she'd barely glanced at him across the table. Then, he'd kissed her so passionately her head had practically exploded off her body.

Definitely not dating.

What were they doing? They'd been circling each other since the first moment he'd stepped into her barn and now what? Where was this unexpected dance leading?

She slowed Buttercup down and brushed her fingers across her lips, still tender and slightly swollen from his kisses. Her eyes closed and she gave a dreamy sigh. Those kisses.

On one level she knew it was dangerous to get involved with him because she could already tell the pull toward him wasn't simply physical. Whatever it was between them didn't feel casual. His strength, his kindness, and his protectiveness had earned her respect. But from the minute he'd stepped into her barn, her orderly routine had been disrupted.

But, he was a nomad; each new movie set his temporary home. She was permanently rooted to her beloved ranch, her horses, the land, the way of life. All of it.

Why would she ever leave? What would she do? Where would she go? She shook her head because it didn't matter. He'd leave and she never would.

He'd tilted her world on its axis and there was no going back. Why was she fighting the attraction? He was on her turf now, however temporary the status. They wanted each other. They were both adults. No strings attached. They would keep it simple. And she'd never been attracted to anyone like this before. Where was the harm in that?

Mind made up, she gave Buttercup free rein and galloped along, savoring the crisp morning air against her skin. Her horse whinnied in pleasure; she always loved to run fast, especially in the quiet early morning hours. When Sam reached the crest of the green hill above the movie set, she gasped at the transformation from twenty-four hours ago. More trailers had arrived, and the crew must have been working nonstop because they'd transformed part of the area into an old-fashioned wood ranch house, complete with a split rail fence, bales of hay, and a few grazing horses. No longer one of the simple Pacific Vista Ranch pastures, the area looked like an authentic homestead from the Wild West.

A Western epic—her dad loved period pieces and making the past come to life. Maybe this explained her dad's fascination with the film and his desire to participate.

Nobody was stirring yet and she peeked at her enormous diver's style watch. It wasn't even 6 a.m. Movies started early, but today wasn't scheduled as a full filming day as far as she knew.

Buttercup's ears pricked a split second before the sound of hooves reached Sam's ears. Warmth crept up her cheeks and her toes curled in her Frye boots when she turned and saw Holt and Rocco's approach. Her lips tingled, would he kiss her again?

"Good morning, Sam." Holt's eyes were shadowed under the brim of his fawn-colored cowboy hat and his voice was flat.

"Hey. Um, you're up early." She smiled and angled toward him. Was that the best she could do? Hadn't she decided to seduce him? Have a fling?

"Yeah, shooting starts at 5:30 a.m. tomorrow so I'm just adjusting to being up early." He sat ramrod straight in the saddle, his gaze locked on the faux ranch house.

"Did you sleep okay?" Her smile faded and she bit her lip.

"Yeah, never better. It's so quiet out here. Slept like a baby." He still hadn't looked at her. He could be talking to himself.

"Well, good for you." She gritted her teeth. Like a baby? Was he kidding? She hadn't slept a wink.

He looked at her for the first time since he'd ridden up next to her, one golden eyebrow quirked. "What's wrong with you this morning? Is there a problem out here already?"

"No, no problem at all." Her fingers dug into the leather reins and she tamped down the pit forming in her gut. They had shared mind-blowing kisses last night and if she hadn't stopped him, neither of them would have slept a wink. He'd been rock hard and ready to go and now he could barely look at her?

"Oh, good. Seriously, it will be like we aren't even here. Your ranch will be left good as new when we're done." He smiled, a friendly stranger.

Who was this bland guy? Where was the sensitive listener? The passionate kisser? Had she dreamed the scene by the pool last night?

"Great. Well, I need to go. See you later." She wheeled Buttercup around and retreated back toward the stables. No way in hell would she allow him to see his indifference bothered her.

Dylan had been right this morning—he probably had an affair on every movie set. So why was he acting as if nothing happened? Seriously? She'd never experienced anything like last night and here he was, nonchalant and unaffected. The bastard. Her first impression was right. As usual.

Fine. Two could play at that game. She'd be polite and cool and calm. If he could run hot and cold, so could she.

CHAPTER 17

NICE GOING, WAY TO BE friendly. Holt rubbed the back of his neck and cursed. Samantha disappeared over the top of the hill; her spine stiff, unlike her customary relaxed riding posture. Damn it. He'd pulled out every iota of his non-existent acting talent to pretend like she was just a kid sister or buddy, but came across more like a rude ass.

But it was the right thing to do. His number one priority was a successful movie shoot and no way would he jeopardize his future because some woman happened to be fascinating. When did she morph from irritating to intriguing? Damn inconvenient.

When Harry offered him the opportunity to make an investment, and technically become a producer, he'd known he would take the risk and sink his hard-earned savings he'd accumulated over the years into this film. Not only was Harry paying him a pretty penny for the stunt work, but he was also offering him his big break.

Instead of saving for another three to five years, he could retire from the career that only became more grueling by the production. Or lose every-thing. The pretty penny wasn't simply extra lining for his bank account; it represented the last contribution to finalize his investment in his new business. His future. His mom's future. His sister's future.

Yes, Samantha stirred him in ways he'd never experienced, but compartmentalizing was one of his major talents.

He'd been doing it his whole life.

Under her tough shell, she had a tender heart. She deserved a man who would be relationship material. As his last girlfriend had very justly informed him, he was a drifter who should stick to casual encounters. Harsh but true.

Although once he started his new business, he wouldn't have to travel like a rock star any-more. Regardless, he wouldn't be settling down on Pacific Vista Ranch. And Samantha McNeill belonged on this ranch.

He belonged in L.A., where all the action hap-pened. Where he could build and leave a legacy to make his mom proud. Maybe she would finally forgive him for not going to college. Wasting four years learning about chemistry or philosophy hadn't appealed. His work ethic had enabled him to save enough money to buy her a house, to send money every month so she didn't have to work, and fulfilled his promise to himself to be the man of the family.

Although contemplating Los Angeles, with its merciless traffic, isolated egotistical show business peeps, and concrete highways didn't appeal either. His stable future would be built in the Hollywood movie industry and he would handle it despite the location.

The crunch of wheels on the gravel road next

to him signaled he was no longer alone. Harry parked his shiny luxury SUV under the shade of a large eucalyptus tree. Holt dismounted from Rocco's back, walked him over to the length of wood fence, and looped the gelding's reins around one rail. Time to get to work. No time to brood.

"Ready to rock and roll?" Harry grinned at him, the eager anticipation of the opening days of filming lighting up his lean face.

"Definitely. This location is going to be perfect. The set designers did an amazing job. How does it look to you?"

"Let's check it out. Was that Samantha riding over the hill?"

They walked toward the pasture where the crew continued to re-create the Wild West.

"Yeah, she was surveying the activity again." Looking like a goddess.

"She's a beautiful woman."

Holt jerked his head and stared at Harry. "She's kind of young for you. She could be your daughter."

"Calm down. I wasn't saying I was attracted to her, but you know I appreciate beauty. She rides like she was born on the back of a horse. What do you think of having her in a scene or two?" Harry studied him, his face impassive.

Holt snorted. "You're joking, right? You're really pushing the envelope with the McNeills. First Chris is directing and now you want Samantha in the film? She'd never agree to it."

"Now you know how she feels? Doesn't she think you're an idiot?" Harry's brows rose over his dark wraparound sunglasses. "I heard about the fluffer comments."

A flush crept up Holt's neck. "Look, I was just joking when I said that. I've gotten to know them all more since I've been staying here. Isn't it enough they are letting you film here? Why stir up more of the past?"

Harry studied him like he was a bug under a microscope. "Huh."

"Huh what?" A dull ache started at his temples and he ground his back teeth. He'd always looked up to Harry, but right now the older man was really starting to piss him off.

"You just seem awfully protective of my friend's young daughter, that's all. It's not like you. I've seen you with other women and you may have liked them, but you never seemed to worry about them." Harry shrugged a shoulder.

"I'm not worried. I'm just—" He just *what?*

"Are you sweet on Samantha?" Harry's black and silver eyebrows drew together.

"No, of course not. She's like a little sister. That's all. I feel bad for what they all went through." So why was he talking so fast?

"Hmmm…protective instincts. Interesting." Harry let out a low whistle.

Holt turned away from Harry's scrutiny, whipped off his hat, and raked his fingers through his hair. "Are we going to get to work or what?" This conversation was off the rails. Time to slam on the brakes.

"Sure. We'll discuss the horses in a bit. Let's head over and survey everything." Harry sauntered over and smacked him on the back. "I just think you're sweet on Chris McNeill's baby daughter.

Never thought I'd see the day you'd step out of casual. That's all."

"Not another word, Harry." Holt shook off his hand and stomped toward the split-rail fence. Sweet on Samantha McNeill, yeah right.

The universe was not conspiring to destroy him because Harry kept his trap shut for the next fifteen minutes while they perused the farmhouse and yard. This morning certainly wasn't unfolding in the way he'd imagined.

Work, his focus was on work. Laser focus was one of his major skills––if he allowed his mind to wander during filming he could die or get seriously injured. No way in hell would he allow his attention to wander.

"Hey guys, how's it going?" Sam's dad asked from behind them.

Holt's shoulders tensed and he forced a casual grin as he turned to face him. "Hey Chris, how's it going?"

"Great, great. The set looks amazing. Great designers, Harry." Chris looked around, his stance relaxed, yet in command. He *looked* like he was in charge.

"I'll let you guys get to it. I'm going to head over and check on the horses." No need to spend too much time with Sam's dad this morning, he wasn't uncomfortable or guilty. Nope.

"Wait one second, let's run my idea past Chris and see what he thinks." Harry said.

Damn it. Holt pivoted back to face the men. Chris looked between them with lifted brows.

"It's your idea, Harry." No way did he support having Sam around even more. No need to create temptation.

"What?" A thread of impatience ran through the ranch owner's voice. Like daughter, like father.

"Well, Holt and I both noticed what an incredible horsewoman Sam is. I could use a talented female rider. How would she feel about being in a few scenes? She wouldn't have to speak or anything."

Chris whipped off his sunglasses and stepped closer to his old friend. "What? Are you kidding me? Hell no, Harry. You're really pushing me too far."

Harry held up his hands in front of him in a protective gesture. "Hear me out."

"Screw you, Shaw. You *know* she was on set when Pamela was killed. What are you trying to do?" A red flush traveled up Chris' neck and his eyes blazed.

Not an opportune time to point out how Samantha's temper must have come directly from her father. Holt kept his mouth shut and observed the verbal volley between the two older men.

"Listen to me." When Chris took another step, Harry's voice rose. "Listen."

Chris paused, his broad shoulders vibrating with temper.

"You helping direct this movie is going to help you move beyond the past. Do you want Sam to suffer from this phobia forever? Maybe if she actually participates in a scene or two, it might help her too? Maybe she'll be able to move past it?"

"What's your deal, Shaw? Are you on a mission of redemption or something to heal my family from losing Pamela? None of us are the same and we never will be." Chris paused and exhaled a deep breath. "My daughters don't have to deal with Hollywood if they don't want to. I know you may have lost perspective, but we do just fine without it here."

"It was just a suggestion. If you don't want me to ask her, I won't. Just an idea. I'm sorry." Harry backed away. "Well, let's get back to work. How about we walk over to the trailers and make sure everyone is arriving on time and we can start tomorrow morning. You still going to observe first?"

Chris didn't move, his jaw clenched. Then, his shoulders softened and he nodded.

"Later." Holt escaped before they could stop him. What was going on with these guys? Harry was pushing the envelope with the McNeills. If he didn't know for a fact the ranch up near Cambria had been damaged due to fire, he might have believed the director had engineered the filming of his Western on Pacific Vista Ranch all along.

Did Harry have some kind of agenda? Holt couldn't forget seeing Samantha sobbing yesterday morning or wiping away her tears last night. Or the feel of her in his arms. He stiffened. Time to head back to the stables and check in on the horses. He'd do his job and keep to himself.

For the first time, he regretted accepting the invitation to stay in the McNeill's guesthouse. Space would be preferable.

Miles of space.

He'd stay out of Samantha's path for good.

CHAPTER 18

"COCOA IS GOING TO BE okay, isn't he?" Sam loved being able to assist her sister in the rehab facility off-season, but hated seeing any animal suffer.

Sam stroked the beautiful brown gelding's dark mane and cooed comforting words in his velvety ear. Cocoa lived on a neighboring ranch and belonged to the Smythe's fourteen-year-old daughter, Ashley. Unfortunately, on a recent outing along one of the winding Rancho Santa Fe riding trails, Cocoa had sprained his foreleg. He needed physical therapy to fully recover before he could carry even the slight load of a petite girl.

"Yes, he'll be fine. The sprain should heal quickly." Amanda smiled at her from the other side of the horse. Cocoa had just been treated to a soothing saltwater bath and was now on the Equisizer to walk and restore his strength.

"I'm so glad. I know the Smythes are thrilled you're the one taking care of him." Their small community held Amanda in high regard for her veterinary skills and practical demeanor.

"I'm happy to help our neighbors. So, what's the latest on the movie? Is the crew all here? Are they filming today?" Amanda asked.

Sam shook her head. "No, it starts tomorrow. The rest of the cast and crew arrive today." She sighed. "Dad was down in the stables and he seems so excited. I still can't really process it."

"I know." Amanda's voice was quieter than usual. "It feels surreal to me."

"I guess I assumed he wanted to be away from it all forever as much as we did."

"We never really discussed it, did we? I mean, we were kids." Amanda monitored Cocoa's pace.

"Nope, definitely not. If the damn media hadn't made our life hell, who knows what would have happened?"

"Dad would still be making movies, you would be a principal ballerina, Dylan would still be an artist, and I would still be a vet. So you and dad are the ones who really ended up on a new path."

"Maybe. I can't think about what might have been——I love the horses and I love this ranch. And dad wouldn't have met Angela." Sam squashed down the memory of her former dreams.

"True. You're amazing at what you do, little sis. Who knows, this might be good for him, heck maybe for all of us. Help put it all in perspective. How do you feel?" Amanda stepped around Cocoa and hugged her.

Sam bit the inside of her lip. "I cried." She blurted it out.

"Oh sweetie, that's normal." Amanda squeezed her in tight to her slender yet strong frame.

"No, you don't understand, yesterday morning I rode over to the set. When I saw it, everything flooded back and it was like mom died yesterday." She pressed her fingers against her eyelids to stem the tears threatening to spill over. Damn it, was she going to turn into a crybaby now? "The pain was just as powerful as it was the day it happened."

"You never cried when it happened. I always worried about you bottling it up and quitting dancing at the same time. Crying is okay." Amanda rested her cheek on the top of Sam's head.

"I hate crying. I even cried in front of——" Oh crap, TMI.

"In front of who?" Amanda stepped back, her emerald eyes wide.

Sam hesitated. Her sisters were her only true confidantes. Maybe Amanda could help her sort out what the hell was going on inside her jumbled brain. And heart. Dylan hadn't been much help.

She stared down at Cocoa's shiny chocolate coat. "Holt, I cried in front of Holt last night."

"Holt? Last night? When last night?"

"Um, after dinner." She dared a glance at her sister.

"After dinner?" Amanda's voice rose an octave and her eyebrows flew up.

"Well, I was upset about dad's announcement and I decided to swim it off. I was doing laps and heard a noise. Holt was down at the cabana." The words tumbled out.

"So how did you go from hearing a noise to crying in front of him? I don't understand." Amanda's eyebrows drew together.

"Well, I snapped at him for being there——" Was it possible she sounded even more idiotic out loud than in her mind?

"Seriously?" Amanda's shoulders shook with laughter.

"I know. I know. Well, he just brings out the worst in me. And then somehow I ended up spilling everything about the paparazzi after mom died and he ended up being really sweet." She rubbed her eyes, making sure they weren't leaking again.

"Hmmmm…" Amanda nodded and tilted her head. "So, what did he do when you cried?"

Sam opened her mouth. Promptly closed it. Tried again.

"He was just nice. But this morning he was back to being cocky Hollywood guy." She cleared her throat and stared over her sister's shoulder. Was he really unaffected? Her gut tightened when she recalled his indifference.

Nothing like the charismatic seducer he'd been at the pool when he'd ignited their passion with his blistering hot kisses and hard calloused hands. Not the arrogant smartass he'd been when he'd invaded her breeding barn cracking jokes. Was he the player she'd initially assumed he was?

"This morning? What?" Amanda's brow creased. "I can't keep up. What am I missing?"

"Oh, I saw him over at the set this morning." Looking like a Greek god carved from marble. And acting just as cold.

Her sister's eyes narrowed. "And was he a jerk?"

Sam ran her tongue around her teeth. Although she'd told Dylan about the kiss, at the time she'd assumed they would continue flirting or kissing or whatever they had been doing. Now he'd morphed into Mr. Ice King and she would rather pretend nothing happened. If she admitted he was a jerk, her astute sister would suspect she was hiding something.

"Not really a jerk. He just seemed sweet last night and this morning he was back to being Mr. Too Hot Hollywood." She shrugged. Time to change the subject pronto.

"Hmmm." Her elder sister pursed her lips, her eyes assessing.

"What are you hmm–ing about?" *Uh-oh.*

"I think Mr. Too Hot Hollywood has a crush on you." Amanda made a few smooching sounds.

"Oh please. He doesn't have a crush on me. He treats me like an annoying younger sister." Well, except for at the pool last night. Warmth crept up her neck, gathering at her nape where his perfect lips had lingered.

Amanda grinned. "Well, you've been *my* annoying younger sister for years and I adore you so…"

"Very funny. Enough about him." She'd already been thinking about him, dreaming about him, and talking about him way too much for comfort.

"Enough about who?" A masculine voice inquired.

Sam jumped and pivoted. Her dad stood a few feet away from them. How much had he heard? He was smiling, so it couldn't have been too much.

"Hi, Dad." Amanda strolled over and hugged their father. "How are you?"

Thank goodness Amanda was so much like their mother—she was quiet and tended to keep her emotions and thoughts behind a serene smile. Her tranquility balanced out their dad's strong energy and also served to distract him from asking too many questions. Sam and her father were too much alike with their hair-trigger tempers and utter lack of patience.

"Good, good." Chris walked over to the Equi-sizer. "Who is this beauty?"

"This is Cocoa, one of the Smythes' horses. He's a real lover. Slight sprain, he'll be fine in no time," Amanda said.

Lover. Sam's cheeks heated again. What if she'd taken Holt as her lover last night? Would he have blown her off like he had this morning?

"Oh, good. Glad it's nothing serious." Chris nodded and focused his gaze on Sam. "Well, I came down to talk to Samantha, but you should hear this too."

"Is everything okay?" Sam's spine stiffened. What now?

"I was just down on set, and it looks amazing. Harry and I were talking and he mentioned he saw you this morning, Sammy?" Her dad was speaking faster than usual.

"Did he? I didn't see him. It was super early and I was on my morning ride. Just checking every-thing out." Sam stared down at her scuffed black boots. Had Harry witnessed the scene between her and Holt?

"Well, he said he saw you and Holt together?"

"Together? What do you mean together?" Her already rigid spine turned to steel. *Crap.*

Chris arched a brow. "Were you with Holt or not?"

"What do you mean *with* Holt?" Now she'd transformed into a parrot. Her brain had closed up shop for the day or possibly forever.

"Sam." Amanda laid a cool hand on her fore-arm. "Dad is asking you if you and Holt were down at the set this morning."

"Oh the set, right." She shrugged. What was *wrong* with her? "Yeah, he was there when I was checking it out."

"Are you getting sick, Samantha? Why are you so flushed?" Her dad asked, his eyes full of concern.

Why wouldn't he be worried? She was acting like a lunatic.

"I'm fine, Dad. Sorry, I'm just starving and you know how I get if I don't eat every few hours. My blood sugar must've dropped. You know how loopy I can get." *Stop babbling or he'll have you committed.*

"Why don't we head up to the house and get you some food. I'll share Harry's suggestion." Her father turned toward the rehab clinic door.

"No, just tell me now." Thus far, Harry Shaw's ideas did not rank among her top ten list. What now?

"I'm curious too, Dad. What suggestion does Harry have now? Filming in the house?" Amanda was rarely sarcastic, so her clipped questions carried weight.

"Girls, please don't be angry with Harry. I owe him."

"You owe him why?" Amanda demanded. "Because mom chose you over him? That was decades ago."

Chris closed his eyes for a moment and the tic at his left temple appeared. "Look, you're right. It is old history. But Harry was in love with your mother, hell, everyone was in love with your mother. I'm pretty sure he never married because it was always her."

"Wow."   Samantha and Amanda exchanged glances.

"It just made things awkward because we all knew it. Harry never held a grudge or anything because they weren't an item when we met. And…" Chris scratched his chin.

"Sorry, Dad, we're not trying to knock you back into the past. We're just trying to understand this whole thing. You have to admit it's all been a whirlwind and we're adjusting as best we can." Amanda's stern expression softened.

"And? Is there more, Dad?" How many secrets were there?

"Well, Harry was the one the media insinuated was having an affair with your mom. He had to deal with that crap too. And when I couldn't finish the movie, he stepped in and did it, even with all the ugliness. He was there for me. For us." Chris closed his eyes again and the grooves around her father's mouth deepened.

"Is that why his name sounded familiar? Why wasn't he at the funeral then?" Sam struggled to keep her voice calm.

"Look, we both thought it would make the media circus even worse, especially at the service. Not like that was possible." He grimaced.

"So what's the question?" Samantha's mind was racing. Her dad had been through enough. Who knew how tough it had been to walk away from an award-winning career, mourn his wife, and raise three teenaged girls?

"Okay. Like I said, Harry saw you riding and he was impressed. Of course." Her father grinned.

Samantha's shoulders relaxed. Compliments on

her equestrian skills were welcome. She gestured with one hand for him to continue.

"So there are a few scenes requiring a female rider—"

Her jaw slackened. "Are you joking?"

"Actually no. There's a rebellious heroine who borrows her brother's breeches and she's kind of reckless." Chris cleared his throat.

"You want me to be in the movie?" Her stomach clenched.

"Dad, you can't be serious." Amanda stepped closer to their father.

"You used to love being on set. The rider he hired isn't as talented as you are. I told him you most likely wouldn't even consider it, but I told him I'd ask you." His eyes shimmered with emotion.

"So like the stunt woman during the horseback riding scenes? But I'm not in the union or an actor or any of it." What the heck was Harry's deal?

"There are loopholes of course. If you wanted to do it, he'd make it work."

Amanda's nostrils flared, her rare, slow burn temper simmering. "But what if something happened? Will Harry not rest until all the McNeills are entangled in his film? What is going on? This ranch is our home and sanctuary. Now, it's been invaded by Hollywood, and you're directing and encouraging Sam to do stunts?"

"Yeah, Dad, none of this makes sense. What gives?" Although she was an incredible rider, no ego there, none of this made sense.

"I told him you'd say no. It's just…" He gazed out the window.

"It's just what?" Sam gaped. Her dad simply wasn't acting like himself.

"You gave up your dreams of being a ballerina. I hate that you paid that price. I know you love what you do now, but maybe having a positive experience on a movie set could help you get past all the awful memories." Chris pinned her with his gaze, and pressed his lips together in a straight line.

"Is that why you're doing it, Dad? To move past it all?" Amanda's voice gentled.

"Maybe. Hell, I don't know." He scratched his jaw again. "It was my life and then it was gone. There's just something in the process that stimulates me like nothing else. And if there's a side benefit of not feeling paralyzed anytime anyone talks about the movie industry, it's not a bad thing, right?" His broad shoulders slumped.

Sam ran to her dad and wrapped her arms around his waist. Would it be so terrible if this movie helped heal a part of him he'd buried? Probably not, but would it make her feel better or worse to be on the set?

She'd locked away the childhood memories because they were simply too agonizing. But the truth was she'd loved every single minute of watching her mom transform into different characters and seeing her dad's masterful orchestration of scenes. Her mom's ethereal beauty, so like Amanda's, filled the movie screen and nobody could tear their eyes away from her for a second.

Before the accident, Sam never questioned her principal ballerina destiny and never shunned the spotlight. After the accident, she ruthlessly packed away her toe shoes and leotards. The horses on Pacific Vista Ranch filled the void and she'd found a new calling as breeding manager and ranch manager.

Was her dad right? Would participating in the movie soften the tightness and dread that arose deep in her chest each time she remembered the day she lost her mother? Although she doubted the scars could completely disappear, if even one layer of buried pain faded, perhaps it would be worth it.

"What do you think, Amanda?" Her sister was like a second mom to her and she valued her opinion.

"At first, I thought it was a terrible idea, but the way Dad explains it, maybe it would help. But only if you're sure." Amanda shifted her gaze toward their father. "It has to be her choice."

"Of course." He looked offended. "You know I've never forced Sammy to do anything, nor would I try."

"I'm assuming I would be riding one of the Hollywood horses?"

"Of course. Remember the lead actress needs to be able to ride the horse too and they selected a mount she can handle." He smiled.

"Would this be a scene you were directing?" It better be.

"I could direct it, yeah. This is assuming it all goes well and I remember how to direct anymore." His grin was wry.

"Okay, tell Shaw I'll do it, but only if you're there and if anything feels weird, I'm out. But what about Amanda?"

"Of course. Remember the ball is in your court. What about Amanda?" Her dad's broad forehead creased.

"Yeah, what about me?" Amanda's eyes widened.

She pointed to her sister. "Well, if I'm participating in this as a kind of therapy, what about her? Shouldn't she do something for the movie too?"

Amanda held up both hands and shook her head. "Oh no, you two aren't dragging me into this scheme. I'm fine."

Sam tilted her head and gazed at her always in control sister. "Are you sure?"

"Of course I'm sure. Dad?" Amanda appealed to their father.

"Amanda knows her own mind. She's my rock, always so steady." Her dad smiled, his hazel eyes bright. "Right?"

Amanda smiled tightly. "Of course, that's me: the reasonable one."

Sam stared at her older sister. Was she really fine? Amanda was tough to read with her level-headed approach to life. But right now something simmered beneath the tranquil surface and Sam was concerned.

"Let's get you some lunch. I don't want you to faint." Chris reached out a hand to her.

"Oh sure. Bye Amanda. Bye Cocoa." She'd forgotten her impromptu excuse. Of course she was hungry as usual, but the blood sugar hadn't been lack of food. Nope, Mr. Too Hot Hollywood had reduced her to a babbling fool.

She stopped suddenly in her tracks.

Her dad looked down at her with raised brows.

"Sam, are you sure you're okay?"

She nodded and hurried along toward the house with him, her pulse thrumming in her veins.

Had she just agreed to ride with Holt in a movie scene?

CHAPTER 19

SAM SWALLOWED THE FINAL BITE of her perfectly crafted tuna melt and popped in the last crisp slice of dill pickle. Her demanding belly was satiated, but her overactive mind continued to wrestle with her suspicions about Holt. Nobody else had been out on that side of the ranch this morning.

"I'm going to head down to the set and let Harry know you've agreed. Are there any days where you won't be available?" Her dad asked.

"Well, I've got piles of boring paperwork and all the usual off-season stuff. Nothing urgent, so I'm flexible." She'd take any excuse to postpone sitting at the computer.

Her dad grasped her hand with his large sun-weathered one. "Thanks for agreeing, Sam. I think this could be fun and who knows, maybe it will be cathartic for both of us."

She turned her palm upward and squeezed. "I hope so, Dad. I still think it's weird he asked me, because I know he wasn't down there on set yet. Are you sure it wasn't Holt?"

"What if it was? Are you two still rubbing each other the wrong way?" His hazel eyes narrowed and his brows drew together.

"No, no, I don't even notice he's there." Sam's cheeks heated again and she stared down at her now empty plate. No, she wouldn't exactly describe last night's make out session as rubbing her the *wrong* way. More like caressing her in all the right ways.

"That's good. He seems like a good kid. Even if Harry saw you from a distance, he'd know you are a gifted horsewoman, just like you're a gifted dancer." Her father's eyes crinkled at the corners and he squeezed her hand again.

"Was a gifted dancer, Dad, was." Twelve years ago she'd been a ballerina. Not anymore.

"You'll always be a dancer, Sammy, maybe just in a different way than we all expected. Anyway, I'm heading down now and I'll see you at dinner." He patted her hand, rose from the table, and sauntered out of the kitchen.

She closed her eyes and exhaled a deep breath. Mr. Too Hot Hollywood had to have been the one to recommend she ride in the movie. What type of game was he playing? Seduce her under the stars and then freeze her out in the unforgiving morning light? He'd made it crystal clear he wasn't attracted to her this morning, so what was his agenda?

Disgusted with her one track mind, she smoothed back her braid and shoved away from the table. Until she uncovered his true motives, she wouldn't be able to concentrate. Color her obsessed.

She slipped out of the house, not wanting to answer any questions regarding her destination. She marched down the path toward the guesthouse, her annoyance burgeoning into righteous anger. She would demand answers. He would comply. He would admit he'd put Harry up to having her be a part of the movie. He would explain why. Her fingers curled into fists.

She stopped mid-stride. Who was she kidding? She was hurt. She'd bared her soul to him last night, shared intimate details about her mom's death, and today he'd been an aloof ass. Could he just flip his emotions on and off like a faucet? Even if he weren't responsible for the movie, he'd answer some questions about his behavior. She wasn't just some random chick, like all his other on-set romances.

By the time she was finished with him, she'd set down the rules for the movie shoot. Rule number one was he would stay away from her. Hands off.

She gritted her teeth. Nobody toyed with her. When she reached the guesthouse, she glanced down and grimaced at her dusty jeans and ancient gray T-shirt. Should she have cleaned up before rushing down to yell at him? She shook her head. Screw it. She didn't need to impress Holt Ericsson.

She raised her fist to bang on the door, but before her knuckles could connect to the wood, a lilting melody caressed her ears. The guitar—— he was playing his guitar. Her fingers relaxed and her hand drifted to her heart as the melancholy notes surrounded her. She recognized the tune, a haunting ballad by one of her favorite alternative rock bands, the Foo Fighters. She leaned against the doorjamb and her eyelids drifted shut. The music filled her heart with its sweet melody.

With a start, she straightened. The song had

ended.

Why was she here again? Her anger had dissipated.

Music really did soothe the savage beast, or the stereotypical redhead's temper, as the case may be.

Did she really need to confront him? Did she have the energy to? Did she even want to anymore? What was the point? He either wanted to be with her or he didn't. She couldn't force him into desiring her. If he were anything like her, the moment she yelled at him, he'd retreat and again: what was the point?

Her shoulders slumped and she pivoted away from the guesthouse to return home. Holt whipped the door open. She angled her head back toward him.

"What are you doing here?" His voice was raspy.

"Nothing. Never mind." She turned away and took two steps, but then he grabbed her wrist and tugged her to a stop. She whirled toward him, yanking her arm from his grasp. "Don't touch me."

"Samantha, you obviously came down here for a reason. What's going on?" His tone softened, leaving just the sexy huskiness.

She swallowed, her throat suddenly parched. Oh my. Once again, his chiseled muscular torso was bare and his smooth tanned skin beckoned to be stroked. He scrubbed one hand over his messy blond hair. His eyelids were hooded.

She crossed her arms in front of her chest. "Fine. I did. Then I changed my mind." So, never mind. Go back to strumming your guitar."

"You heard me playing?" His piercing silver

blue eyes widened.

"I did." She dug her fingers into her triceps. *And you playing one beautiful song calmed me down.* No way she would admit it. Her pulse was racing. He was just so damn pretty. No, not pretty. Gorgeous.

He leaned against the doorjamb and raised his brows.

"You were playing one of my favorite songs. Why aren't you a professional musician instead of a stuntman?" The words tumbled out. *And the schoolgirl babbling commences again.*

His square jaw dropped. "You're kidding, right?"

"Oh don't fish for compliments. I heard one song and you could be on any stage in the world and you know it. Just say thank you." Please, like he didn't know it.

His mouth snapped shut. "Okay, thank you. But you're exaggerating. I just play for myself."

If she stretched her arm toward him, she could touch the expanse of golden skin. Flashbacks from his kisses last night heated the blood in her veins. Dangerous. Being this close to him was dangerous. If she were as smart as her sister Amanda, she would keep their relationship all about business and forget about last night.

Definitely not as smart as her older sister.

"Cat got your tongue? If I'd known my guitar playing would stop you from yelling at me, I would have serenaded you weeks ago." One corner of his sculpted lips quirked up.

"Ha ha. Serenaded me. I'm not the kind of girl who gets serenaded, that's my twin." Damn it, why did she have to reveal her insecurity? But it was true—Dylan was floaty and feminine.

Before she could react, he wrapped his fingers around her shoulders and pulled her into his warm bare chest. He gazed down at her, and his pupils dilated, "You're beautiful, Samantha."

She froze. Her feet were glued to the spot, and her knees wobbled. Heat flooded her cheeks, but she couldn't tear her gaze away from his.

"You don't believe me?" His eyes narrowed and he frowned. "What would it take?"

"Take?" Her pulse drummed in her temples and the unsteadiness in her legs spread through her entire body.

"Yes, Samantha McNeill, what would it take for me to convince you?" His strong hands slid up her arms, leaving a trail of goose bumps in their wake. His large calloused palms gripped her shoulders.

She stepped back, but his hands tightened and she couldn't retreat. No man had ever looked at her the way he did. Sure, she knew she cleaned up okay and she had to be halfway good-looking since she had the same face as her twin sister, but beautiful?

Where was her usual supply of one-line zingers? Clever snappy retorts? Her lips parted, but nothing emerged.

His gaze dropped to her mouth. His muscular arms banded around her, enveloping her in the heat from all his smooth skin.

"I guess I'll just have to show you." He lowered his head and captured her lips in a demanding kiss, the pressure coaxing her lips apart.

She moaned and wrapped her arms around his

waist, digging her short fingernails into his bare back, for once wishing she indulged in manicures and had long, sexy fingernails to scrape along his muscles.

Her mind blanked and her eyelids floated shut. Each swirl of his tongue drew him deeper inside her. His breath tasted minty and cool. Heaven. When his hands slid up to frame the sides of her face, and he changed the angle of the kiss, she was lost. Lost in the sensations shooting down every inch of her body. *This.* This magic was what she'd been missing.

He tilted his head back for a moment and she almost cried at the separation. "You're beautiful and I want you."

Her pulse kicked and she stared into his heated gaze. When his lips brushed against hers again, she couldn't stop the moan.

Wasn't this why she'd come down here? To demand why he'd kissed her this way and then ignored her? To discover if last night was a fluke or if this attraction was beyond anything she'd ever experienced?

Definitely not a fluke.

She needed Holt.

Now.

"Yes," she replied against his lips, unwilling to break their connection.

He growled deep in his throat, swept her up in his arms, and carried her over the threshold of the guesthouse. Their lips remained fused together. He kicked the door shut behind him and when he released her legs, she slid down the length of his body. Every single rock-hard inch.

He dragged his hands down from her shoulders to her hips; trailing liquid fire everywhere he touched. He cupped her bottom in his hands and lifted her up and placed her on the kitchen island counter. He stepped in between her legs and yanked her in close, never breaking their kiss. She wound her legs around his waist and raked her hands through his messy, sexy hair. Her center liquefied and she wiggled to create some friction where they were joined together.

As he continued his assault, he freed her hair from her braid with one hand. He leaned back for a moment and thrust his fingers into her hair, fanning it out around her so it cascaded over her shoulders and down her back.

"I love your hair. Your face." He nipped at her jaw and nibbled along her neck, holding her in place. "You've driven me crazy from the moment we met."

She giggled. "Well, I don't know if that's really true. I think you wanted to throttle me more than kiss me, right?"

He flashed his white teeth, "Well, maybe so. I prefer this kind of insanity."

"Me too." She stroked an errant strand of hair off of his tanned forehead and smiled shyly. *Since when was she shy?*

"Let me show you, Sam." He leaned in again and clasped her head in his hands, holding her immobile.

His kiss grew tender now, teasing. Suddenly, his hard palms stroked up her naked back. She shivered and pressed closer to him. He had pulled her shirt from the waistband of her jeans and somehow he'd unhooked her bra at the same time. Air brushed against her bare skin when her shirt and bra sailed toward the middle of the room. He drew her against him and the moment her sensitive breasts touched his hot silky skin, she melted.

His hands slid up to her shoulders again, and held her arms' length away from him. He gazed down at her naked torso. Instinctively her arms began to rise to cover herself. She'd always been self-conscious over her tiny boobs, but didn't want him to stop. Didn't men, especially the Hollywood ones, love those big, plastic store-bought boobs?

"No." He caught her arms and held her still. "Let me look at you."

She struggled not to squirm under his hot gaze. At least her stomach was flat thanks to her jack-rabbit metabolism and her demanding job. She bit her lip. Couldn't they turn off the lights and get to it?

His gaze lifted and now his eyes were molten blue flames. He released one arm and caressed her breast. Keeping his gaze locked with hers, he leaned down and grazed her taut nipple lightly with his teeth.

She held her breath and the jolt of sensation rocked her. Finally, he lowered his head and stroked her other breast with his tongue. He brushed his lips from one erect nipple to the other in an unrelenting assault. Sparks danced along her skin. Flames were engulfing her at his studied attention and she grasped his shoulders so she didn't collapse.

He slid up from her breasts and captured her

lips once again. This time, his kiss was wild. Her mind blanked. Her whole body burned.

"Can you feel what you do to me, Sam? You are perfect." He scooped her up and she wrapped her denim-clad legs around his waist and he carted her into the bedroom where he tossed her on the bed and then dove in after her.

"Oof, and you're heavier than you look." She giggled again as his weight settled on top of her. What was with the giggles around him?

Immediately, he propped himself up on his forearms, shielding her from taking all his weight. "Did I hurt you?" His brows knit together.

"No, no. I'm just teasing you." His weight felt delicious on top of her.

"No more teasing." He captured her lips again and shifted them so they were on their sides facing each other. One hand stroked down her waist and curved possessively around her hip.

For a moment suspended in time, they simply stared at each other. She reached up one fingertip and stroked it along his high cheekbone, down the hollow of his cheek, and brushed across his sculpted, perfect lips.

How had she landed here, half-naked? With the wicked archangel Holt who she had wanted to kill when he interrupted her in the breeding barn?

He captured her hand, turned his head, and kissed her palm. A starburst of sensation tingled from his mouth straight to her center. She slid one finger between his lips. He inhaled harshly and then bit down, lightly scraping her knuckle with his teeth.

"Holt." Her vision blurred. He tugged her closer

and captured her lips. His hands turned demanding. Her belly clenched when he stroked her back
and forth over the waistband of her jeans.

"So tight, so smooth. Baby, your body is insane."
He managed to unbutton her jeans, yank down
the zipper and slide her pants off while still kissing
her. A finger looped around her cotton thong and
ripped it off with the jeans. "Let me look at you."

Somehow, she was on her back again and he
was above her, his gaze reverent. Like she was the
most incredible woman he'd ever seen.

He growled and trailed kisses along her collarbone and across her breasts, down her ribcage
and lingered at the hollow of her navel. His hands
were stroking, caressing, alternately firm and
feather light. She was burning up and she writhed
beneath him. She needed...

His hand cupped her and she arched off the bed.
He stroked once. Again. She moaned, her hips
moving of their own volition. He circled her most
sensitive spot with his thumb and stroked her with
his fingers.

"You're ready for me." He breathed against her
hipbone.

"Yes. Please. I need you now, Holt." Uncontrol-
lable shivers racked her from head to toe.

"Patience is a virtue." His lips curved against
her skin and he remained where he was, his breath
hot along her hipbone.

"Holt." She grabbed his hair, but he wasn't playing along.

He shifted and pinned her hips with his hands.
He gazed up at her, his gaze hot and his smile
wicked. "I have to see if you taste as delicious as

you look." He bent his head and licked her center with one long, hot stroke.

She bowed off the bed and cried out. He kissed, licked, and drove her wild. Almost instantly it seemed, the tremors escalated and her climax slammed through her like a lightning bolt. He stayed where he was, enjoying every second of her orgasm. Once she lay still, limp, and satiated, he rolled to the side and removed his jeans.

He smiled and reached into his jeans pocket and pulled out a condom from his wallet.

"Help me put it on." He whispered.

Her fingers fumbled as she unwrapped the package. She reached over and stroked him and he jolted. He was hard as steel with satiny skin. Together they smoothed the thin layer over him and he rolled onto his back, taking her with him.

She straddled him, his arousal throbbing against her. He lifted her hips and with excruciating slowness, lowered her inch by inch until he was buried inside her. She blew out the breath she had been holding and worked to adjust to the fullness. She leaned forward and placed her palms on his pecs as her hair tumbled forward, creating a curtain around them.

"Ride me. Please." His voice was raw and gravelly.

His hands gripped her hips and she began to move. It was natural. Wild. Free. She reached her arms up and grasped her hair as she rode him. The headboard creaked, and their heavy breathing punctuated every stroke. He released her hips and captured her hands, threading his long fingers through hers.

"Yeah, just like that." He released one hand and reached to the point where they were joined together. Stroked and caressed. Another climax built and blazed through her and she fell forward, desperate to feel his lips against hers. The moment her mouth met his, she exploded and rocked against him.

"Sam." He groaned her name and grasped her hips once again, holding her in place. He stroked two, three, four more times and whispered her name again as he climaxed. He pulled her down and wrapped his arms around her, keeping her pinned on top of him.

She collapsed on him and couldn't move. He kissed her hair and then she was asleep.

HOLT'S EYELIDS WEIGHED A HUNDRED POUNDS. He forced them open and swore. The late afternoon sun slanted across his face, the bright light momentarily blinding him. Disoriented, he rubbed his hand across his face and tried again. When he turned his head, a pair of inscrutable, velvety chocolate eyes watched him. Her small hands were tucked underneath her head and her long slender legs curled up into her chest.

"Hi." Oh yeah, that's why he was waking up in the middle of the afternoon.

"Hi yourself. Did you know you smile in your sleep?" Sam's rosy lips curved up.

"I don't think I've stopped smiling since you came down here and kissed me." Unable to resist, he stroked his hand along her silky auburn hair.

"Kissed you? You kissed me first." Her eyes

widened.

"Don't argue. You came down here because you wanted me to kiss you. Is that better?" His chest tightened when her delicate little nose wrinkled. Teasing her was so easy.

"I did not come down here for you to kiss me. I came down here to——" Abruptly, she clamped her lips shut and the now familiar lovely pink flush crept up her cheeks. She couldn't hide from him. Her fair skin gave her away.

"To what? Kiss me, right?" He laughed and reached out and tickled her slender waist.

She scrambled back toward the other side of the bed. "Don't!"

He grabbed her before she could escape, sat on her, and tickled her until tears streamed down her cheeks. "Admit it and I'll stop."

"Stop." She twisted from side to side and snorted between bursts of laughter. "Please I can't take anymore."

"Admit it and I will. Just say 'I came to kiss you.'" He wouldn't relent. Couldn't stop laughing with her. He needed to hear her admit she wanted him.

"Fine. I came down here to yell at you for being so cold this morning." She bit her lip. "But I really did want to kiss you."

He froze. "Really?"

She shoved him off of her, scooted out of reach, and yanked the sheet up to her collarbone. Damn king-sized bed. "Yes really. Happy now?"

"Huh." Every muscle in his body stiffened.

"Well, why were you so cold this morning? You acted like the kiss never happened last night and

I'd decided to…" She bit her plump lower lip.

"Decided to?" He struggled to focus on her words, but her proximity was making it damn hard. All he wanted was to kiss her again.

"You go first. Why did you act like that?" Her dark gaze grew serious.

"Damn it." He sat up and raked his fingers through his hair. "Look I'm attracted to you, but this is complicated. The movie. Your family. The ranch. All of it. I thought it would be smarter if we kept it on the friend level." *Shit. Damn. Shit.*

"Well, we definitely weren't friends before." She swung her legs over the edge of the bed and began braiding her hair. "I should go."

"Sam, wait. Let's discuss this like two adults." *Damn it, he'd messed up again.* Her slender shoulders were stiff and her tone was neutral. Too neutral. Why couldn't he seem to remember under her tough shell she had a soft center?

"It's a little late for adulting now, right?" She kept her beautiful back to him and scanned the room for her clothes.

"Your shirt is in the kitchen, remember? Come on, we need to figure out how to handle this." What the hell had he done?

She stood and whirled to face him, sparks of temper shooting from her eyes. "We'll just act like nothing happened. Easy." She located her jeans and stuffed one leg into them.

"Will you stop and listen to me for a minute?" He ground his back teeth together and leapt out of bed.

She hopped on one leg and managed to stick her other leg into her jeans. She yanked the zipper closed and bolted out of the bedroom.

He shook his head and followed her. Why was she so damn stubborn? Couldn't she give him a chance to explain?

"Sam."

She stuffed her T-shirt into her jeans, keeping her back toward him.

"Will you listen to me?" Why was he the one asking these questions?

"Fine. Talk." She turned to face him, hands on her narrow hips, her expression mutinous as a child forced to eat her vegetables.

Her jaw was set and her eyes burned into him. He stepped toward her and grasped her shoulders again so she wouldn't run away.

"I don't have a damn playbook for this. You'll agree it's complicated, right?" Wasn't that an understatement?

She nodded.

"Will your dad want to kill me?" Holt wasn't used to having dads of the women he dated around. Hell, this movie had turned into a truly tangled web with all the intersections here between his job, Harry, Sam's dad and Sam.

Her jaw softened. "No. At least I don't think so. You're right. It is complicated." She looked off over his shoulder and then caught his gaze. "I'm not sure what to do either."

"See, we can agree, right?" He leaned in and kissed her soft lips.

"I don't know. This is new ground for me. It probably would be smarter to keep it on the down low." Her eyebrows drew together, but her voice softened.

"So you think you can sneak out of the house later tonight without getting caught?" The words came out before he could stop them.

Her mouth dropped open. "Tonight? Do you mean after dinner?"

He nodded and grinned at her surprised expression. Hell, he wanted her again right now.

"So, we're going to keep doing…this." She gestured with her hands between the two of them.

"This?" He laughed now. Her cheeks were flaming pink.

"You know. This." She laughed too, the smile lighting up her beautiful face. "Hot monkey sex in the afternoons."

"At night is better. Once we start filming, I'll be on set all day." He pulled her tight little hips in close against him.

She leaned in and slid her arms around his neck. "You're right. Tonight? Again?"

"Or now?" He was rock hard and ready to go.

"No, I need to get back to the house. I'll come back after dinner." She rubbed herself against him.

He captured her mouth and dove into the kiss. "Leave your hair down for me."

"Mm-mm." She licked her lips and backed away toward the front door. "Bye." She gave an awkward half-wave.

When the door clicked shut behind her, Holt rubbed the back of his neck. He was playing with fire. He couldn't afford to piss off Chris McNeill and lose this job. They would just have to be very careful. Hell, he made a living performing dangerous maneuvers and being careful was in his DNA.

Besides, he'd jumped off cliffs before and come out unscathed, right?

CHAPTER 20

"SAM, AREN'T YOU COMING DOWN for breakfast?" Her dad's voice boomed from directly behind her.

She jumped and turned to face him. "You startled me. Since when do you sneak up on people?" She swallowed, her throat suddenly parched.

"I didn't sneak up on you, silly girl." He tugged on her braid. "Are you hiding something?" His eyes scanned the pile of papers on her desk.

"Hiding something? Of course not. Just double checking all the vaccination records are in order before hitting the kitchen." Heat crept into her cheeks, damn it. No way could her father suspect she'd crept back into the house a mere thirty minutes ago.

Could he?

His tanned brow creased. "You sure everything is okay? Is it the movie?"

"Fine, I'm fine. Let's get breakfast." She pivoted and strode to the door, unwilling to allow her dad to look too closely.

No doubt her cheeks were still pink from Holt's five o'clock shadow and her lips still swollen from his passionate kisses. And her eyes were probably bloodshot too because she hadn't gotten much sleep. Okay, no sleep.

Not that she was complaining. She smiled dreamily when a hot memory from their shared 3 a.m. shower popped up. She'd never view the guest house bathroom quite the same way again.

"Sam?"

She shook herself back to the present.

Her dad.

Breakfast.

"Sorry, sorry. I didn't get much sleep last night. I just need coffee." She dared a glance at him and he was peering at her like she'd sprouted a uni-corn horn.

Thank god they reached the kitchen. Tears of joy sprang to her eyes when the cinnamon scent of Angela's French toast reached her nostrils. She hurried to her step-mom's side and gave her a quick hug.

Her dad leaned in and kissed his wife's cheek. "French toast. Perfect."

Sam filled her plate with three thick slices of the mouthwatering sourdough French toast. Once she'd slathered soft butter over each one and dumped half a bottle of syrup on top, she got to work. She was ravenous.

"Are you headed down to the set this morning? When are you filming?" Angela asked.

"Uh-uh." She grunted and chewed her toast. She wasn't ready to see Holt in the light of day quite yet. At least with other people around.

"I'll be going down later this morning to check on everything," her dad said.

She was contemplating whether to snag one or two more slices when her father's phone buzzed.

He picked it up and frowned at the screen.

"What's the matter?" Sam straightened in her seat.

He laid one hand on her forearm. "Nothing is the matter. Except Harry is damn high-handed. He made dinner reservations for tonight with the two lead actors, Holt, and us at the Inn. Thinks it's a great idea to start out the movie."

"The Inn? Tonight?" The Inn at Rancho Santa Fe was not just the historic, beautiful hotel smack in the center of town; it was also the hotspot where the locals gathered for cocktails or a meal.

But dinner with Holt? Tonight? Her heart thundered against her ribcage.

"Yeah, at 7 p.m." Her dad's eyebrows drew together.

"Maybe it will be good for you to meet the leads and for all of us to have a nice evening together. It will also give you the chance to share with them what the ranch means to us and emphasize it's not just another movie set." Angela, always the voice of reason, smiled across the table.

"You've got a point. I can lay out some ground rules for them." Sam nodded, warming to the idea. "Make sure they're discreet about the location. Maintain everyone's privacy. Tell them the movie is off if they screw up."

"Sam, no need to be hostile. The contract is iron-clad. These aren't two newbies and I'm sure they don't want to be mobbed by paparazzi either," her dad cautioned.

A little reminder to keep their traps shut couldn't hurt anyone, right? "Who said anything about hostility? I just want to make sure they get it. And they need to be super respectful of the property. Are they staying at the Inn?"

"Yes, they're at the Inn. You know the staff there is discreet. Harry reserved one of the back tables in Morada. Will someone tell Amanda?" Chris said. "Where is she, by the way?"

"Already down at the rehab center," Angela said.

"I'll swing by and let her know." Sam stacked her dishes in the sink and escaped from the kitchen. The minute she reached the hallway she exhaled a shaky breath. Operation Clandestine Affair was still a secret.

Now she needed to fly under the radar of Amanda's eagle eye. Would she be able to keep the ridiculously smug, satisfied expression from surfacing?

And how in the world would she act normally at dinner with her family and Holt?

HOLT NODDED AT HARRY, ALTHOUGH HE HAD NO frickin' clue what he'd said. He kept his eyes glued on his boss and studiously worked not to keep staring at Samantha, who walked with her sister in front of him. Beads of sweat popped up on the back of his neck, and his gut tightened. *Focus man, focus.*

Damn, Sam looked incredible tonight. Her fiery red hair spilled down her back and he would swear she smelled like the wildflowers from the ranch. His hand itched to stroke down the silky length of her mane. She had on some tiny scrap of black fabric and some type of high-heeled sandals that made her toned legs look a mile long.

Was she trying to kill him?

Would she wear the shoes and nothing else for him later? His step hitched and he adjusted his suddenly uncomfortable dark jeans.

"Holt. Did you hear a word I just said?" Harry did not like being ignored.

"Sorry. Just admiring the view." Would he survive this meal?

"That's what I was saying about The Inn. I'd love to film here sometime. Doesn't it remind you of the Ahwanee?"

He managed to tear his gaze from Sam's chiseled calves and focus on the lobby as they entered the building. He whistled below his breath. The soaring wood-beamed ceilings, huge roaring fireplace, and dramatic chandelier in the lobby did remind him of the old Ahwanee in Yosemite, more of an old-style grand mountain lodge than the boutique-y L.A.-style hotel he'd expected. Nice.

"Yeah, pretty sweet."

The place was like something off a movie set. A fire blazed in the enormous woodburning fireplace. A low slung leather couch and several comfortable chairs clustered around the hearth. An elegant older couple sipped wine in a pair of brown low-slung aviator style armchairs. The silver-haired gentleman waved at Chris and Angela, who returned the gesture.

He was out of his league here. The place reeked of money and privilege. He was just the hired help.

A glamorous young hostess in all black, who

could have been in Hollywood or New York City, greeted the McNeills by name and quickly escorted them to the restaurant. They crossed through the Morada Bar, a high-ceilinged, comfortable lounge area with high top booths, a few tables, and an L-shaped buffed zinc bar.

A slick-looking bartender, who was shaking martinis in a shiny silver mixer, called out, "Hey Sam and Amanda."

"Hey Max." Samantha waved and sent him a playful grin.

Holt jerked to a stop and glared at the guy.

What the hell? Who the hell was this guy and why was Sam all flirty with him? Where was his bad-tempered boss lady? He squared his shoulders.

His lady? Where had that come from? The only thing he called his own was his guitar.

"Holt, keep moving buddy." Chris said from directly behind him. "We need to get to the table sometime tonight. You can check out the bar later if you want."

"Uh, sorry." He was an idiot.

They finally reached the back corner of the restaurant where the lights were dim. Jack and Ella, the stars of the movie, were already seated on the far end of the high-backed booth, so you couldn't see them unless you were standing in front of the table. Private and discreet. Perfect.

Although he'd learned many celebrities lived in and visited The Inn at Rancho Santa Fe, A-list movie stars were commodities to be protected. This wasn't Hollywood, after all.

Amanda and Sam were smiling at Jack, *People Magazine*'s Sexiest Man Alive. Why was she suddenly so friendly? She definitely hadn't smiled at him like that when they first met. He clenched his jaw. For god's sake, was he actually jealous of her looking at the movie star?

Harry made introductions and then somehow Holt ended up sitting next to Samantha in the enormous shadowed booth.

He jolted when a strand of her long hair brushed against his forearm when she leaned forward to chat with Jack and Ella. Her hair's clean fruity fragrance assaulted him. Her bare skin, all of her creamy skin, was inches away. If he reached his hand over he could run a finger down her lightly muscled shoulder. He grabbed his napkin and dropped it on his lap. He needed the camouflage since he'd apparently morphed into a horny teenager.

But did Sam have to beam at the movie star quite so intently?

Hard to hate the actor and actually, he really liked Jack Hanson. They'd worked well together back on the daredevil flick where he'd been his stand-in. Jack was the kind of guy men wanted to be buddies with and women just wanted.

"Holt?" Harry stared at him from across the table, his salt and pepper eyebrows raised. "Did you hear a word I just said?"

"Uh, no, sorry." Damn it. Way to sound like an idiot. Again.

"Please tell me you aren't getting sick or something. We were just talking about tomorrow morning."

"No, no, I'm good. Go on." He nodded.

Harry continued and Holt forced himself to

keep his gaze trained on his boss.

He jerked up straight in his seat. Sam's fingers stroked up his thigh underneath the long table-cloth. He grabbed her hand and stopped her progress before he groaned.

From the corner of his eye, he caught the smirk on her full lips. Brat. Her dad was only a few feet away from them. Sweat popped up on the back of his neck.

"Hello everyone, have you had a chance to peruse the menu? Mr. and Mrs. McNeill, shall I bring your regular cocktails?" A tall waiter asked from the edge of the table.

"We'll have a bottle of Cristal for the table to start, Matthew, and then we'll let you know," Chris answered.

"Very good sir." The waiter rushed away.

"Thanks so much for letting us film at your ranch, Mr. McNeill, we're all so excited about being a part of this movie and you made it possi-ble." Ella, the current It girl in Hollywood, smiled at Sam's dad.

"Yeah, thank you. I'm looking forward to a closed set and some peace and quiet. The media has been a royal pain. The more privacy the bet-ter." Jack smiled.

"No problem. I'm glad it all worked out." Chris nodded.

"Are you both planning on keeping a low pro-file while you're here in Rancho Santa Fe or are you spending time around San Diego county?" Sam asked, her voice casual, although her death grip on his thigh under the table belied her tone.

"Well, I love San Diego and the beaches are

amazing, but we've got a really tight filming schedule, so I doubt we'll leave Rancho Santa Fe much. We want to make sure we finish in the time frame you gave us," Jack said.

Sam's talon-like grip softened and she smiled at the movie star's reply.

"Great. It's discreet here in the Ranch, but all bets are off if you go to the beach or into downtown San Diego. We value our privacy." A hint of warning threaded through Chris's deep voice.

"Don't worry, I won't let you down. Once we've finished filming, it will be like we were never here. You'll see." Harry clapped his hand on Chris's shoulder.

"Excuse me." The waiter stood at the edge of the table, a magnum of champagne in his hands. A deeply tanned, skinny brunette, holding an ice bucket and silver stand, stood by his side. Her eyes widened the moment she recognized Jack and Ella, but her face remained impassive. "This is Suzanne and she's in training. She'll be shadowing me tonight."

Once the champagne was poured, Harry offered a toast. "Here's to shooting a top-box office winner."

When they clinked glasses, Holt caught the waitress-trainee staring at Jack and Ella again. Although Matthew's service was impeccable, something about the woman caused his instincts to kick into overdrive. He shook it off. If the McNeills thought the restaurant and Inn were discreet enough to dine in with the famous actors, it had to be, right? Confidentiality was essential to them and they wouldn't jeopardize their own blessed and hard-won privacy.

He had enough to worry about sitting in such close proximity to Samantha. Here's to a chilled drink cooling him the hell down during dinner. Her fresh scent surrounded him and each time she turned her head, a silky strand of flame-colored hair brushed him, causing him to clench his jaw on more than one occasion.

In profile, her beauty––the curve of her creamy cheek, the fullness of her cherry red lips, and the sweep of her impossibly long lashes over enormous doe eyes, blew him away. He tried not to check his watch more than every two minutes, but if he had to sit through one more course before he could drag her back to the guesthouse he might explode.

When half the table ordered after-dinner drinks and dessert, he cursed under his breath. How much longer could he keep shifting in his seat? He jolted when Sam's hand curved around his thigh again and inched higher up his leg. Not cool at all. He moved her hand back onto her own leg. When he looked up, Angela was watching them, a shrewd half-smile gracing her lips. Damn it, she suspected something.

Act nonchalant. He asked Amanda about the latest horse he'd seen going to her rehab facility, hoping to allay Angela's suspicions. He was just being friendly to all the McNeills. Personal discretion. Professional discretion. Deflect. He wasn't ready to admit to himself what he was feeling about Ms. Samantha McNeill and he certainly didn't want to be questioned about it by her family.

No, for now, he would try to make it through the rest of the meal.

Minute by excruciating minute.

CHAPTER 21

"HELLO?" HOLT HAD LEFT THE door unlocked for her, so where was he?

Silence greeted her when she wandered into the guesthouse. Suddenly, her throat was parched and nerves skittered down her spine. Water, she needed water. Maybe he was in the kitchen?

Nope, the room was empty. She grabbed a glass out of the cabinet and stuck it under the stainless-steel refrigerator water dispenser. She guzzled some of the cool liquid and then rubbed the chilled glass against her overheated cheeks. She closed her eyes. What was she doing here?

At dinner she'd felt seductive and womanly in her borrowed cocktail dress and sky-high stilettos, confident in Holt's attraction to her. Now, all her old insecurities rose to the surface. She was too boyish, too awkward. What did she know about seduction?

Her prior relationships, if you could call them relationships, had been casual and convenient. Not one of her guy friends had ever made her angry or even intrigued her.

After flirting with Holt at the restaurant for the last few hours, she'd been ready to pounce on him. She missed half the dinner conversation and truth be told, hadn't paid a whit of attention to the Hollywood heartthrob across the table. In fact, when she'd studied his golden god looks, all she could do was compare him to Holt.

They could have been brothers, but Holt's cheekbones were a little more chiseled, and his jaw slightly more square.

Where Jack Hanson's eyes were a cerulean blue, Holt's eyes had a shimmer of silver, giving them a more mysterious look.

Jack's face was flawless, but Holt's pale scar above his left eyebrow saved him from being too pretty.

And although the movie star's voice was deep and sexy, Holt's voice had a raspiness to it that sent chills down her spine. Not to mention how the sound conjured up vivid memories of him whispering passionate demands in her ear.

So here she was.

Irresistibly drawn to him.

Where the hell was he?

"Make yourself at home." Holt's husky voice murmured against her ear.

She jumped and the rest of the water sloshed over the edge of her glass onto the floor. "You're like a cat—how do you always manage to sneak up on me like that?"

"Me sneak? You're the one breaking into my house, drinking my water." He nuzzled her neck and her body went limp against his muscular one. Sparks shot down her spine and goose bumps popped up on her arms.

"I wasn't sneaking. You left the door open." Her heart knocked against her ribcage. She leaned back into his rock hard torso and her hands reached up to grip his powerful sinewy forearms.

He spun her around and grasped her shoulders. His pupils were dilated, rendering his blue eyes almost black. His sculpted lips were parted and he stared intently at her mouth.

"What punishment does such a bold intruder deserve?" He murmured and moved to stand between her thighs.

"Punishment?" Had she really squeaked? How could her voice even work when all her attention was focused on his eyes, his lips, his powerful leg nudging hers apart, and his obvious arousal pressed against her center?

"Maybe a spanking?" His lips were a breath away from hers.

"Spanking?" Outraged, she jerked back only to find the unforgiving granite countertop impeded her movement. "You've got to be joking."

"Do you want me to be joking?" He didn't allow her to escape, his warm minty breath mingled with hers, but his lips still hadn't touched hers. All she needed to do was shift forward a centimeter to end the torture, but she wouldn't. Spanking—seriously?

"I do." Although her skin was on fire and her pulse hammered, it was just his proximity, not the suggestion of getting kinky. "Not my thing."

"Hmmm...I love how fast you react—I'm sure I can come up with something. Maybe I'll tickle you again." He brushed his mouth against hers between each word, torturing her with the softness of his lips.

"No. Just kiss me." She thrust her fingers into his hair and yanked his head down to meet hers.

His lips descended upon hers with satisfying pressure and their tongues danced together in perfect harmony. She stroked her fingers through his thick silky hair and pressed herself closer. His bare chest was hot, singeing through her thin tank top and spiking her own already over-heated skin.

Lost in his embrace, she reveled in his possessive kiss. His strong hands slid down her waist to grasp her hips and then back up her ribcage and cupped her breasts. She moaned and arched into his calloused palms. She couldn't seem to get close enough to him. Suddenly, a cold breeze hit her and her eyes flew open. He'd stepped back a few inches and without his heat, the temperature plummeted.

He wound his fingers through hers and smiled as he led her to the bedroom. Bemused, she followed and allowed him to lead her to the massive king-sized bed. His touch was gentle as he eased them down onto the bed together and he cradled her in his arms and rolled them so they were lying facing each other. He stroked one hand down from her shoulder to her waist and curved around her hip possessively. His eyes were heavy-lidded and his lips curved into a lazy smile.

His intense gaze pinned her in place. She couldn't move. His kiss was tender this time. Gentle. He tugged her tank top from her denim shorts and helped her slide out of her clothes.

"You're exquisite." He whispered against her collarbone. "I'm going to worship every single inch of you." He nibbled along her skin and burned a trail of kisses down her body.

When his tongue found her navel, her eyes

blurred and her head dropped back onto the pillow. She could barely breathe. Her skin glistened with sweat, the sheets rustled as they moved, and his clean masculine scent surrounded her. He traveled lower, dropping feather light kisses on her hipbones before smiling up at her. He lowered his head and kissed her most sensitive place, continuing his torture until she was a quivering mess, and only when he'd pleasured her until she'd lost track of any sense of time or place did he slide up her body.

"Look at me, Samantha." He hovered over her, braced on sinewy powerful arms and his gaze locked on her face.

"Holt." The connection between them was beyond. Beyond anything she'd had before.

He didn't release her gaze as he entered her with exquisite slowness. Only when he was buried inside her did he groan and close his eyes.

Tonight, they made sweet, beautiful love. Somehow his gentleness and attention slayed her more than their passionate first encounter. Nobody had ever taken such care with her, given her such attention before. When he brought her to the edge one more time, they both shattered together.

Satiated not just physically, but somehow utterly relaxed mind and heart as well, she drifted off to sleep in his arms.

SAMANTHA EASED THE FRONT DOOR SHUT AND tiptoed through the still-dark house. Nobody needed to know she hadn't spent the night in her own bed. She stretched her arms over her head and grinned. Holt's sweetness last night had caught her by surprise. Every time they were together, another layer of his personality was revealed. Beneath his sexy, cocky exterior resided a complex, fascinating man.

"Someone looks like the cat who swallowed the cream," Amanda said from the doorway to her room. "Where have you been?"

Drat. Why had she lingered in the hallway daydreaming about her incredible night with Holt? In front of her big sister's doorway no less. The sun hadn't risen yet, but Amanda was a habitual early riser.

"Um, in the kitchen for a snack?" Maybe she could escape her sister's scrutiny with a teeny white lie.

Her sister snorted. "Right. More like snacking on the stud of a stuntman. I thought the two of you were going to burst into flames at The Inn last night." Amanda leaned against the doorjamb, her blonde hair mussed and her sensible white cotton robe belted tight around her narrow waist.

"Oh crap, do you think anyone else noticed?" Wouldn't her dad have said something? Although, she hadn't been aware of anyone or anything except for Holt.

"No, I don't think so. Dad and Harry were engrossed in discussing the movie with Jack and Ella, who were both really nice by the way. Angela doesn't miss much so she probably did. So spill––what is going on with you two? Were you down at the guesthouse?"

Sam bit her lip. She had never been able to hide anything from her sisters. At work, she had to be strong and a leader so masking her emotions wasn't difficult. Most people at the ranch or those she dealt with for the breeding business had no clue what she was truly feeling beneath her often-tough exterior. Her college friends knew her to a point. She'd created her outer shell to only reveal what she wanted to reveal, except for her family.

"I like him." She blurted it out.

"Like him? Like *like* him?" Amanda's eyebrows shot up to her hairline.

She nodded. "Yeah, *like* like." She hugged her arms around her waist and the imprint of his long tanned fingers circling her ribcage flashed through her. What those hands could do.

"Wow, you two were fighting like dogs up until recently. What changed? It's almost like little kids at the playground——you are mean to the one you like best." Amanda's tone turned serious.

"I'm not sure. One minute he was annoying me beyond belief and the next he was making me laugh. He is actually really funny. He has this dry sense of humor and cracks me up. I thought he was the typical cocky L.A. type and he's actually humble and hard working. And he's so smart. And he takes care of his mom. Who knew he would be anything but a pretty face? And he plays the guitar like a professional. He could be a musician if he wasn't a stuntman. He's so talented and his hands…"

Amanda gaped at her——her jaw slack and her eyes wide. "You are gushing. You're in love with him."

Sam's mouth fell open. "In love? You're crazy. I just like him and our chemistry is beyond smoking hot." *Love? No way.*

"Smitten kitten. Infatuated lady. Head over heels in love. Whatever you want to call it. Samantha Michele McNeill, you have never, and I mean never, talked about a guy this way before." Amanda's green eyes were full of wonder.

"Of course I have." She paused and scratched her head. *What was the guy's name in college she'd dated for a few months? Matt? Michael? Marty?* Her stomach clenched.

"Oh crap, I haven't, have I? No, I'm not in love." She shook her head vigorously. "Don't be ridiculous. I just like him, that's all. It's way too fast anyway." She nodded her head to emphasize her point.

"Uh-huh, sure. Keep telling yourself that and bobbling your head. But from your description, he sounds like someone I know." Amanda crossed her arms across her chest and smirked.

"What? Like me?" She sputtered. "No. Look, we're having a good time. I've just never met any-one like him. But I'm not dumb enough to fall in love with a man who is on the road two hundred days of the year and lives in Los Angeles the rest of the time." Of course she wasn't in love. Maybe attracted. Intrigued. Hot for.

But definitely not in love.

"Not that I have a clue, but I remember mom saying you don't choose who you fall in love with. It just happens. And if you two are falling in love––" Amanda patted her chest with both hands.

"Stop saying love. We are not falling in love, okay?" Sam hissed the words and her fingers curled into fists. Although their dad and Angela were in the east wing of the house, she couldn't risk anybody eavesdropping on this whopper of a conversation. "Look, I can handle this. I can handle him. I'm not Dylan." Her tummy flip-flopped again. She *could* handle him, couldn't she?

"Dylan wears her heart on her sleeve, but yours is just as sweet and vulnerable, even if you do a great job of hiding it." Amanda held up a hand. "Let me finish. I just want you to be careful. He's a stuntman and is doing dangerous and life-threatening things every day at work. He's based in Hollywood—everything you've tried to avoid since we moved here. I'd just hate for you to fall for him and something happen to him and…" Her sister frowned.

"I know. I know. Don't you think I realize all of that? Although now the movie crew is here, I see how much Dad misses it and if I'm honest, I always loved it too." The morning on the hill overlooking the set, she'd been forced to admit it to herself.

"You did love it. You and Dylan were always with mom." Amanda's smile was wistful, her eyes misty.

"Didn't you? I know you weren't there as often because you worked so hard in school to get perfect grades." Her older sister had been a serious student.

"I did, but you two had the artistic genes, not me. It was easier for me to let the show business world go." Amanda shrugged.

"I've just tried not to think about it at all. But I did love it." Even if she wanted to continue to suppress it, the floodgates were now open.

"I was so surprised."

"Yeah, me too. I'm not sure why I agreed, but maybe this whole movie thing will be a way for us all to move on from the past. A positive experience to erase all the bad memories. I think it's important for Dad." Her dad loved what they'd created at the ranch, but nothing sparked his excitement as much as the adrenaline rush of being on a movie set behind the camera.

"You have a point. He does seem happy about it. It's tough not to worry, but it all seems like it will go smoothly and fast. And like Harry said, once they are gone, it will be like they were never here."

Sam's breath caught in her throat. Amanda's words pierced her. Like they were never there? Would Holt walk away when the job was done and never return? Why did the vision of him disappearing into the sunset leave a bitter taste in her mouth?

"Like I said, we're just having fun. No expectations. No strings. When the shooting is finished, I'll probably never see him again." She forced her voice to be casual, but the hollow words stuck in her throat. *Never see him again?*

But, she'd be fine. She always was.

Amanda stepped out of the doorway and wrapped her into a warm hug. "Just be careful, okay? I don't want to see you get hurt. He seems like a good guy, but this whole situation is complicated."

Sam squeezed her sister's deceptively fragile frame and closed her eyes. "It's impossible. I know. I'll be careful."

"Okay, run back to your room before dad catches you looking like something the cat dragged in." Amanda gave her a gentle push toward her bedroom.

"Hey––I thought I was the cat? Now I'm the bird?" Did she look so disheveled?

"The cat with the bird's nest hair. Just scoot. I'll see you later." Amanda smiled at her and retreated back into her room and shut the door in her face.

Sam crept down the hallway past Dylan's empty bedroom and reached her own. She closed the door behind her and sagged against the solid wood.

In love? Was she falling for Holt? Each hour she spent in his company confirmed to her how much she'd misjudged him. Sure, he was cocky, but she needed a man with a strong ego who wouldn't be threatened by her own powerful personality.

She hurried into her bathroom, shucking her shorts and shirt on the way. She flipped on the light and muffled a scream at the red-haired Medusa reflected back to her in the enormous mirror. Her hair looked like she'd been stranded on a desert island for months or maybe stuck her finger in an electric socket. She'd never get the tangles out.

Holt hadn't batted an eyelash when he'd walked her to the door. Was he blind? Or guilty because he was the one creating the rat's nest on her head?

Damn it, all of this was new. She'd never acted the way she did around him. Excited. Nervous. Giggly.

And when she wasn't with him, she was day-dreaming like a tween over the latest rock star du jour.

She was infatuated with him. She was twen-ty-seven years old and had never been in love. A little romance and infatuation was fine. She could handle it.

What could possibly go wrong in a mere few weeks?

CHAPTER 22

"CUT." CHRIS YELLED THROUGH A bullhorn from across the pasture. "Come on in, Holt."

Damn it. Not again. If he had to do another frickin' take of this scene, he'd melt off the horse. Holt wiped the old-school red bandana across his forehead, mopping the sweat that seemed determined to pour into his eyes and blind him. Not ideal when he was supposed to be galloping across the pasture like a rocket shooting into the stratosphere.

The unseasonable Santa Ana winds were back again and it was hot as hell outside. This breeze didn't cool you down––no, it was more like when the smoke from the barbeque blew in your face and made you feel like you were the hamburger on the grill instead of the chef. His stomach growled.

"What's the problem?" He was a professional and would re-shoot a scene a thousand times if it was required. Not that it ever was. He prided himself on performing in one or two takes unless something else was going on. As this was the fifth cut of the afternoon, he sure hoped it was something external.

"The light is off. We've tried adjusting the cameras ten times and just can't get the scene right with the glare. And it's boiling hot out here. Damn Santa Ana winds in July." Chris's face was red and he looked as steamed as Holt felt right now.

Holt leapt off the horse and sauntered over to Chris and Harry. "Okay. Do you want to try at sunset or first thing in the morning?" The light was usually the most favorable at dawn or dusk. The middle of the day, like what they were attempting now, created too many shadows and glares unless you could shoot from certain angles. Although it shouldn't have been a big deal in this scene because he wasn't filming any close-ups, just riding toward the cabin to save a damsel in distress.

Hell, Jack probably didn't even need him to stand in for this scene, but Chris insisted upon it. When Holt had suggested Jack could handle it, Chris had bitten his head off. No way would the director risk Jack getting thrown from a horse on his watch. Holt would use his horsemanship in all scenes requiring any pace faster than a trot. Once Holt was almost to the cabin, he would slow the horse's pace and hand the reins over to Jack. Straightforward, or so he'd thought when they started filming today.

"Should we just start the next scene in the cabin and you guys can handle this in the morning?" Jack, clad in identical buckskin breeches and white long-sleeved linen shirt, sat on a director's chair with an open script in his lap.

"Sounds good to me. Chris? Harry?" Holt prayed one of them would say yes so he could ride back to the guesthouse and plunge into an ice cold shower. Or maybe dive into the pool and stay underwater for as long as he could hold his breath. Not to be a wimp or anything, but even the bottoms of his feet were sweating in the oppressive heat.

"Yeah, it makes sense. Damn it. Waste of time." Harry yanked his dark sunglasses off and pinched the bridge of his nose—one of his characteristic tells when he was pissed.

"It's okay, Harry. We've got time." Chris shrugged, seeming unperturbed by the delay in the filming.

"Now you don't care about timing?" Harry glared at him. "We've got a lot of other scenes we can film, so we shouldn't get behind unless this damn heat doesn't break. Holt, we'll shoot it right after the sun comes up. The light will be better."

"Anything else for me today?" His eyelids were drooping and his back was tight. Either he really was getting old and retirement was definitely the right path, or last night with Sam had sucked it out of him.

Every muscle in his body stiffened as a vision of falling asleep tangled in her fiery mane jolted through his system. Definitely time for a freezing cold shower. And not just for the damn wasted afternoon sweating his ass off on the back of his horse.

"Nah. You're good," Harry said. "Now, Jack, get ready to earn your Hollywood paycheck." He slapped the actor on the back and together they headed toward the cabin, the camera crew trailing behind.

"Everything okay, son? You look a little wiped

out." Chris asked over his shoulder as he followed the others toward the makeshift cabin.

"I'm fine. Just going to head on up." The last thing he needed was Samantha's father wondering why he looked like he was rode hard and put away wet, besides the weather.

"Okay. See you later." Chris waved and kept going.

Had Chris been scrutinizing him more than usual? Or was he paranoid? He hadn't said a word and from what Holt had learned about the patriarch, the man was forthright and didn't hold much back. Just like his youngest daughter.

If he'd suspected his baby girl had spent the night with him last night, Holt would probably be carried back to the house in a body bag, not canter off into the rolling hills. If Harry found out there would be hell to pay.

Why was his simple life plan suddenly so problematic?

A few weeks ago everything had all seemed crystal clear. Biting the bullet and dumping his savings into the movie had been a safe bet. Harry would create a blockbuster and they'd laugh all the way to the bank. Film the movie, which would be a blast because who didn't love the Wild, Wild West and he also enjoyed working with Jack. Bonus.

Earn his highest paycheck to date and use it, along with his investment payout, for the final funding he needed to launch his own stuntperson agency. Transition into a position where he would finally be able to earn his living without risking life and limb. Ensure he'd be able to take care of his mom forever and even his sister if she needed his help.

No distractions.

Nothing holding him back.

Then came Samantha. At first he'd seen her as simply an obstacle to overcome. If anybody could have convinced Chris McNeill to reject Harry's request to film on his property, Sam was the one. Thank god McNeill had listened to Harry and overruled the protests of his family.

He urged his horse into a canter toward the guesthouse, and prayed the heat would break. A burst of light caught his eye and he reined in to a stop. He shielded his eyes with one hand and scanned the horizon. The powerful hot winds rustled through the trees and the air smelled dry, if it were possible. Ideal fire weather. He sure as hell hoped the McNeills had a foolproof plan in case a blaze broke out.

A few flickers of light from the direction of the ranch's perimeter alerted him something wasn't right. His pulse accelerated and he gripped the reins. Were they flames popping? He sucked in a deep breath, but the acrid odor of smoke didn't materialize. What the hell was it? Another light-ning quick series of flashes popped again. What the hell?

He dug his heels and sped toward the high pri-vacy fence shrouded in tall, dense trees. His gut clenched as adrenaline flooded his veins. Some-thing was wrong. The crackling wind and pitiless sun scorched his skin, but he kicked up his pace.

Something was happening in the trees or on the fence. He ground his teeth when the suspicion hit him.

He yanked the reins and halted at the base of an enormous elm tree. He shoved his cowboy hat back and peered up into the dense, thick branches. Maybe he had heatstroke because nothing was there. He rubbed his jaw and looked around. Nothing.

Another series of lights flashed.

Son of a bitch.

He leapt off the horse and scaled up the tree trunk. A skinny pale arm attached to a scrawny body held an enormous camera. The little slime was perched on one of the branches that ran parallel to the ten-foot high solid wood fence.

"Hey, what the hell do you think you're doing?" He shouted and the parasite perched precariously on the tree branch jolted and almost dropped his camera.

The skinny weasel slithered back along the branch, heading toward the fence. The weasel might be slippery, but Holt did this kind of shit for a living. He scrabbled along the branch and made a swipe for the camera and actually felt it brush his fingertips.

Before he could find purchase, the rodent managed to reach the fence and slide off toward the street. Holt reached the edge, just in time to see the photographer snatch back a collapsible aluminum ladder and foil his pursuit.

Holt had lost the guy. By mere seconds. He slammed his fist against the sturdy branch and cursed. How could he have been too slow to catch the guy?

"If you publish any photos, you will be sued for

everything you and any rag you try to sell them to have. Do you hear me?" He yelled at the retreating figure. The little shit hoisted the ladder into the back of a silver SUV and gunned off without a word.

Holt punched the thick tree branch again. It was the first frickin' day of filming and already the vultures were swarming. How the hell had the press been tipped off they were filming the movie at the ranch? Who had betrayed their trust?

Most people in the industry knew if you were dumb enough to cross Harry Shaw, you were committing Hollywood suicide.. The penalties in the crew's contracts were stiff and Holt had personally checked out everyone single person involved, at Harry's request. His gut told him it wasn't someone from the inside. But who?

He crawled back towards the base of the tree and jumped back to earth. He mounted his horse, wheeled him around and stared out over the rolling green pastures. What now? He rubbed his jaw and took a few deep breaths. Damn, he so did not want to tell Harry and Chris the media were on to them.

Chris McNeill would be furious and Harry's head would probably detonate. Damn it, the entire movie could be jeopardized by a leak to the press because McNeill could tell Harry to go to hell and choose his family over a favor to an old friend.

What if Harry had to cancel the rest of the ranch shoot? But his boss had too much riding on this film's success. Changing locations would necessitate hemorrhaging money they couldn't afford to lose if this movie could have any shot at being a big box office success. But if Chris kicked them out, they were screwed.

They couldn't stop filming. The movie couldn't be postponed indefinitely. This shit couldn't be happening on the first damn day. Without this movie, he would lose all his savings and who knew when he'd be able to stop beating his body up and start running a stable business.

He gripped the reins so hard the leather bit into his palms. This movie was supposed to be his last. This paycheck was vital. He couldn't start his new venture without it. He couldn't convince his mom and sister to move to California without it. He couldn't find true security without it.

His horse whinnied and he leaned down and whispered in his ear. "Shhh boy. Give me a second."

Screw it. He rode toward the guesthouse. Logically, he should wait and see and maybe nothing would come of it. The photographer had been so far away. Ella was safely tucked away in her trailer and Jack had been sitting under the make-shift awning with a cowboy hat shielding his face. How far could those damn lenses film anyway? What could he possibly have seen?

Him riding a million takes on the horse?

A shadow of Jack peering at the script?

The cabin and yard, making it obvious the movie was a historical?

Or simply blurry shadows?

Probably only blurry shadows, right?

What good would it do for him to tell everyone now? The fact Harry was filming a Western wasn't a secret. But the location was supposed to be. Damn it.

Was the media aware the movie was filming there and trying to get photos of *People*'s Sexiest Man Alive and Hollywood's highest paid actress? Sometimes early on set photos would titillate the public's excitement for a new film and up the box office results. But Harry had sworn to keep the set location under wraps.

Or was somebody clever enough to find out it was Chris McNeill's ranch and sense a juicy story?

Either way, they'd figure out it was McNeill's ranch and the tabloids would have a field day excavating the decade old tragic story. Pamela McNeill's death had changed the course of the McNeill family's life forever. Altered the course of Samantha's life forever.

His gut clenched. Oh shit—Sam. She would go ballistic if she heard photographers had been here. She would try to convince her dad to move the production off their land before it was too late. More importantly, she would be devastated if the headlines read *Chris McNeill Back on Set for the First Time since his Wife's Tragic Death.*

"Sorry boy." He tightened the reins and cursed under his breath. Rocco angled his head back, his brown eyes questioning.

"We can't go back to the house yet Rocco. Sorry." Holt couldn't play the wait and see game with the paparazzi. He wouldn't risk hurting Sam.

If he alerted Harry now, the most powerful man in Hollywood might be able to kill the story before it appeared. And even if it meant postponing his own plans to retire and start his business when this movie was done, so be it. Even if it meant losing all his savings he'd invested. A sour taste rose in the back of his throat and he expelled a shaky breath.

He'd be damned if the paparazzi would screw up the movie or worse, destroy Sam and her family's peaceful refuge.

He changed directions and urged Rocco back down the hill to once again share news nobody on Pacific Vista Ranch wanted to hear.

So much for a leisurely swim or a cold shower.

CHAPTER 23

I REALLY DON'T HAVE TIME FOR an impromptu family meeting. I'm elbow deep in rehabbing the McCullough's mare. What do you think this is all about?" Amanda huffed, her usually soothing voice exasperated.

"No clue. Maybe the location isn't working out after all and they want to film somewhere else?"

Why did her heart constrict considering Holt leaving before the end of the month? Once his taillights disappeared and the gate closed silently behind him, she'd probably never see him again. Well, unless she was watching an action adventure movie and scanning the dangerous scenes for any glimpse of him. And wasn't that just pathetic?

"Your dad said they'd be up to the house in five minutes. I've got some fresh lemonade and some new local IPAs. We'll be covered whatever the news might be." Angela set down the drink tray on the dining room table, the official family meeting space.

Her sister paced back and forth across the hardwood floors, her generally stoic nerves nowhere in sight.

"Sit, Amanda. The clicking of your boots is driving me nuts." The tick tock pattern of her walking reminded her of the old Poe story, The Telltale Heart. A sign of impending doom? Why did everything feel ominous right now? If one of the horses was hurt... Her temples began throbbing in time with her sister's steps.

Chris burst into the house and strode to the table with Harry and Holt trailing behind him. His jaw was clenched, his tic was pulsing, and his face was flushed. Three clear signs he was spitting mad. "Angela, girls, let's sit down."

Sam couldn't read Holt's expression and Harry could win the World Series of Poker with the impassive look on his face.

Okay, so they weren't going to waste any time on pleasantries. What in the world had happened this afternoon?

"Are the horses okay?" She couldn't sit down and have a civilized discussion if something had happened to her animals.

"The horses are fine. Everyone, please sit." Her dad sank into his customary seat at the head of the table. His tone was clipped.

Once they were all seated, he turned to Holt. "Why don't you share what you saw? And, everyone, please let him tell the whole story before you ask questions." He turned and narrowed his eyes at her.

"Fine." She crossed her arms and hunched into the dining room chair.

"I hate to be the one bearing bad news——" Holt snagged her gaze for a brief moment before looking around the table.

Holt's crystal blue eyes caught hers again for a second and he arched a brow. "Here's what happened. I was riding back toward the house and saw some bursts of light in the trees by the far fence. It's so hot and hazy and at first I thought maybe flames were breaking out on the property. A fire." He hesitated.

"I couldn't smell any smoke so I rode over to see what it could be. When I got closer, I realized it was the flash from a camera." He paused again.

Sam shot to her feet. "A camera?" She whirled on her father. "Dad, cameras over the walls? Paparazzi?"

"Samantha, sit down. Please. Let him finish." The grooves around her dad's mouth deepened.

She plopped back into the chair, but her entire body was vibrating and heat raced up the back of her neck. The pounding in her temples increased to a death march.

"I climbed up the tree and there was a little sleaze ball with one of those long-range lenses snapping photos. I tried to grab him but he managed to get over the fence. The jerk had a ladder. I yelled at him not to publish anything or he'd get sued, but he peeled out in some crappy truck." Holt's posture was rigid and his sculpted lips compressed into a tight line.

Sam ground her back teeth together and struggled to slow down her rapidly escalating breath. She would not lose it.

She had full control of her temper. Of course she did. Hyperventilation notwithstanding.

She would keep quiet until the story was finished if it killed her.

"How in the world did they find out about the movie so soon? What happened to the air-

tight security? The ironclad privacy agreement?"
Amanda glared at Harry, her creamy skin ghastly
white.

"I'm going to find out. Everyone I hired is fully
aware of the privacy and security. They also know
damn well if they violate the contract their careers
are finished. They won't be able to work at the
concession stand of a movie theater in Juneau,
Alaska, if I find out they talked to the press. I
don't think it was anyone on set." Harry's jaw was
set and his eyes were glacial obsidian chips.

"Well, who the hell was it? Someone obviously
alerted the press the movie was being filmed here.
We've been here over a decade and never once has
a photographer climbed the wall." Sam slapped a
hand onto the rustic wood table and glowered at
the director.

Nobody spoke.

"Dad?" Her stomach churned and bile rose in
her throat. *Not again. Please not again.*

Chris raked his fingers through his hair and
shook his head. "I have to agree with Harry. All
these people care about is making movies. They
wouldn't be dumb enough to risk their careers by
crossing him. I just have no idea who would do
this."

"Is there anyone here on the ranch who might–
–" Holt looked around the room, brows raised.

"Nobody on the ranch would do this. They
are loyal, they make a great living, and are dedicated." Sam declared. Nobody would betray the
McNeills or endanger the ranch's profitable operations.

"She's right. We have a small staff, but most of

them have been with us since the beginning. I doubt they'd want to have any harm come to the ranch. It's in their best interest to keep things as they are." Angela nodded her head.

"What about the neighbors bringing their horses in for rehab? Outside people?" Holt asked her sister.

Amanda shook her head, her skin still sheet-white, her eyes shards of bottle green glass. "No, I don't think so. I've never discussed the movie with anybody and the rehab facility is near the main ranch entrance. The horses come in via trailer and never go beyond the clinic area. There's no way they could know the movie equipment or filming would be happening on the other side of the ranch. We've got over two hundred acres, remember?"

"What if someone saw the eighteen-wheelers and trailers arriving? Would those stand out on the single lane roads here?" Holt rubbed the scar on his forehead.

Amanda shook her head. "It's not uncommon to see big trucks and trailers through here. Remember, everyone has horses in Rancho Santa Fe."

"She's right. It isn't any of our people and my gut tells me it isn't the movie crew either. So how in the hell did the stupid photographer end up in one of our trees?" Her dad bumped his fist on the table; the tic in his temple giving away his barely veiled temper.

"Well, however it happened, we can all agree the paparazzi wouldn't be here unless the movie was here." Sam snapped out the words and gripped the table so tightly her knuckles ached. "So, the filming here needs to end. Today. And Harry you need to quash this story and photos." Cut. The End. Sayonara baby. It's a wrap. They all had to leave.

"Hold on." Harry held both hands up. "Hold on. Let's not be hasty. Let me make some calls. I'll make it crystal clear there will be major consequences if one single photo of a blade of grass from this ranch shows up anywhere. I can fix this. Chris?" He looked at her dad.

Her dad's brows drew together. "Damn you, Harry. You swore everything would be simple. You had it all under control. We haven't even shot one full day and already the press knows a movie's being shot here. How the hell can I trust you now?"

"Look, both Jack and Ella have rabid fans. The photographer probably just got wind they were here and wanted to be the first to snap photos of them." Harry looked around the table, reverting back to the charming Hollywood dealmaker.

"How do you know? How do you know they won't dredge up everything? Do you think they won't do the research and see this is our ranch? What if they dig up the story about our mom's death? The accident? The scandal?" Sam shot to her feet and tightened her grip on the table with both hands. Her temples were pounding, her heart was racing, and she had the urge to toss her glass at Harry's dumb pointy head.

"Everything with your mother happened a long time ago Samantha——" Harry's tone was one used to address rabid animals or sociopaths wielding AK-47s.

"You weren't at the funeral with reporters screaming at us or at our house when the helicopters were swarming, when reporters were camped in front of our gate, Harry," Chris turned toward his old friend. "Those bastards followed the girls to school." He closed his eyes and exhaled.

"Chris, I'm sorry about it, believe me. I think we all need to calm down for a moment. I'm sure I can fix it."

Chris stood, his voice deadly calm and his hazel eyes flashing. "I'm not happy about this, especially since I'm the one who agreed to allow the filming. So here's what we're doing. Harry—make some calls and report back in an hour. Amanda, go back to the rehab center and try to focus on work. Sam and I will ride around the ranch and make sure all the fences are secure. Angela, do you want to ride with us or stay here?"

Everyone was silent for a moment, the tension in the air as thick as the Santa Ana haze lingering outside.

"I'll stay here."

"I could ride out with you guys." Holt stood.

Sam shook her head. "No. This is family business."

He looked at her with brows raised over hot eyes.

"It's okay, Holt. It's something Sam and I should do together. Thanks for the offer." Her dad shook his head.

"Yeah, thanks for the offer." Sam avoided looking at Holt. "Dad, let's go."

The headache and stomach pain intensified and she prayed she wouldn't barf all over the kitchen.

Her mind told her this wasn't Holt's fault—he had a lot riding on this film and wouldn't risk losing it. Logic wasn't leading the way now, however.

Family preservation was all that mattered and anybody who wasn't part of the McNeill clan... she couldn't be around right now. Not even Holt.

Especially Holt.

Everything about him was intertwined with this movie. His smart-ass sense of humor, their off the charts chemistry, and his surprisingly tender side. Right now she needed to focus on protecting Pacific Vista Ranch and forgetting about this movie.

His presence was a painful reminder their lives, as they knew them, could be over.

CHAPTER 24

HERE GOES NOTHING. SAM HESITATED, her hand gripping the doorknob, the cool smoothness a balm against the turmoil twisting inside her. She opened the door without bothering to knock. No need for manners at this point.

"Holt." She strode into the great room and jerked to a stop. Swallowed to moisten her suddenly dry throat. He was sprawled on the dark leather couch, sporting a pair of running shorts and nothing else.

Could this man ever put a shirt on?

"I figured you'd be by. Did you guys find anything?" He shifted to a seated position, the sleek muscles in his chiseled chest and abs rippled; oh lord those abs. His smooth bronzed skin made him look like he was carved from caramel. She loved caramel.

She licked her lips and stared.

"Sam?" His dark blond brows arched.

Her well-rehearsed speech evaporated. Every last brain cell popped and disappeared. "Do you mind putting a shirt on? It's hard to have a serious conversation with you when you're naked."

"Naked?" His perfect white teeth flashed and he powered up off the sofa. He took two strides toward her and halted when she put a hand out.

"Shirt. Please. We need to have an adult con-versation." Humiliating or not, she genuinely could not look at him right now and remember the gravity of the situation.

He was just too damn tempting. Now she knew the silkiness of his skin under her hands. The clean masculine scent and the slightly salty taste of him. Dangerous. A shiver shot down her spine and her pulse quickened.

He laughed and grabbed a t-shirt off the back of the armchair next to him. "Come on Sam, are you saying you can't control yourself around me?" He took another step toward her.

"Shirt. On. Now." At least she hadn't yelled the words.

Focus. Why was she here again? Wasn't she angry? Determined? Hell, his sheer physical pres-ence made her forget anything but the feel of him. She shook her head.

The movie.

The paparazzi.

Disaster.

He pulled the white t-shirt over his head and now she wanted him to peel it off again. Damn him. Before she could react, he swooped in and wrapped his arms around her and captured her lips. When she kept her mouth firmly closed to him, he nibbled and coaxed until her lips parted on a groan and she sank into his delicious kiss. Sensation took over and she savored the minty fla-vor of his warm breath and the sheer heaven of his rock hard body against hers.

When his hands slid underneath her shirt and

stroked up her overheated skin, she tore herself away from him and stumbled back a few steps.

"Stop. We need to talk." And obviously speech wasn't possible when he touched her. Or was in her line of vision for that matter. Her brain dissolved into a puddle, just like every other part of her body.

"Play now, talk later?" His grin was mischievous.

"No." She forced her smile off her face. They had to be serious and she needed some answers.

"You're tough. Fine. I'll sit on this side of the sofa and you sit in the chair. Is that safe enough for you or should we build some kind of barrier so you don't pounce on me?" He exhaled, plopped down and crossed his arms, the golden hair glinting on his sinewy forearms.

"I'll do my best to restrain myself. You are such a smartass. Just stay on your side." Maybe then she'd have a chance of remaining on track with her decision.

He scooted one inch closer to her. "Is this still my side?"

She snorted. Damn him. He made it impossible to remain angry and she was angry, wasn't she? Why couldn't she remember why she came here in the first place?

Focus, girl. "We need to talk." Nobody had ever thrown her off the way he could, simply by being.

Holt frowned. "I told you everything I saw. Everything I could think of. Until we hear from Harry, I don't know if there's anything else to discuss about the trespassing scumbag."

"Well, things have changed now. My dad hasn't

decided yet, but it's possible he's going to call it quits on the film. You guys will have to leave. Harry is just going to have to deal with it." Everything had changed.

"Seriously? Look, Harry can put the nix on any story. And even if a photo or two of the actors surface, there's nothing we can do about it now. We can up security, make some changes, but it doesn't make sense to stop filming now." Holt squared his shoulders and shifted back toward the other end of the couch.

"Look, why do you care so much? I understand it's your job and you invested in the movie. But you'll still get to make your movie. It might just get delayed until you find another ranch to shoot on. That's business. This is impacting our entire life. Jeopardizing our privacy and our home. Can't you understand that?" Her belly twisted.

"I understand that Sam. It's not that simple though. I think you're over-reacting. It was one photographer, Harry will handle it, and everything is going to be fine." He crossed his arms and his mouth thinned.

"Don't mansplain to me 'everything is going to be fine' and pat me on the head like a good little girl." She surged to her feet. "It is absolutely not fine, damn it. You don't understand what it was like."

"Samantha, I know you're upset but Harry will handle it. It's going to be—" His tone turned soothing, which fanned the flames of her temper.

"I told you it's *not* fine, damn you. Do you even understand what we went through when my mom was killed? How hard it was to start over? What do you know about having a home? To finally be able to rest because someone created a safe haven for you and to see it threatened over a stupid movie?" The last words came out dangerously close to a scream.

He leapt up from the couch, his eyes now a frosty ice blue. "You have no clue what I've done for my family. All you think about is your own little world and damn anyone who might jostle you out of your complacent little bubble. There's a big world out there, beyond these gates and you can't just pretend it doesn't exist. You can't control everything. You can't spend your whole life hiding out."

"Bubble? That's rich coming from you, Mr. Hollywood. You're the one living in a bubble of camera, lights, and action. What happens when the cameras are shut off? Do you even have a life outside of it? And you're right, I don't have a clue about what you've been through because you haven't told me anything. You're in the middle of my family and know all our secrets. From what I can see, you're basically a drifter, living from movie set to movie set." The words tumbled out, the dam had broken open and she couldn't control the ugly deluge. Anger was easier to navigate than sorrow. She ought to know.

His jaw clamped shut and suddenly his entire expression was as glacial as his eyes. "You've got me all figured out. I drift from set to set and that's all I am. This is all just another job to me until I drift onto the next one. I've got some things to do." He pivoted and strode out of the room.

The slam of the bedroom door echoed through

the house and Sam pressed her hands against her churning gut and released a shaky breath. Her infamous McNeill temper had struck again.

But the truth had come out. This *was* simply a job for him. His hooking up with her was simply a side benefit. A side benefit he probably took advantage of on every movie set.

"Fine." She whispered the word, a hollowness filling her where only seconds before anger had consumed her. Getting the last word offered no solace.

Falling in love. Hardly.

More like hot monkey lust. Heat. Sparks.

Undeniable physical chemistry. Nothing more.

Although he wasn't the total jerk who had mouthed off the first day in her barn, he wasn't relationship material. Who was she kidding? She wasn't really either––she'd never cared about a relationship, figured the right man would show up once she'd achieved all the goals she had for Hercules as a top stallion and Pacific Vista Ranch. And when had the concept of love and commitment come into play? Who was living in the land of make-believe now?

Sure, he was funny. Kind. Talented. Smart. Gorgeous.

She pressed the heels of her hands against her eyelids. Now wasn't the time to catalog all his positive qualities. What was the point? She'd been nasty just now and a sliver of remorse filled her. When would she ever learn to cool off her temper before opening her mouth? Taking back words didn't work too well. Drifter might have been a little bit harsh. She needed to apologize.

She took two steps toward the bedroom.

Stopped.

Not tonight. What was the point? She would never see him again when the movie wrapped and the movie could stop filming tomorrow. She turned and walked to the door, an unbearable weight dragging down her shoulders.

She was rooted to the ranch and Holt had been working in the film industry since he was eighteen years old. He'd never really had an attachment to a place, so how could he understand how much this situation hurt her? Pacific Vista wasn't just where she laid her weary head at night. It was everything. And she didn't need to fall any deeper in…lust…like…whatever…with a man who had no clue what roots or family meant.

He would be fine and move on to the next movie and the next woman. She'd be fine. They'd only known each other a short time and spent a few nights together. People did it all the time. Great sex, some laughs, and move on.

The end.

So why did her heart feel ripped out of her chest?

CHAPTER 25

"THERE YOU ARE. YOU SNUCK out without breakfast, but I've kept some pancakes warm for you, my girl. Your favorite: strawberry banana." Angela pulled her in for a hug.

Sam's cotton shirt was plastered to her back and damp tendrils of hair itched the back of her neck. She sank into her stepmom's warm embrace. What would she do without her soothing presence?

"Definitely my favorite. These crazy Santa Ana winds are really stressing me out. The fire hazard is so high and I had to check all the stables and make sure trailers are ready for the horses and ensure our evacuation plan was firmly in place." She mumbled the words into Angela's shoulder, unwilling to relinquish the comfort of her arms.

"The darned things literally kicked up again blowing overnight. Did you meet with all the grooms and ranch hands?" Angela didn't seem to mind hugging a sweaty mess.

"Yes, the evacuation protocols are set in stone should a fire erupt near the ranch. The poor horses hate fire so much. Hopefully if one does start nearby, we can get them on the trailers and to safety before they panic. Once it's smoky, all bets are off." If the animals' vision and breathing were impaired from smoke, efficiently moving them became tricky, at best.

"And do the ten visiting movie horses have their own trailers?" Angela released her and moved to the shiny stainless steel stove.

Sam nodded. "They do. Our ranch hands know to follow the same emergency protocol with them too. For now."

Angela sighed. "That's a relief."

"So, where's Dad?" She leaned against the blessedly cool granite countertop. Her tone was casual, right?

"Did you mean to ask is he down on set and what's going to happen with the movie?" Angela raised her brows.

Sam smiled sheepishly. "Exactly. So glad you understand me."

"Sit down and let me bring you a plate and we'll discuss it." Angela bustled around the stove and loaded up a stack of pancakes and a pile of crispy bacon.

Sam sank into one of the seats in the breakfast nook and dumped half a pitcher of syrup on her plate, crunched a piece of perfectly crisp bacon, and began stuffing some fluffy pancake goodness into her mouth.

Angela would speak at her own pace. Her stepmom joined her at the table, a turquoise blue ceramic coffee mug cradled in her capable hands.

"Well, he is down on the set. He went to talk to Harry." Angela held up one hand when Sam started to talk. "He hadn't made his decision before he left."

"What do you think he'll do? Doesn't he think

the risk is just too much? Seriously, none of us can go through what we endured in L.A. again. It was hell and the press is even more ruthless now because of social media." Her belly clenched. "I won't have a good night's sleep until this is over."

"Oh sweetie, I know. And I know you aren't sleeping for a variety of other reasons." Angela's warm dark eyes didn't reveal her thoughts.

"What do you mean?" She swallowed.

"This whole situation with the paparazzi, what did you think I meant?" Angela raised a brow, but her gaze remained impassive.

Sam stared at her stepmom. Hell, the woman could win the Texas Hold 'Em Poker tournament with her ability to appear neutral and unruffled.

"Sam, believe me, I know. I may not have been there with you, but I was here when you all were recovering. I know how much it scarred you all." Angela's brow furrowed.

"I'm not scarred." She reared back. "I'm just cautious and don't want to live through it all again. It's different."

"Sweetie, you all have scars. It's natural after what happened. You just don't want to allow the scars to prevent you from living your life. Living from a place of fear is no way to live." Angela laid her cool hand on hers. "Your dad will do the right thing."

Sam dropped her fork onto her plate, her legendary appetite evaporated. "Do you really think I live my life out of fear? I don't."

"You're a brave, beautiful person, Samantha. You are an incredible success and we're all so proud of you. I do think you keep people at arm's length sometimes and I worry you might chase off happiness that way. Sometimes being vulnerable is being strong." Angela smiled at her, her brown eyes warm.

Her brows rose. "Keep the paparazzi at arms' length? That makes no sense." What was Angela implying?

"Of course not the paparazzi. Nobody wants them here. Or anywhere. But we can't live our lives controlled by their actions either. I meant Holt."

"Holt? What do you mean?" She cleared her throat and shifted in her seat.

"I know you, sweetheart. I've seen you two together. He makes you laugh. He challenges you. And he's certainly handsome." Angela waggled her eyebrows.

"What? I don't know what you—" No smart comeback materialized.

"Luckily everyone else was distracted at dinner at The Inn, but I sat across from you two and couldn't miss the sparks flying." Angela fanned one hand in front of her face.

"Oh, you're probably imagining it. You're right. He just cracks me up sometimes. That must be what you mean." Heat flooded into her cheeks. Thank god Angela hadn't been able to see below the table. She hoped.

"No, It's not what I mean and you know it. I saw you sneaking into the house the other morning." She paused and Sam bit back a retort. "You two are actually a lot alike. I like him for you. He sees the real Samantha. He's a nice boy."

"A nice boy?" She choked. "Nice *boy?* He's not

a boy. But it doesn't matter because he's a drifter and he's leaving."

"He's not a drifter and I hope you didn't call him that. Don't be so judgmental. You're better than that." Angela's brown eyes narrowed. "And who knows what the future holds? Would you have ever predicted we'd have a movie filming on the ranch?"

"Never. And look how it's turning out." She rolled her eyes. "How do you know he isn't a drifter? He flits from movie to movie, he has no idea about how important family is——it could never work between us." Why did that make a pit form in her belly? Why did it matter?

Angela's large eyes widened. "He hasn't told you about his family?"

"His family?" How did Angela know anything about it?

"What do you two talk about?" When Sam's cheeks flamed again, Angela laughed. "Okay, don't tell me. He has family back in Colorado and he's very close with them."

"He did mention his mom and sister, and something about his dad leaving, but no details. When did he tell you about them?" He'd told Angela and hadn't bothered to tell her?

"When I showed him the guesthouse, we had a chance to talk. Sure, he has a crazy career now, but I got the impression he was working toward something and he'd be able to take care of his mom and sister and move them out to California."

"Huh." He'd mentioned his mom, but made it sound like he never saw her. She'd assumed they weren't particularly close.

"Huh indeed. So don't jump to conclusions. My gut tells me he's a good man and I suspect yours did too or you wouldn't have let him close to you." Angela raised a brow.

"Well…" She bit the inside of her cheek and stared down at her half-eaten breakfast.

Angela rubbed her shoulder. "All I'm saying is don't cut things off because you are afraid he's going to leave you. You don't know what's going to happen next."

She pinched the bridge of her nose. "Umm…it may be a little late for that. My sweet, calm nature and all that. But what about the movie? If it ends now, it kind of makes it all a moot point."

"Did you get into an argument with him?"

"Something like that." She hunched down further into her seat. She'd been positively awful to him.

"Well, you apologize if it is warranted. You and your dad have your quick fuse tempers. As for the movie—your dad is more excited than I've seen him in years. I never realized how much he missed the business. It was his passion, his life for so long." Angela's smile faded.

"I know. I can see it too. We all loved it. I'll even admit I feel the sparks too. I used to love being on set. But it just seems so risky." Her dad was jazzed and she hated to see his joy be yanked away from him. Again.

"Well, Harry could enforce the contract and it could get messy if your father breaks it. Maybe the wisest thing is to wait and see if anything pops up from the photographer. For now, they are here, they are filming, and maybe it will all just go away." Angela shrugged, but her somber expression belied the confidence in her tone.

"Maybe. That's what Holt said too." She smoothed back the loose strands of hair tickling her forehead. "Well, I'll wait and see what dad says. For now, I'm going to head to the office and try to finish up some more of the never-ending paperwork."

"Aren't you going to finish your breakfast?" Angela's mouth dropped open. Sam left food on her plate——exactly never.

"Nah, I'm full. But thanks for the breakfast and the talk. You're the best." She forced a smile, but her chest ached as she left the kitchen.

Despite wanting to run outside and scream, Sam forced herself to walk to the office in the other wing of the house. So Holt was close to his mother and sister. And what exactly had happened with his dad? Her sharp words echoed in her mind and she cringed. Damn it. He made such a good show of being Mr. Casual.

Why the hell wouldn't he bring it up? Lord knows she'd cried in front of him at the pool. He knew everything about her family and what, was she just supposed to be a mind reader? How could she when he didn't bother to tell her anything?

She halted in the office doorway. Had she ever bothered to ask for any details? It wasn't like they had been on the classic dating path where you asked about family on date number two or anything. But still. Denial was a beautiful thing.

She closed her eyes and sighed. She would indeed have to suck it up and apologize to him for her nasty tirade. Ugh. She hated apologies.

Later. For now, the thrilling world of vaccination protocol reports called. She had to ensure each and every one was not only billed in the system, but also make sure the horses were scheduled for their next set of vaccines. The sooner she started them, the sooner she could escape the dreaded computer. And go find Holt to apologize.

She'd just plopped into the comfortable leather desk chair and powered on the desktop when her dad strode into the office. He approached and gave her a quick hug.

"So?" She gripped her hands together and held her breath.

"You ready to discuss this?" His hazel eyes were bright and he smiled at her.

"Sure." Her stomach tightened and her shoulders tensed.

He dropped into the chair opposite the desk and crossed one denim-clad ankle over his other knee. "Okay. First, Harry made some calls. He made it clear to the press there would be serious repercussions if a story broke."

"And do you think he can control it?" She gave a quick nod, but she doubted anybody could control all of those money-hungry, amoral parasites.

He shrugged his broad shoulders. "Who knows? He's really influential and most people know it's better to stay on his good side. I'm sure there are some unscrupulous people out there who just want to make a buck and cause trouble. Like we know." The grooves around his mouth deepened.

"Okay. So what did you decide? Is it worth it to you, Dad? Aren't you worried for the repercussions?" Her breath lodged in her throat.

He leaned forward. "Well, I want to film the movie. I love it. I'm sorry, Sammy."

They looked at each other for a few moments. Sam released a shaky breath.

"Don't apologize, Dad. I know you are passionate about the horses too, but I think I'm finally realizing how much you gave up to provide a different life for Amanda, Dylan, and me. I guess I never really thought about it too much." She shrugged. More like never thought about how tough it must have been for him to end his career.

"Why would you? You were fifteen years old. I wanted to get away from L.A., from all of it." He gripped his thighs. "I do love our life here, don't get me wrong. This is home and nothing will change it. But maybe I took it all too far. Maybe isolating us here made us hold onto the pain instead of processing it. I don't know."

Sam swallowed the fear creeping up from her heart. Was Holt right about her living in a bubble? Of being scared of the outside world? "I don't know either. But what if the media brings up mom's story again? Throws all the ugliness in our face?"

He surged to his feet. "Damn the media. I refuse to live my life in fear of someone possibly bringing up the past. It is the past. It's our tragic past and your mom deserves to rest in peace and we all deserve to live our lives however we want."

"And you deserve to direct a movie if you want." Pain, sadness, and anger flitted across her beloved father's face. He had lost the most. His wife. The mother of his children. His long-time career. Their entire family had been forever altered by the freak accident that cut Pamela McNeill's life tragically short.

"Damn them. If a story breaks, a story breaks. We'll be fine. If one more camera or reporter comes within a mile of our ranch, believe me there will be consequences." Her father's jaw clenched.

"Okay. Okay. Should we tell Dylan all this is happening or allow her to remain in ignorant bliss in Paris?" Worry tickled the back of her neck. Dylan would be hysterical.

"There's no need to upset her or anyone until if or when something actually happens. And if worst-case scenario, something does happen, we'll deal with it then. Not put our lives on hold anymore." Her dad walked over and pulled her up out of the chair into his familiar, powerful bear hug.

"Do you really think we've put our lives on hold? I feel like we've created an amazing success-ful ranch." She'd dedicated her adult life to the horses and her family.

"No Sammy, our lives haven't been on hold, but I worry maybe we've all held onto the idea that anything outside of Pacific Vista Ranch could harm us. There's a difference between privacy and isolation."

Her shoulders softened, but her belly remained in knots. On one hand, her dad was absolutely correct, but the quarter horse breeding industry was cutthroat. Scandals could impact their busi-ness. Hercules was on the brink of being the top stallion in the country and the reputation and security of Pacific Vista Ranch secured. But, what if it were all ruined by some capricious, stupid story?

The McNeills valued their life on the ranch and the lack of drama. What if they lost their privacy and tranquil lives?

What if was right. Damn them. She'd never been a chicken and despite what Angela had implied, she didn't think she'd been putting her life on hold or operating from a place of fear. No she hadn't. And she wouldn't start now. She squeezed her father tight.

From the moment Holt Ericsson blew into her barn, everything changed.

Nothing would ever be the same again.

She stepped back from her dad and squared her shoulders. She would apologize to Holt; it was about the only thing she could control.

Whether he would stick around to accept her apology was a whole other issue.

CHAPTER 26

"YES, MOM." HOLT CRADLED THE phone between his ear and shoulder as he picked up his guitar and carried it back to the couch.

"No, Mom." He sank into the leather cushions, gently placing the Martin beside him. Unfamiliar emotions were pulsing through him and music was the only hope he had of expressing them.

His gut was tangled in knots. His eyes were gritty from lack of sleep, and he alternated between being pissed off and feeling guilty. He'd failed. He should have been faster and caught that photographer. Stopped this disaster.

Playing his beloved guitar was his only opportunity to process the thoughts and daydreams about his current obsession.

Damn Samantha. He was still angry after her tirade yesterday. She was just so quick to pounce on him.

And not in a sexy, playful way.

But he hadn't really shared the nightmare of quitting high school to work after his dad bailed, or any details of his mom's cancer and fragile health. How would she know? He'd perfected his fast and loose persona and she'd bought it.

He *had* been a nomad.

Currently was *still* a nomad, after all, wasn't he staying in her family's guesthouse? No roots? But drifter sounded like loser and he didn't appreciate the implication. He had plans. Big plans.

"Holt? Holt? Are you still there?" His mom's wavering voice drew him out of his ruminations.

"Sorry, Mom. What did you say?" Now he was being a bad son.

"I just asked if you'd be able to come see us when your movie wraps. It's been too long."

His mom never asked for anything or made him feel guilty for his unpredictable lifestyle. But he did feel remorseful. She'd been devastated when he'd chosen to seek his fortune in Hollywood instead of earning a college degree.

But earning money to make sure she never wanted for anything, at least financially, motivated him more than some piece of paper.

"Of course. When the movie is finished, I've got a few things to do for my new business first. But then I'll be there. I really want to move you and Jenny out to California. This weather will be so good for you. No more of freezing snow one day and sweltering heat the next." Although it was balls hot with the unrelenting Santa Ana winds right now.

"Oh honey, you know the weather is great here in Littleton. If you don't like the weather in Denver——"

"Wait fifteen minutes. I know, I know." He hated the annoying refrain everyone in Denver made about the mercurial climate. "That's the thing. Consistency will be better for you. You can be outside every day here, without bundling up like an arctic explorer."

"We'll see. So next month for a visit?"

"Yes, we should be done by then and I'll catch a flight out." His mom's persistence was one of her primary strengths.

"Anything special on this set? Rancho Santa Fe is part of San Diego, right? I hear it's gorgeous."

"Yeah, it's gorgeous. This ranch is unlike anything you've seen. You'd love it." He rubbed the back of his stiff neck, willing the muscles to relax.

What would his mom think of Sam?

Although the odds of his mother meeting Samantha were slim. Hell, he wasn't sure if he and Sam would ever talk again, much less play 'meet the parents.'

The odds of Samantha apologizing––well, he wouldn't bet on it.

The chance they could find any common ground––doubtful.

Even if they made up, they had no future.

She belonged on Pacific Vista Ranch and he belonged... hell, he didn't really belong anywhere.

"Okay, sweetie. Try to have some fun too. You sound distracted. Call me when you have some dates. You know I'll be here. I love you."

"I love you too, Mom." His mom was his anchor, even if she was hundreds of miles away.

He hated how delicate she sounded these days. Getting her out of the Colorado weather would be great for her immune system. She'd never fully recovered from the brutal chemotherapy and radiation treatments all those years ago. They'd weakened her bones, left her feet numb from neuropathy, and eradicated her ability to fight off infection. Moving her to California would be the best for all of them.

He grabbed the guitar and placed it across his lap. His eyelids drifted shut and he began to strum. The dark, intense notes flowing from his fingertips conjured a vision of Sam's cameo perfect face. His eyes flew open.

Sam's beauty as she cantered on Princess Buttercup.

Sam's fiery energy when she wore her boss hat and expertly ran her breeding operation.

Sam's love and loyalty to her family.

Love. His chest tightened and his fingers froze on the strings.

Love?

He was in love with Samantha McNeill. The most challenging, difficult, exasperating, amazing woman he'd ever met. His heart knocked against his ribs and sweat popped up on the back of his neck. The trilling of his phone interrupted his impending panic attack.

Sam smiled when she answered the Skype call from Dylan. "Hi Dylan. I miss you." They hadn't spoken all week.

"Sam." Dylan croaked her name.

"Oh my god, what's happened? Are you okay?" Dylan's face was deathly pale and tears flowed down her cheeks.

"Am *I* okay? What about you?" Her twin's damp eyes widened.

The hair on the back of Sam's neck prickled. "I'm fine. What's going on?"

"You mean you don't know? How can you not know? Where's Dad? Amanda?" Her sister's voice rose and bubbled on the verge of hysteria.

"Everyone's working. You're freaking me out. Tell me what has you so upset." The blood thrummed through her veins as her sister's emotions penetrated through the phone screen.

"You haven't seen the news? Social media?" Dylan's mouth dropped open.

Sam shook her head. Her heartbeat thundered in her chest. Oh no. It couldn't be. Dylan was in Paris. Please let it be something else. Anything else.

"Our ranch. The movie. Newsflashes of an 'old Hollywood tragedy.' Everything we feared. How did it happen?" Her twin's voice rose two octaves.

Heat flushed through her body and every muscle along her spine tensed. "Are you kidding me? I thought Harry had been able——"

Dylan sprang. "You knew this might happen and you didn't warn me?"

"Slow down. Slow down. Where did you see this?" She drew in a deliberate, steady breath, fighting against the fury bubbling up from her gut. Her fingers curled into her palms. *Stay calm.*

"Everywhere. It's trending on Twitter, for god's sake. Hashtag McNeill Tragedy."

Bile rose in her throat. *No. No. No.* "What?"

"Hashtag McNeill Tragedy. Old photos of mom. Photos of Jack Hanson and Ella Roche. Pacific Vista Ranch. Dad's disappearance from the movie business." Dylan sobbed the words.

Sam squeezed her eyes shut and held her breath. Counted to one. Two…

"Damn it. I knew it." The adrenaline pumped through her veins, and she shot to her feet. Harry Shaw was toast.

"So you did know?" Her twin whispered, shock and betrayal written across her face.

"Look, I don't have time to explain. I need to find Dad now." He was toast too.

"Don't you dare hang up until you tell me something, Samantha." Dylan demanded.

"Somehow a photographer found out about the movie and Holt tried to catch him, but couldn't get up the tree in time. Harry swore he'd do damage control and threaten the world if anything leaked. Obviously, his reach isn't as powerful as he claims. I'm glad you're in Paris and not here. I need to find Dad." She powered off the phone before Dylan could respond.

Her sister was safe thousands of miles away. She could deal with her later. Now she would fix this disaster before it raged any further out of control. Time to deal with the fallout.

Sam stuffed her phone into her back pocket, grabbed her cowboy hat, and sprinted out the front door to the stables. The heat slammed into her like a concrete wall. The Santa Ana winds whipped against her, impeding her progress. Leaves were ripped off branches and floated around in the simmering air like ravens of doom. The hot air had to be screaming around fifty miles per hour.

Day from hell indeed.

She released Princess Buttercup from her stall, saddled her, and leapt up onto her back. She clucked and urged her to a gallop. Together they flew across the rolling green hills to the far side of the ranch. Sweat dripped into her eyes and she shook it away.

Her Dad and Harry better be in one spot.

Harry Shaw would get his ass in gear and fix this. Pronto.

She hadn't even bothered to pull up the story on her phone. What was the point? If Dylan was seeing it in Paris, it had blown wide. Filming on Pacific Vista Ranch was done.

When she crested the hill, she saw the cameras, lights, and action. The hero cradled the heroine in his arms, apparently shooting a tender love scene. Her father and Harry stood to the side, intent on the actors.

Too bad.

As she slowed Buttercup's pace, her dad turned and lifted one finger to his lips, urging her to be quiet.

Too damn bad. Quiet time was over. The scene was over.

"Harry." She yelled as she reined in Buttercup and slid to the ground. "Get over here."

The actors froze, their mouths hanging open in comically identical expressions of amazement and horror. Nobody interrupted a scene when Harry Shaw was filming.

"Sam, what are you doing?" Her dad frowned and took a step toward her.

"What the *hell* do you think you're doing?" Harry snapped out the words.

"Oh, you were going to fix it." She made air quotes. "Well, I just got a call from Dylan in Paris and stories about the McNeill tragedy and Pacific Vista Ranch and the movie are trending all over the Internet. Great job, Wizard of Oz. You're full of hot air. Damn you." Her hands curled into fists.

Her dad's jaw dropped. "Please tell me you're kidding." His tone indicated he knew her too well to know she wasn't. He pivoted toward Harry. "Harry?"

Harry cursed. "The story is international? Damn it all to hell."

"That's all you've got?" She narrowed her eyes. "What happened? I thought you had it handled? Now what?" She swiveled toward her dad. "Dad? Now what? Dylan is devastated."

"Did you read the story?" Her father's broad shoulders sagged.

"No, I rode down here as soon as I heard. I thought Mr. High and Powerful had fixed it. Got it under control. We should have known better than to trust you." She glared at the director.

Nobody moved. The actors and crew looked like statues on their marks. The heavy winds stirred the heat up, but otherwise everything was silent.

"Well?" Mr. Movie Mogul had no retort?

Harry and her father exchanged glances.

"Harry. We need to deal with this now." He angled toward the set. "Take a break, everyone. Don't leave the ranch. We'll text you when we know what's next."

Her father's long stride ate up the ground toward where his horse was tied. "Sam, with me. Harry, meet me at the house. Now." He leapt up onto his horse and rode off without another word.

Sam hopped on Buttercup's back and raced to catch up with him. Her t-shirt clung to her skin and her pulse pounded in her temples. The air was oppressive now, the heat punched up so it felt like Death Valley at noon in the height of summer. She wished she were diving into the swimming pool, instead of what promised to be an ugly scene with Harry in her father's office. Were the winds kicking up even more now? Mother Nature was angry too.

She caught up with him at the stables and tossed her reins to Marco. She hurried to catch her dad and wished for the millionth time she was taller and had longer legs.

Without breaking stride, her dad knocked on the guesthouse door and yelled, "Holt, meet us in the office. Now."

The door flew open and Holt appeared in the doorway, his full lips compressed into a tight line and his eyes flinty.

She stopped. "You knew, didn't you?" Why else would he look so grim?

"I just got a call from a buddy in L.A who told me. Wait a second. Let me grab a shirt and I'll be right up."

Her eyes descended from his face to his chiseled golden chest and flat, sculpted abdominals. Of course he was half naked. Something other than anger curled in her belly.

"Do you want me to wait for you?" The words escaped. Damn her mouth for always opening before her mind engaged. She'd been so nasty, he probably didn't want to be within a mile of her.

His artic blue eyes warmed. "Please. I'll be right back." He turned and strode into the house.

Angela's admonition returned to her and she

pressed one palm to her lips. When would she learn not to snap out the words without thinking? She owed him an apology, even if he didn't ever care to speak to her again. Whatever his family situation, she shouldn't have basically called him a worthless drifter.

First, business.

Apology later. She wouldn't let him leave the ranch without at least apologizing. He deserved it and her conscience dictated it.

"Let's go." Holt appeared and was tucking a navy t-shirt into his faded jeans.

She turned and they marched up to the house together. For once, words eluded her.

"How did you find out? Online?" His husky voice was gentle.

"No, Dylan called me from Paris. She knew about it first, if you can believe it." She forced her tone to match his.

He whistled under his breath. "The damn Internet."

"Right. I was shocked. She said the story about our family is trending on Twitter." She sighed and shook her head.

"And she went all that way to stay out of the situation and she gets it dumped on her anyway. I'm sorry." Holt frowned.

"Yeah, she was devastated and surprised I didn't know about it. I just hadn't gone online today—— I'm not a big fan of social media anyway." More like hate all media, social media included.

Holt paused next to one of the enormous date palm trees lining the path. He grasped her arm and turned her toward him, his eyes filled with concern. "Are you okay?"

Goosebumps popped up along her arms, despite the broiling heat. A shiver of awareness danced along her skin where his strong hand remained. For a moment, she forgot about everything except for him. He was so damn gorgeous and now he was being sweet, even after her nasty attack yesterday. He dropped his hand by his side.

She shook her head. "I'm furious. But I just want to do damage control now. I won't let these jerks ruin our lives again." Harry. Paparazzi. Disaster.

"I'm angry too. I'm sorry I underestimated how much the press would be interested in your family. If only I'd caught the little weasel." He shrugged one broad shoulder.

"We'll deal with it. We always do. Don't apologize. You tried." She cleared her throat. "I'm the one who needs to apologize to you." Miracle—she didn't choke on the words.

Holt's brows arched. "I'm sorry, what did you say? Because it sounded like you said you owed me an apology, but that can't be right."

"Very funny. I was a total bitch yesterday and you didn't deserve it. Sometimes I just can't seem to shut up." She cleared her parched throat again. "Words roll out and I regret it right after. It's one of my biggest flaws. I shouldn't have said things about your family. And its not your fault the media found us." Huh, hell hadn't frozen over.

He averted his gaze, not meeting her eyes. "Do you really see me as a drifter?"

"No. I know you aren't a drifter. I don't really understand how you can live on the road all the time and not really have a home, but I shouldn't have said that. I am really sorry." Why had she said such a thoughtless comment?

When he didn't reply, she reached up one hand and touched his chest. "Holt? Can you forgive me? I'm so sorry."

"We both said some things we didn't mean. I'm sorry too. I wanted to protect you and I couldn't."

Her heart knocked against her ribs. He *had* tried to keep her and her family safe. She smiled, every muscle in her body softening.

His eyes blazed into hers and he grabbed her and crushed her against him.

Her arms were trapped between them and she slid them up and wound them around his lean waist. Everything else faded away and her lips parted as she stared up at him.

He slid his hands up and clasped her face. His eyes burned into hers and her pulse raced.

"Please kiss me." Had she said it out loud?

He smiled and lowered his golden head to hers. His sculpted mouth pressed against her lips and she moaned. She drove her fingers into his thick hair and opened to him.

Tingles traveled down her spine, then her hip vibrated. At first, she ignored it. Couldn't care less who would be bothering her right now. Then she remembered.

She broke off the kiss and grabbed the phone out of her back pocket.

"Where the hell are you? Get up here now." Her dad's text was all caps.

"Oh crap. My dad. We have to go." She breathed out the words, struggling for composure.

"Oh yeah. Let's go." He smoothed back the hair

from her face and threaded his fingers through hers.

They strode together up the path to the house.

"Holt." She halted in her tracks and stared down at his long tanned fingers intertwined with her slender pale ones.

"Yeah?" He gazed down at her, all nonchalant.

"We're holding hands." She lifted her gaze to his and her belly took a long, slow roll.

"Yeah. Yeah we are. You okay with it?" One corner of his beautiful mouth hitched up.

"I...I'm not sure. Probably not the best time with everything going on." Her hand tightened on his, loving the feel of his calloused palm covering hers.

"But later? We need to talk, Samantha. I have some things to tell you." His blue eyes were twin flames and it wasn't just intense desire flickering behind his eyes. *Things to tell her?*

"Tell me?" She swallowed. "Okay." And that's all she had. For once her impulsive mouth didn't run away with her. Nope, she didn't have the words. But warmth filled her, a different type than the sun frying the back of her neck.

"No comment? That's a first." He flashed his white teeth. He brushed his fingertips along her cheek with his other hand and tugged her hand and continued up the path.

She pulled on her hand, but he wouldn't release her.

"I'll let go at the door." He smiled down at her.

She followed because she wasn't sure what else to do. Wait, that wasn't quite true. She kept her hand in his because it felt right. His strength, warmth, and calmness fortified her and made her feel protected. Who knew what they were doing, but he sure seemed to be confident.

When they reached the front door, she paused.

"No matter what happens, I'm here for you, Sam." He drew their joined hands to his mouth and kissed her fingers before he relinquished her hand.

Drawing courage from his quiet strength, she turned the knob. "Let's go do this."

CHAPTER 27

CHAOS ENSUED. AMANDA GLARED AT Harry and her customarily calm voice was urgent. The director was holding up both hands in front of him and nodding his head. Angela, her dark brows drawn together, flanked her dad. Her father's knuckles were white where he gripped his massive oak desk.

"Sam, Dylan called you? Is she okay?" Amanda caught sight of them standing in the open office doorway. Her skin was flushed and her eyes flashed with fury. Although her sister didn't share her lightning fast temper, when she was angry, her McNeill blood showed.

She nodded and marched into the office and Holt followed. "She'll be fine. She just couldn't believe I hadn't heard yet. Insane. So Harry——any answers yet? Who was the leak? What are you doing?"

"Yes. I made some calls on the way up from the set. There will be no further stories. The idiot who started the first one has been fired and won't be able to get a job reporting on the corn growing in Iowa. Trust me." His jaw was tight and his eyes cool.

"That's what you said before." Amanda crossed

her arms across her chest and glowered at him.

"Yeah. Excuse us if we don't feel confident in your word right now." Sam crossed her arms, mirroring her sister. Holt stepped closer to Sam's side. His solid presence bolstered her nerves.

"Look, while I can't get the story already out there removed from the news stations and social media, there won't be any more. Period. I've got it handled." He jutted out his chin and scanned the room.

"But what does that matter? It's already out there and the damage is done." Sam piped in.

"Girls, we can't do anything about the stories already out there except to ignore them. It's done." Her dad's hazel eyes flashed and he nodded when nobody replied.

"I will be damned if I allow the media to dictate what I do with my life and how any of us act ever again. We changed our lives once and I'll be damned if I'll do it again. I'm done." He caught Angela's hand and pulled her in closer to him.

"Here's how everything will move forward from now on. First, we'll step up security. We will finish this film on time and on budget. We will ignore any news reports. If anybody is stupid enough to ask us for comments, the response in No Comment. Are we agreed?" He scanned the room.

"Your father is right. It's done. We'll live our lives like normal. The story will die down quickly, there's too many other crazy things going on in the world for it not to. We won't hide. Girls?" Angela hugged her dad as she spoke, always the source of comfort.

Sam covered the two steps to embrace her sister. She sighed out the breath she'd been holding. Amanda's shoulders were stiff, but the heat in her eyes had cooled. Her calm, cool, and collected persona was firmly back in place.

"Girls?" Her dad asked.

"I guess we don't have a choice. But you're right. It's just talk and we can ignore it. We'll get through this. Now that it has come up again, I think it's time for us to dig out all the photo albums and the movie posters and stop pretending like that part of our lives didn't exist." Amanda nodded.

"I'd love to do that. And while I'm not happy about it, I agree we can't hide out anymore. Won't hide out anymore." Samantha linked her arm with her sister's. "And dad, now we understand how much you missed this and I don't want to stand in your way."

"Thank you. We'll get through this together, like we always do." Her dad's eyes were bright.

"Who was the leak, Harry?" Sam asked. Curiosity won out—she was willing to move on, but needed to know.

Harry grimaced. "The damn waitress who was training at The Inn. Apparently when she saw Jack, she tipped off a reporter at one of the tabloids. The tabloid put two and two together when they learned Jack was with your family. Then the idiot reporter dispatched the scumbag photographer."

"The Inn? Our Inn? They are known for being discreet. Damn it." Chris slapped his hand on the desk.

"She's been fired. They are also planning on prosecuting her for violating her employment contract there. I guess some people don't care about breaking privacy clauses—" Harry shook his head. "I'm sorry. I know I pushed this on you."

"You did, but you were right. I'd say we're even now. You helped me by finishing the film after I couldn't do it and it's all come full circle. And we both had to deal with those rumors."

"It wasn't ever about evening the score, but I'm glad it all worked out." Harry nodded.

"I'm glad it wasn't anyone you hired, which is a positive. And we'll finish the movie. Like I said, I won't play into this crap ever again." Her dad shook his head. "Let's get back to work. Text the leads and let's finish up this scene today. We're on a schedule." Her dad looked around the room." Holt, can you come down in an hour?"

"Sure. I'm ready." Holt nodded.

"Let's do this." Harry whipped his phone out of his pocket.

Sam hesitated, and then looked at Holt. He winked at her and she couldn't prevent the smile from spreading across her face or the tingle down her spine. She turned to file out of the office. Maybe today wasn't Armageddon after all.

Before anybody could exit, Owen, the stallion manager, burst into the room.

"We've got to evacuate. There's a fire just across the canyon behind the north wall. They've already called for mandatory evacuations."

"What? When did it start? Mandatory evacuations?" Amanda and Sam cried at once. "We've got to move the horses."

"The ranch hands are all down at the stables and moving on evac protocol. The winds are so intense right now, the flames are moving crazy fast." Owen threw up his hands. "After the Witch Creek disaster, nobody is taking any chances. We need help though. We've got to get the horses out before the smoke gets too heavy." Owen turned and ran down the hallway.

"Everybody stay calm. We've been through this before. I'll take care of packing up the valuables from the house. You go help with the horses." Angela hurried behind her father's desk and started whipping open drawers.

Chills shot through Sam's body and for a split second she couldn't budge. They had one hundred and fifty horses and taking them all to safety was no easy feat, protocol or not. She'd created the foolproof plan herself, but if the fire was moving so fast the evacuations were already mandatory, what if they couldn't save them all? Horses were so incredibly sensitive and freaked out at smoke and fire.

Her mind flashed back to 2007, when the fires jumped across Del Dios Highway, and the flames destroyed everything in their path. Some residents hadn't been able to move all their animals in time and had freed the horses from the stables to give them a chance of beating the fire. Pictures of towering flames buffeted by vengeful Santa Ana winds and horses galloping wildly in circles, whipping their heads from left to right, seeking an escape from the hellish inferno flashed through her mind. The fear. The loss. The horrific tortuous death.

No. Not again. Not here. She squared her shoulders.

"Sam, Dad, Holt, let's hit the stables. Let's make sure the irrigation is on full blast around all the buildings and the near pasture. Angela, you keep working in here and start packing up the cars." Amanda morphed into her efficient self and barked out the orders nobody considered refusing.

"I'll drive back down to set and get the crew and everyone out of here. We've got three or four horses down there, and we have their trailers. I'll have the crew load them up and drive them out. Where's the best place to take them?" Harry asked.

"We'll be taking ours over to the Del Mar Fair-grounds. It's only a few miles away on the other side of the 5 and it's a safe place with enough room to house all the animals. Have your crew take them there as soon as possible. Don't forget their papers if you have them." Sam offered the directions as she retreated out of the office.

"Done. I've got a ten-bedroom house in Encin-itas. Once you've taken care of your horses, grab your stuff and everyone can stay there until it's safe to return." Harry said. "Do you need my help once I've cleared out the actors and crew?"

"Come back up to the house and help me load the cars, Harry." Angela asked.

"Will do." Harry waved and jogged toward the front door.

"Sam, you okay?" Holt asked as they ran down the stone path to the stables together.

"I'm fine. I'm fine." The adrenaline pumped triple time through her veins; but she forced her usual work ethic to take over.

The acrid smoke assaulted her nostrils. How had it burst up so quickly? The distinct grey tendrils were darkening up the formerly blue sky off in the distance. The howling wind spread the heat and it all seemed to have appeared within seconds. The fire couldn't have begun more than an hour ago. Or had it?

Had she been so wrapped up in her fury over the media leak she'd missed the early signs of fire? Talk about perspective on what was important. Now they were facing a true threat to everything that mattered: home, horses, even their lives.

"We'll get the horses out in time." Holt grabbed her hand and squeezed it. His firm touch gave her one more layer of strength.

Of course they would get the horses out on time. They had a plan. And Holt was by her side.

The stables were a hive of activity. Ranch hands were loading the horses into the trailers lined up along the paved lane. Thank god she had checked and double-checked that everything was ready to go earlier. The whole process was an expensive endeavor, but no way would Sam lose a single animal.

So far, the horses looked relatively calm except for a few whinnies and Sam prayed they'd stay that way. The scorching winds rocketed around them, ruffling the horses' manes and tails. Amanda was leading two of their horses down to the waiting trailers and her dad was helping load others.

"Buttercup?" Sam asked her sister.

"She's already been loaded into the first trailer. She's fine." Amanda called over her shoulder.

Sam expelled a breath of relief. Buttercup was her baby.

"What do you want me to do first? Stay here or go to one of the other stables? Just tell me," Holt offered.

"Come with me and we'll start there." Sam strode toward the second stable. "Yes, our number one priority is evacuation. We'll move them all to the Fairgrounds, which should be open since we're under mandatory orders. I'm hoping they'll be able to contain it fast, but with these winds, I'm not taking any chances."

"I'm taking one of the trailers down to the rehab center and getting those horses. Dad, can you come with me?" Amanda asked as she ran toward one of the trailers on the end of the line.

"Yeah, I'm with you." Her dad and Amanda hurried away.

Holt and Sam jogged to the next building. They worked in tandem. Words were unnecessary, but his support and dedication were palpable. The Santa Ana winds continued to pump dry crackling air, bits of hay swirled around them, and a few of the horses whinnied. Sweat poured down both of their faces and Sam's fingers ached. It didn't matter. She whispered sweet nonsense to each horse as she escorted them from their respective stalls and led them to the waiting trailers.

As they continued to methodically empty the stable, sirens blasted the air and two fire trucks sped up to the stables and stopped.

An enormous guy with close-cropped black hair and a goatee jumped out from the driver's seat of the first truck and landed lightly on the pavement.

"Who's in charge here?"

Sam paused and handed Holt the reins of a dappled gray mare. "I'm the ranch manager."

The firefighter approached and Amanda came running up toward them. His dark eyes widened when he saw her, but then he turned his back and addressed Sam, his face impassive.

"The fire is moving fast. How much longer before you can you get the horses off of the property?" His deep baritone voice was brisk.

"We've got about a quarter of them loaded up now. We've got enough trailers for almost all of them. We'll have to drive some of them over to Del Mar, unload, and come back for the rest. I'm about to direct them off now so they can be back for the rest as soon as possible." She exhaled and wiped her sweaty palms on her jeans. "What's going on? Where did the fire start?"

"About a half-mile down the road. Cause unknown. Nothing contained yet. These damn winds. I've got ten trucks on it now and we're waiting on help from the air. I've got the whole Covenant on mandatory evac. We can't have another Witch Creek." He shook his head.

"We've got irrigation for the main areas going, but the buildings may need additional protection. How many trucks can you get here?" Amanda demanded.

"The priority is getting the fire contained. We'll have trucks here too, but I can't give you a number yet." He continued to address Sam, not glancing at her sister. Odd, most guys drooled when they saw her.

"When?" Amanda's brows drew together and

she stared at the guy.

"I'll keep you posted. Once you have the horses out, I'd take your valuables and cars and get to safety. We'll let you know when you can come back." He narrowed his eyes.

"I'm not leaving here until every one of my horses is safe," Sam declared. No way in hell.

"Me neither." Amanda turned on her heel and marched back to the stable to help Holt.

"Look, Ms. McNeill, I'm new in town, but I'm aware of who your family is and the size of your ranch. We'll do our best to protect you, but remember what matters." He watched her sister stride away.

"Thanks. But, the horses are our first priority. We're on it. Thanks for coming out." She didn't have time to reassure anybody. Her horses needed to get to safety, pronto.

She looked up at the harsh sky and muttered a small prayer to Mother Nature to snuff out the fire before it was too late.

CHAPTER 28

SAM'S SHOULDERS SAGGED, HER EYES were stinging, but her horses were safe. The last twenty horses had just been transported to the Fairgrounds. Thank goodness. Nothing else mattered.

She trudged the last few steps to the guesthouse and Holt flung the door open before she could knock.

"Samantha, you okay?" Holt stared at her, his gaze intense yet unreadable. He stood with his guitar under one arm and his duffel bag slung over his other shoulder. His hair was stringy and sweaty, his face red, and his eyelids hooded. And still he looked gorgeous. An exhausted archangel.

She could only nod and stare.

During the madness of evacuating the animals, her mind had been completely focused on the task at hand. Now, all she saw was him. Everything between them rushed back to her. The man. The sweet tender lover. The cocky stuntman. The protective, caring man. The soulful musician. The first man to ever engage all of her senses. The first man she'd ever truly loved.

"You ready? Let's get out of here and go to Harry's." He tilted his head and offered a weary half-smile.

I'm in love with Holt Ericsson. Oh my god. "Are those all your belongings?"

"Yeah."

"That's it? Everything you own?" How could his life fit into two canvas bags and a guitar case?

"I've always traveled light and we won't be at Harry's for long. Stuff doesn't matter to me, never has. My mother and sister are important. My guitar matters. You matter the most." He stepped closer and she felt his warm breath fan across her cheek.

"Me?" Was that her voice squeaking? All breathy?

He dropped the duffel bag on the ground and leaned the guitar case on top of it. He pulled her against him and enfolded her in his muscular arms. "Yeah, you."

He kissed her, and the world fell away. The media. The fire. The world. His embrace was her only world now. Lips parted, tongues tangled, and heat sparked through her veins. Him. This overpowering connection was what mattered.

"Holt, I——" *I love you.*

"Shhh. We'll talk after we get your things and get to safety. Angela packed for you and is already on the way to Harry's. I wanted us to go together." He placed one finger on her lips.

"No damn it. Wait a second." She huffed out a breath. "I have something to say and you'll listen. We have another minute."

"Sam, we should go." He started to reach for his guitar case.

She grabbed his arm. "Wait. Holt, I've never

said these words before, but I'm saying them now to you." She sucked in a deep breath. "I love you." Her breath lodged in her throat and she stared into his deepening blue eyes.

He chuckled and before she could respond to his surprising reaction, he swung her up into his arms and spun her around. "Hey world, Samantha McNeill loves me."

"You're crazy, Holt. Put me down." Her breath hitched in her throat. "And don't you have something to say to me?"

He laughed again and set her lightly on her feet. "Thank you?"

"Thank you?" Her jaw dropped and she shoved him, although he was so damn big and stubborn he didn't budge. "Are you kidding me? Thank you?"

"Yes, thank you for loving me." He leaned in and kissed her nose. "I appreciate it."

"You appreciate it?" Was he kidding? She bared her teeth.

"Because I love you Sam and I want to be with you." He pressed a gentle kiss to her cheek.

"You do?" Her heart thumped against her ribcage. "Be with me? What does that mean?"

He held her shoulders and stopped laughing. "It means I love you and I want to spend my life with you. I want to figure out a way we can make this work."

"But I belong to the ranch, Holt, and I can't ask you to give up your career for me." The fluttering in her belly hardened into a knot. What was she thinking? How could they be together? She hadn't thought beyond her burgeoning feelings.

Running the ranch was her life, everything she'd worked toward for the last several years. His work was on the road.

She couldn't leave.

He couldn't stay.

"I don't have to give up my career and neither do you. I've been saving to start my own business. My body can't take stunt work much longer and this movie was actually my last planned gig. Your dad said the fire department called and the ranch will be safe and we can finish the movie once the fire is contained. With this paycheck, I'll have enough to start my own stunt person agency and once it is set up, I can run it from just about anywhere." He smiled.

"Really? Anywhere? Like here?" Her heartbeat accelerated.

"Yeah, like here. It will take a while to get it going and it will have to be based in L.A. But, once it's up and running and I hire a great manager, I won't have to be there so much. For now, I can commute between L.A. and Rancho Santa Fe. We'll make it work. That is if you want me around?" He stroked one strong hand along her cheek and she turned to press her lips to his palm.

Joy flooded through her. He'd adapt around her career? Her beloved ranch? Could she really have it all?

"Oh Holt, I feel like I'm dreaming. Yes, absolutely yes." She started to wrap her arms around his neck, but he caught both her hands.

He dropped to one knee and kept a firm grip on her fingers. "I don't have a ring Sam, I want to pick one out together, but I have the words. You are one of a kind. From the first moment I walked in on you and the fluffer, my life changed. I won't say it was love at first sight, but it's definitely love now. I love you and I want to marry you. Spend our lives together." His silvery blue eyes held her captive.

Her entire body trembled and her lips curved upward. "Yes, absolutely yes! You'll have to put up with my temper, but it will be a fair trade because I have to endure your smartass self."

"Deal." He stood, yanked her in close, and lowered his mouth to hers. "Let's go."

He grabbed his stuff, and they walked hand in hand to the main house.

Smoke sat on the horizon and assaulted their nostrils with pungent fumes, but Sam smiled anyway. She trusted the fire department to contain the fire, she trusted her horses would remain safe in their temporary sanctuary, and most of all she trusted the man by her side to love her forever.

EPILOGUE

Seven months later,
Pacific Vista Ranch

SAMANTHA MCNEILL STARED AT HER father and huffed out a breath. What had she been thinking? How in the world would she dismount from Princess Buttercup without tumbling over her voluminous skirts and landing in a heap of tulle? She should have worn trousers and this whole make-an-entrance-as-bride-to-be would be a whole lot easier. The cool February breeze caressed her unbound hair and the Southern California sunshine warmed her bare shoulders.

She looked across her favorite pasture, transformed and filled with people dressed in fancy clothes, to where Holt stood waiting for her under the flower-covered arch, an enormous grin on his handsome face.

Chris McNeill reached for her with his strong arms. He looked dapper in a charcoal grey tuxedo, boots, and his wide-brimmed cowboy hat. "Come on, Sammy, I've got you. You can do this."

"Here goes nothing." She sighed and as gracefully as she could, swung her legs to the side of her horse. So far, so good. The layers of shimmering ivory gown shifted with her, and she leaned down to grasp her dad's broad shoulders.

He caught her waist and lifted her to the ground. The moment her favorite boots touched the brilliant green grass, the crowd applauded. Her knees wobbled and her pulse kicked in. This was it.

"Are you ready for your Hollywood ending, my sweet beautiful girl?" Her dad clasped her hand in his warm one.

She drew in a deep inhale, savoring the clean afternoon air. She smoothed down her dress, and exhaled. She was ready.

She handed the reins to her step-brother Grant and he led Buttercup to the special rail they'd set up for her to observe the wedding. Then Dylan and Amanda were handing her a giant bouquet of pale pink roses, the same shade as their silk bridesmaid dresses. Amanda kissed her cheek. "You're glowing, Samantha. Savor every moment."

Her sisters glided down the flower petal strewn aisle and took their places opposite Holt at the altar.

The guitarist began playing a beautiful tune and tears sprang to Sam's eyes when she recognized the song Holt had written for her. When he'd first played it for her, back when they'd first declared their love for each other, she'd shed tears of happiness. She didn't want to cry today, she only wanted to smile and laugh and celebrate the beginning of their new life together. Her heart tightened in her chest and she squeezed her father's arm.

Each step led her closer to this wonderful man, this man who'd challenged her, made her laugh, and most importantly, made her feel. After the successful completion of the movie, he'd retired and started his business, as promised. They were now living in the guesthouse together, so she could run the ranch and he could have a true home base. Holt was now officially an integral part of the McNeill clan. She couldn't stop grinning. Her dad pressed a kiss on her forehead and joined Angela in the front row of chairs set up on the grassy hill.

Holt came to her, both hands outstretched. He grasped her hands and squeezed. His silvery blue eyes were glistening and full of emotion. "You're look so beautiful, Samantha. I'm the luckiest man in the world."

"You look beautiful too. I love you." Warmth flooded her from head to toe.

Together they turned to face the wedding officiant, who smiled and addressed them and all of the guests. "Today we are here to celebrate Holt and Samantha, who from what I understand had a quite unique first meeting here on Pacific Vista Ranch." Familiar with the story, the crowd laughed.

And so it began.

~THE END~

THANK YOU!

THANK YOU FOR READING *NOBODY Else But You*! I hope you loved Samantha and Holt's story as much as I loved writing it. The next book in the Pacific Vista Ranch series is *The Very Thought of You* and is an unrequited love story featuring Amanda McNeill and sexy firefighter Jake Cruz. http://www.clairemarti.com/mybooks.html

To find out about new books, book signings and events, and receive exclusive giveaways and sneak peeks of future books, sign up for my newsletter: http://www.clairemarti.com

If you love steamy beach romances, check out my award winning Finding Forever in Laguna series. You'll find previews of *Second Chance in Laguna*, *At Last in Laguna*, and *Sunset in Laguna* here: http://www.clairemarti.com/mybooks.html

And if you have a moment, please leave a review for *Nobody Else But You* on your favorite book site.

OTHER BOOKS BY

Second Chance in Laguna
At Last in Laguna
Sunset in Laguna

AUTHOR BIO

CLAIRE MARTI STARTED WRITING STORIES as soon as she was old enough to pick up pencil and paper. After graduating from the University of Virginia with a BA in English Literature, Claire was sidetracked by other careers, including practicing law, selling software for legal publishers, and managing a non-profit animal rescue for a Hollywood actress.

Finally, Claire followed her heart and now focuses on two of her true passions: writing romance and teaching yoga. She lives in San Diego with her husband and furry kids.